STATE OF DECEPTION

VIRGIL JONES MYSTERY THRILLER SERIES
BOOK 4

THOMAS SCOTT

Copyright © 2017 by Thomas Scott. All rights reserved. No part of this book may be reproduced in any form or by any electronic or mechanical means, including photocopying, recording, or by any information storage and retrieval system without written permission from both the publisher and copyright owner of this book.

This book is a work of fiction. No artificial intelligence (commonly referred to as: AI) was used in the conceptualization, creation, or production of this book. Names, characters, places, governmental institutions, venues, and all incidents or events are either the product of the author's imagination or are used fictitiously. Any resemblance to actual persons, living or dead, businesses, companies, events, locales, venues, or government organizations is entirely coincidental.

For information contact: ThomasScottBooks.com

— **Also by Thomas Scott** —

The Virgil Jones Series In Order

State of Anger - Book 1
State of Betrayal - Book 2
State of Control - Book 3
State of Deception - Book 4
State of Exile - Book 5
State of Freedom - Book 6
State of Genesis - Book 7
State of Humanity - Book 8
State of Impact - Book 9
State of Justice - Book 10
State of Killers - Book 11
State of Life - Book 12
State of Mind - Book 13
State of Need - Book 14
State of One - Book 15
State of Play - Book 16
State of Qualms - Book 17
State of Remains - Book 18
State of Suspense - Book 19

The Jack Bellows Series In Order

Wayward Strangers - Book 1
Brave Strangers - Book 2

Visit ThomasScottBooks.com for further information regarding future release dates, and more.

This work is dedicated in loving memory to my late grandfather, David Claude Whiteman, who speaks to me often. Truth lies in fiction, folks. Bank on it.

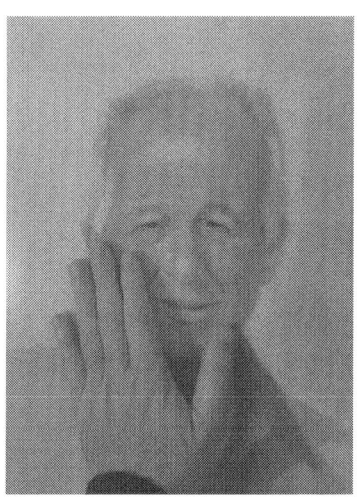

de·cep·tion
 dəˈsepSH(ə)n

> The action of deceiving someone.
> A thing that deceives.
> "A range of elaborate deceptions."

Deception is a state of mind, and the mind of the state.
—James Jesus Angleton, CIA Counterintelligence

"Don't deceive yourself, Son."
—Mason Jones

CHAPTER ONE

FOUR SECONDS AGO

The deception didn't happen quickly, like a magician's trick or a back alley grifter taking down marks with a game of three-card Monte. It developed incrementally over time, the disparate parts so small and segmented no one knew how to fit all the pieces together until it was too late. The answers were all right there…the problem was—someone would later say with ironic hindsight—nobody had bothered to ask the right questions.

When it all became evident what was really happening and they finally did put it together, none of them had any real faith they'd be able to fix it, the hastiness leaving them little chance of success. But it was their only shot and they meant to take it. By then, they simply didn't have a choice. They were out of time. And the history of it—

one buried deep and all but forgotten—had now resurfaced decades later and it remained just short of... unbearable.

Virgil Jones held the Glock with a firm grip, his hands steady, the barrel pointed straight at the other man's head, a choice now, and without question, a price to be paid. He leaned forward, his knees slightly bent, his weight rotated up on the balls of his feet. When he slipped his finger into the trigger guard he asked for forgiveness, though he didn't know to whom he was speaking, or if they were even listening.

He took a breath, the inhalation something like acid in his lungs, and when he could inhale no more he locked eyes with his best friend and brother, Murton Wheeler. The look on Virgil's face remained a conveyance of everything that couldn't be said aloud, a lifetime of memories, brotherly love, their victories, their mistakes, and then...

This:

Murton nodded at Virgil, his mouth a thin hard line, his jaw flexed tight. The nod was nothing more than a quick tip of his head, one that said, get on with it then.

When Jones pulled the trigger, Wheeler's head jerked away and he fell to the ground, dead before he hit the floor, his body bent in an awkward position, blood leaking from the gaping hole in his forehead. His eyes remained open and seemed to register surprise, as if maybe the last thought his brain processed was disbelief that his death would come from the hand of the one person he least suspected capable of pulling the trigger.

But it had, and in that instant Virgil knew in many ways his life would never be the same.

As Virgil's late father, Mason, was fond of saying: *Stay tuned.*

CHAPTER TWO

FOUR WEEKS AGO

THE PROBLEM WAS, EVERYONE HAD SOME SORT OF problem, and Virgil Jones, lead detective of Indiana's Major Crimes Unit didn't like problems. He liked solutions. Nice simple solutions that made everyone's problems go away so he could live his life in a calm, peaceful manner outside the chaotic whirlwind of what his wife, Sandy, had come to call—her tongue firmly embedded in her cheek every time he brought it up—Opps.

Other people's problems.

For example: The MCU now had its own facility, an old post office building just south of the city's not-so-infamous Spaghetti Bowl, a series of never-ending loops, on-ramps, exits, and city streets, that, when viewed from above looked like an actual bowl of spaghetti. They'd managed to take most of the kinks out of the spaghetti over the years, a major construction project that straightened some of the loops and disposed of the ghost ramps and exits. It didn't look much like a spaghetti bowl anymore…it looked more like a few pieces of overcooked Fettuccine stuck to the plate after three bottles of red. But the name lived on, simply one of the city's quirks. If you said 'down by the spaghetti bowl' to an Indy native, they knew where you meant, no matter what the noodles looked like.

The new facility would serve as the main hub for all investigative operations of the MCU. They'd have their own lab and dedicated crime scene crew, individual offices for everyone on the squad, and a research department with access to every crime database in the country. Ron Miles was the director of operations for the entire unit. With the expansion of the MCU, Ron's job had naturally transitioned into mostly administrative tasks, the tasks themselves a waste of his talent and resources. Miles was up to his neck in it and he didn't like it. It was, he'd tell anyone who'd listen, state government at its finest, his voice thick with sarcasm, the disdain open and apparent to anyone who'd listen. After a while the listeners began to drift away.

Virgil formerly held the job until he was sacked by the governor due to a drug problem he'd developed a couple of years ago. The drug problem was something of an aftereffect…in that *after* he'd been kidnapped and had the snot knocked out of him, the *effect* was he'd gotten himself hooked on Oxycontin during his recovery. He ended up beating the Oxy back—no small task—and the governor later re-hired him, but it came with a twist. Miles would remain as the unit's official leader, while Virgil and Murton would take the lead on the most difficult cases, reporting to the governor through his chief of staff, Cora LaRue.

Virgil and Murton were, for lack of a better way of looking at it, the governor's official fixers, even though the whole thing was sort of hush-hush and as unofficial as it could get. They were a part of, yet apart from the MCU, running their own caseload, directed by Cora.

The entire situation caused more than a little friction between Virgil and Miles. The friction naturally carried over to Murton Wheeler, Virgil's best friend, brother, and co-worker. And if that wasn't enough, because Virgil and Cora had worked together for many years, if the friction happened to work its way up the chain of command it rubbed off on her. Since there weren't many links in the chain to begin with, when Cora had a problem, it landed on Virgil to straighten things out. The bottom line was this: The entire situation continued to chase its own tail—Miles would complain about something to Cora who in turn would tell Virgil to take care of it.

Ultimately it left Virgil in the untenable position of

having to have a talk with his official unofficial boss and tell him to cool his jets. Miles didn't like it.

But Virgil had other problems. So…

THE OTHER PROBLEM WAS THE LAND. TWO THOUSAND acres of prime farmland sitting along the Flatrock River in Shelby County, Indiana. Every single acre of the land now belonged to Virgil and Company.

Virgil and Company—an actual legal entity—was set in a trust, the trust itself wholly-owned and controlled by Virgil and Sandy. They took possession of the land almost by accident after discovering their adopted son, Jonas Donatti, was heir to a fortune. So they called their lawyer, formed a corporation, dumped the land into the trust and spent most of the winter celebrating their good luck and their newly formed family. Control of the trust would ultimately be passed on to their two sons, Jonas and Wyatt, who, years from now, after completing their respective educations, could do with it what they pleased. It'd be up to Virgil and Sandy to make sure they raised the boys with a set of values that'd keep the money pointed in the right direction, which they both agreed was outward, for the good of…something. They'd let the boys decide what that something was when the time came. For now, they were simply stewards.

The press tried to make a stink over the land and the

money it would generate, specifically how it ended up in Virgil's lap, but the stink didn't stick. They'd already adopted Jonas before they discovered his connection to the former owners of the land, owners who'd been killed during Virgil's previous case. It also helped that Virgil had publicly vowed never to frack the land. On principle, Virgil didn't have a problem with natural gas extraction. The problem was the methodology used in its removal. If and when he sold the land, he'd hold on to the mineral rights, ensuring the poison would stay out of the ground.

They formed the trust and put a name to it for two reasons: One, the lawyers and accountants told them no matter what they ended up doing with the land—there was no shortage of options—it'd be less of a tax hassle if they did it from a business perspective as opposed to a personal one. The other reason was simpler: They were all tired of referring to it as 'The Land.'

So Virgil and Company was born, which ended up making scant little difference. They still had tax issues to deal with, actual mounds of paperwork that sat on Virgil's desk growing higher by the month, and no one called it Virgil and Company. They all kept calling it 'The Land.'

Virgil was at home, sitting at his desk reviewing one of the mounds. Wyatt, now four months old, was tucked in a bassinet next to his desk, his arms batting playfully at the tiny multi-colored stuffed animals that hung from a mobile that swirled out of reach. Every once in a while he'd let out a little giggle and it made Virgil smile.

Virgil and Wyatt were alone in the house. Their live-in housekeeper and nanny, a fine lady by the name of Huma Moon, was at the movies with Jonas. Sandy was at the doctor getting what they hoped would be her final checkup before having her medical restrictions lifted. She'd been restricted because of the surgeries she had after Wyatt was born.

An Indiana National Guardsman Virgil had been hunting had viciously attacked her. The soldier, a guy named Decker, had injured her so badly that she had to have a field C-section on the floor of their own living room. During the procedure she almost bled out, but was saved by a last-minute blood transfusion from the governor's pilot, Richard Cool, as he made an emergency run to the hospital in the state helicopter. All together, the entire ordeal put a whole new take on the saying 'Keeping up with the Joneses.'

Anyhoo…the land.

The problem with the land wasn't so much the land itself, it was what to do with it…and when. The 'when' part of the equation turned out to matter. Spring was right around the corner and over the holidays Virgil and Sandy had entertained a number of offers from farming operations both large and small, some of whom Virgil knew from his previous case. The list had finally been narrowed down to two entities. Sunnydale Farms was one. The other was the remaining members of the Shelby County Co-op.

As the 'when' part of the equation crept closer by the

day, they knew they had to make their decision soon or the land would simply sit there all year earning them absolutely nothing. That was entirely unacceptable because Virgil and Sandy had to mortgage their house to pay the inheritance and back taxes on the land. If they didn't get someone to plant for them this spring, Virgil and Company would be no different than most any other farmer: Dirt-poor and land-rich. They could already feel the pinch.

It was an odd sensation to him…the money. While he had no actual money, he did have the land which appraised close to eight thousand dollars an acre which meant Virgil and Company's assets were close to sixteen million dollars. The thought of it made his head swim. They'd put it on the market almost immediately, but there hadn't been any serious offers…yet. So in order to minimize his tax bill, Virgil would have to declare himself a farmer—something that Murton seemed to enjoy to no end—to qualify for the farm tax credit. And because Virgil didn't know winter wheat from Shredded Wheat, it meant he'd need to get someone to plant and tend the harvest for at least one year. Maybe more. And it had to be someone he could trust. It was either that or they'd slowly go broke.

So. Virgil sat at his desk reviewing the proposals. The bids were all based on yield—how many bushels of corn, beans, wheat or whatever that could be harvested per acre—minus expenses. The yield mattered because it set a baseline for the future. If he could find a buyer who wanted to farm the land, he'd net roughly eight to ten million dollars after taxes.

But if he sold the land for other uses—housing, retail commercial ventures, industrial warehousing and manufacturing—then the value of the land would skyrocket. He wouldn't be looking at a sale amount of eight thousand an acre. He'd be staring down the barrel of thirty thousand per acre or more. And that math *really* made his head spin. He wouldn't only have money…

He'd have fuck-you money.

VIRGIL WAS SO CAUGHT UP IN LAND MANAGEMENT ISSUES that he didn't hear Sandy come in. She had her blonde hair pulled back in a ponytail and wore a colorful sleeveless spring dress and a pair of white Chuck's with no socks. She slid up behind him, placed her hands on his shoulders and ran them down inside his shirt, all the way to his stomach, then bit him on the earlobe.

Virgil relaxed back into his chair. He was so deeply in love with his wife he sometimes thought he might burst. But he wasn't beyond having a little fun with her, either. He dropped the papers on his desk, grabbed her arms and said, "Huma, I'm a happily married man. We can't keep going on like this."

He thought it was hilarious.

Sandy almost bit his ear off. "Very funny, mister. Maybe the three of you should run off to the islands together."

Virgil spun his chair around. "The three of us?"

Sandy sat down in his lap and wrapped her arms around his neck. "Yeah. You, Huma, and that big toothy weather person you never miss in the morning."

"There is nothing wrong with a little morning meteorology to start the day, especially since it looks like we're going to be farmers."

Sandy shook her head at him. "Then get up at four in the morning and start watching the Farm Report. Virgil, I love you. You're good at whatever you put your mind to. But we are not going to be farmers."

"We are on paper. Need to be for the tax credits. And don't let Murton hear you say that. I don't think he's had this much fun since…ever."

"He'll get over it." Then, "Ask me about my doctor appointment."

"How did it go?"

Sandy smiled at him. "He lifted the restrictions." Then, as if she'd not quite made her point, she added, "All the restrictions, Virgil." She bit her lower lip and raised her eyebrows at him.

He stood from the chair with Sandy in his arms.

"What are you doing?"

"I'm doing what any other farmer in my position

would do," Virgil said as he carried her over to the sofa. "I'm going to plant some seeds."

She almost rolled her eyes at him, the remark was so corny. But it *had* been longer than they'd ever gone without sex, spring was in the air, and the bottom line was this: Farmers or not, it was time to plow.

CHAPTER THREE

Patty Doyle, a senior at Indiana University in Bloomington, decided to skip her final class of the day, a three-hour mind-numbingly tedious lecture on the ethical and moral ramifications of ancient archaeological excavations. She'd spent the past three-and-a-half years learning everything the school had to offer regarding archaeology and was almost done. She'd received a fine education, and now, in her final semester before graduating, she was winding down.

Patty thought the class itself was a joke. For three years they taught you everything you needed to know to be part of a team that traveled the world, exploring and recovering artifacts from places that hadn't been seen for thousands of years, then, right when you were about to graduate, they hit you with a full semester of ethics and morals.

The class may as well have been called *Here's how to do it and why you shouldn't-101*. The premise of the entire class was elementary, both in substance and presentation. Modern archaeology was about history, but it was also a bit of a money grab. The grab usually went something like this: The major digs were funded through grants, a tomb or historical site with some significance was revealed, the site packed with precious metals and jewels often valued in the hundreds of millions of dollars. These finds were pulled out of the ground and then out of the country, carted off to various museums and universities, usually in the U.S. But plenty of money managed to change hands along the way.

So what? Patty thought. Isn't that why they called it capitalism? Her job dealt with the discovery, not the political or social-economical ramifications of what happened afterward. She'd let others worry and debate the ethics of the whole affair. The space program had managed to turn the moon into a giant dumping ground but no one accused NASA of littering, did they? In any event, no class today. Besides, the point had been made during the first hour of day one. Everything else had been so repetitive Patty thought she might have to wear a neck brace and prop her eyes open with toothpicks to stay upright and awake.

So instead of going to class, Patty decided to take some time to herself. She had a package coming in at the post office and it needed her signature. She'd take care of that and then go for a run.

She dressed in her running clothes, got in her car and headed out to the woods. She often did her workouts on the city streets around the Bloomington area, but every once in a while she enjoyed the extra challenge of the beautiful wooded trails Brown County offered. Today was one of those days. Besides, the homeless population in and around Bloomington had gotten to the point that if you were out on the streets for five minutes you got hit up for food or money every half-block. No thanks. Today was going to be enjoyed the way it should…in the woods, with Mother Nature.

The way it turned out, Patty Doyle should have stuck to the streets and dealt with the mendicants and moochers. Or better yet, gone to class. After her stop at the post office—the package still hadn't arrived—she headed out of town toward the Yellowwood state forest not far from the quaint little town of Nashville. She failed to notice the vehicle following her. She might have if she'd been paying better attention, but she had too many things on her mind, chief among them, how to gently, but effectively rid herself of her boyfriend, Nate Morgan. That was another thing that was winding down. It had in fact, already unwound. Nate, god bless him, hadn't noticed.

SHE DID FIVE MILES THROUGH THE WOODED TRAILS, barely breaking a sweat. She was in the prime of her life and in the best shape ever. It hadn't always been that way. By the end of her first year she wasn't worried about the so-called freshman fifteen—the extra fifteen pounds that everyone says freshmen put on from bad food and too much beer—she was worried about the freshman fifty. So she buckled down, started eating healthy, and took up running. It'd taken her two years to get the extra weight off and now she not only felt great, she looked it too. Patty Doyle would turn your head if she happened by.

She liked it...her ability to turn heads. Nate Morgan didn't like it at all. Patty thought Nate was an okay sort of guy, but it wasn't like they were going to get married. He'd been there for her when she'd struggled with the weight and that mattered to her. But he was going to be a doctor—a general practitioner, no less—and she was going to travel the world. Not a good mix. Plus, ever since she'd lost the weight and gotten herself in shape, she wasn't only turning heads, she was getting offers. Serious offers. She liked it; the attention.

And Nate, well, he was a whiner. Every time another man even looked her way, Nate would whine about it in his nasally voice. She was so tired of it she wanted to scream every time he opened his mouth. They were going out to dinner tonight. She'd do her best to let him down easy.

He'd still whine though.

Whatever. Time to move on. Their lives were moving

in different directions and it was time to get up and get on with her own.

But when Patty Doyle got back to her car, she suddenly discovered she wasn't going anywhere, at least not right away.

She had a flat tire.

She leaned against the side of her car, opened her water bottle and drank the entire container dry. Might need the hydration after all.

Her car was parked outside the entrance to the state forest and no other vehicles were in sight. When she unlocked the glove box and checked her phone she couldn't get a signal. Who would she call anyway? Nate? No thank you. He'd whine about missing class and the fifteen-mile drive out to get her. Then he'd whine about changing the tire. He'd whine until Patty slit her own throat so she didn't have to listen to it anymore.

Easy Patty, she told herself. Slit your own throat? Maybe she'd waited a little too long to give Nate the old heave-ho. She'd skip dinner and talk to him as soon as she got back.

She'd never changed a tire before, but how hard could it be? She'd seen her uncle do it more than once. She unlocked the trunk with her keys and then removed the jack, lug wrench, and spare. The jack was some sort of scissor contraption with a nub that stuck out on one side. She placed the jack behind the wheel and turned the nub with her fingers until the jack expanded and met the frame. But there was a problem. The lug wrench didn't fit the nub, and even if it had, she'd only be able to twist it a half-turn at a time. That couldn't be right. Wasn't there supposed to be a crank to raise the jack? She thought so. When she dug around in the trunk she discovered she didn't have it. Now what?

She checked her phone again. Still no signal. She was about to put everything back in the trunk and start jogging down the road when an old pickup truck turned in and stopped next to her.

Her first thought was she could be in real trouble here…out in the middle of nowhere, alone with a flat tire. She held the lug wrench in her hand and gave the truck a hard stare, half of her wanting it to continue on its way, the other half glad it stopped. There were two men in the truck. The driver rolled down his window—the truck was so old he actually had to crank the window down by hand, the gears inside the door creaking as the glass screeched into the door frame. The noise reminded her of Nate's voice.

With the window down the glare of the sun against the glass went out of her eyes and she could see the men clearly and almost laughed at the absurdity of her own thoughts only moments ago. If she'd ever seen two more harmless looking men than these, she couldn't recall where or when.

"Looks like you've got a little problem," the driver said. He smiled when he spoke, his eyes fixed on the flat tire. "Take some help from a couple of old geezers?"

Patty relaxed her grip on the lug wrench, embarrassed by the hard stare she had given the men when they pulled over to help. "I guess I'm not in much of a position to say no. Don't ask me how, but it looks like I'm missing the crank for the jack."

The driver's smile remained in place, his eyes occasionally checking the rearview mirror. The passenger seemed to be looking at everything in sight except Patty. He stepped out of the truck without saying a word and walked around the front of the vehicle and inspected the tire.

When he returned from the rear of the pickup he carried a hydraulic floor jack, the kind you see in an automotive repair shop or on pit-road during a NASCAR racing event. He set it under the frame, inserted the handle and began to take the weight off the wheel. When Patty turned to watch him work, the driver stepped out and moved to help his partner. He looked at Patty.

"Mind if I borrow that lug wrench? Got to loosen the lugs before the tire comes off the ground. I'd use my own, but the lugs on the truck are sized differently than yours. Miss?"

Patty glanced at the truck's wheels. Were they sized differently? She couldn't tell. She suddenly had a funny feeling. She didn't want to give up her only means of protection and at the same time she didn't want to offend the very men who had stopped to help her in her time of need. She looked at the wrench in her hand as if the answers she sought were there instead of her gut. Then she thought, give it a rest, girl. The world is full of kind and decent people who only want to help. Two of them are demonstrating that right now. Besides, both men had to be at least sixty-five years old. If nothing else she'd be a half-mile down the road before they could turn their truck around.

"Sorry. Here." She held the wrench out. The driver took it gently, winked at her, then started in on the lugs. Five minutes later the tire was swapped out. The truck's passenger twisted the handle of the hydraulic jack and Patty's car settled down to the pavement.

"There you go," the driver said. "Fit as a fiddle. Boy, that makes me sound old doesn't it? What is it kids say these days? Good to go, or something like that? Come on, let's get the flat in your trunk and you can be on your way. I don't see any sidewall damage. You must have picked up a nail along the way. I'll bet they can patch it up and you can use it for your spare. The tire we put on looks brand new. Still got the teats on it. Might want to think about getting a crank for that scissor jack, too."

The driver of the truck was a talker, Patty thought. The other man hadn't said a word the entire time. Maybe he had a speech impediment, or something. No matter, she was grateful for the help. "Thank you, I will." She grabbed the useless scissor jack, moved to the rear of her car and tossed it in the trunk.

The driver of the truck let out a chuckle. "Hold on there," he said, placing the lug wrench and flat tire on the ground behind him. "The tire's got to go in the wheel well first. If you don't, everything will rattle around back there and make a hell of a racket every time you hit a bump or turn a corner." He reached in and pulled out the jack and handed it to her. The other man was putting the floor jack back in the bed of the truck.

The driver picked up the flat and centered it in the well of the trunk, then grabbed the jack and set it in the center of the wheel before closing the lid.

Patty turned and looked at the ground. Where was the lug wrench? Had he placed that in the trunk already? No, she was sure he hadn't. A sickness rolled through her gut with tremendous speed. Patty realized the sickness had been there all along. She simply hadn't been paying attention. She reached for her phone but it was too late. The passenger of the truck was on her, moving much faster than a man his age should have been able to move. When he finally spoke, Patty feared it might be the last words she ever heard in her life.

"Trying to find this?" he said. The look on his face was unmistakable.

When Patty turned to run he swung the lug wrench

across her lower back and she dropped to her knees, her phone skittering away under the car. The pain was so intense no sound escaped her throat, the look on her face like that of a woman who'd walked through a plate glass window. Then she took a kick in the stomach and fell forward, rolling onto her side. Two minutes later she was gagged, taped, and strapped down under a tarp in the bed of the truck. The passenger of the truck pulled Patty's keys from the trunk lock, got in her car and fired it up. He nodded to the truck driver as they drove away.

And just like that, Patty Doyle was gone.

CHAPTER FOUR

Wyatt slept through the plowing, which both surprised and disappointed Virgil. He said something to Sandy about it as they were getting cleaned up. "Maybe we should take him to the doctor and have his hearing checked."

Sandy, in keeping with the pre-festivities farm theme gave him a flat stare and said, "Maybe your implement isn't as big as you think."

"Hey…"

"Relax, Mr. Green Jeans. I'm messing with ya. Your implement is perfect. In fact, if it was any bigger, I probably wouldn't be able to walk." She fanned her face with her fingertips and with a mock southern accent said, "Why, I can barely stand as it is."

Virgil waved her off. "Yeah, yeah. Keep talking." He turned to leave but Sandy chased him down and jumped on his back, wrapping him up with her arms and legs. They fell on the bed and rolled around laughing like a couple of kids. They weren't very loud, but the noise woke Wyatt.

And Virgil thought, *hmm…*

SANDY WENT TO GET THEIR SON AND AS VIRGIL WAS pulling on his boots his phone buzzed at him. He grabbed it from his pants pocket, checked the screen and saw it was Delroy.

Delroy Rouche was Virgil's partner and manager of the bar they owned, a joint called Jonesy's Rastabarian in downtown Indianapolis. It had always been called Jonesy's, but when Delroy and their head chef, Robert Whyte, both Jamaicans, came to work for Virgil and his late father, Mason, they turned what would have otherwise been a local tavern into one of the hottest authentic Jamaican themed bars in the city, if not the entire Midwest. On weekends during the summer months, they drew crowds from as far away as Chicago and Cincinnati. When Mason died, he left his share of the bar to Virgil, Murton, Delroy, and Robert, making them all partners.

Virgil knew that Delroy and Robert were the draw, so when Delroy suggested the name change, Virgil said yes. He didn't really have a say in the matter, as he and Murton didn't devote much time to the daily operations since he'd gone back to work for the state, taking Murton along for the ride.

"Hey, Delroy. What's up?"

"Dat what I'd like to know, mon. Too bad nobody tell me anyting these days."

Virgil learned a long time ago that when speaking with a Jamaican you had to let them get to the subject at hand in their own way…and on their own timetable.

"I'm not sure what you mean."

"Delroy not surprised. Maybe you should come over. Murton's back."

"How is he?"

"It getting worse every time he go away, mon. Robert and me, we talk about it. Afraid if he keep going, one day he leave and dat be dat. No more Murton."

"He seemed fine to me, last time we spoke."

"When was dat, mon?"

Good point, Virgil thought. He ignored the question. "I'll be there as soon as I can. Don't let him leave."

He thought Delroy might give him a smart-assed Jamaican response, something along the lines of, 'How I do dat, me?' But he simply hung up.

VIRGIL FROWNED AT THE PHONE FOR A MOMENT, THEN kissed his wife and infant son good-bye, fired up his Ford Raptor and headed downtown. Once he was on his way, he pulled out his phone and punched in the number for Paul Gibson, an agent for Homeland Security.

A few months ago, after wrapping up their case down in Shelby County, Gibson had delivered a message to Murton. He had, in fact, done much more than deliver a message…he'd brought in agency cleaners and disposed of the body after Murton had tracked down Decker and killed him. If that wasn't enough, the cleaners took care of Decker while Murton and the governor of the state of Indiana sat in a limo and talked about current events.

Gibson didn't answer his phone, so Virgil left him a voice message and asked him to call back as soon as possible.

The message Gibson delivered to Murton had been, in typical federal form, cryptic. An envelope got passed, the contents nothing more than a residential address in Louisville, Kentucky, and a photograph of Murton's long lost father, Ralph Wheeler.

According to Gibson, a group of Russians had been backing the play in Shelby County in support of the now-defunct fracking operation. Also according to Gibson, the same group of Russians were supposedly involved in the theft of nuclear pharmaceuticals from a compounding company out of Louisville. Virgil spent the better part of a month trekking across the state from South Bend to Evansville and all points in between looking into the theft, checking hospitals and university research facilities, matching actual inventory to shipping records. In the end, it turned out to be nothing more than a line item clerical error on an inventory management spreadsheet.

Virgil had gone to Louisville, hooked up with his Kentucky counterpart and friend, a state detective by the name of Jack Grady, and read the riot act to the pharmaceutical company's executives. After a bit of toe-in-the-dirt apologies from the executives and their promise of repayment to the states of Kentucky and Indiana for expenses incurred during the investigation, Virgil and Grady went away.

"I would have been satisfied with an apology," Virgil said. "I can't believe you got them to agree to pay for the investigation."

Grady shrugged. "I took a shot. My boss wanted me to. Little surprised myself, tell you the truth. Too bad I won't see any of that money. A bonus would be nice."

Virgil laughed. "Yeah, like that would ever happen."

"Go ahead and laugh. Easy for you, isn't it?"

They were walking out to Grady's car. He'd give Virgil a ride back to the airport where Cool was waiting with the state helicopter. Virgil stopped. "What do you mean, easy for me?"

This time Grady laughed. "You're kidding, right?"

"What are you talking about?"

"You're the talk of the Tri-state, Jonesy. Everyone in the department knows you've got fuck-you money."

Virgil waved his hands. "That's what everyone thinks, but I don't. I have the land, but there's a big difference.

It's not as simple as it sounds. The land is *costing* me money. I'm about to go broke."

"Yeah, yeah," Grady said. "My heart bleeds. You've got it made. You've got the land, you've got a state helicopter at your disposal, your wife is hotter than anything I've ever—"

Virgil looked at him. "Easy, Jack. You're getting a little wound up."

"You know when the last time I got to fly on Kentucky's State helicopter? Wait, don't answer. I'll tell you. Never."

"Does Kentucky have a state helicopter?"

"I don't know. They won't tell me. Hey, speaking of state helicopters, how is that Cool motherfucker these days?"

Like that, all the way to the airport.

As Virgil drove to the bar, his thoughts remained focused on the photo of Murton's father. He thought, though he couldn't prove, Agent Gibson had an agenda, one he was not yet ready to divulge. In the meantime he was dangling bait in front of Murton's nose, waiting for the perfect opportunity to yank the rod and set the hook.

Enough already.

It was, Virgil thought, time to cut bait and motor back to shore.

An hour later he went in through the back kitchen entrance, said hello to Robert and his sous chefs, then made his way out to the main bar. The patron area of the bar was long and narrow with high-back mahogany booths along the entire length of one wall. The bar itself sat opposite the booths with an aisle-way between the two sides. The aisle was wide enough for a row of four-top tables that ran in a single line, front to back. A large mirror filled the entire wall behind the bar and made the whole place look bigger than it actually was. Small stained glass light fixtures hung low over the booths and a soft blue neon sign above the bar mirror advertised 'Warm Beer & Lousy Food.' An elevated stage at the back between the kitchen entrance and the restrooms provided enough room for the Reggae house band that played from midweek through the weekend.

Delroy was tending bar and when he saw Virgil come in he tossed a rag over his shoulder, walked over and bumped fists with him. "Respect, mon."

"Respect, Delroy." Then, right to it. "Where is he?"

Delroy was bald, wore small hoop earrings and had dark brown eyes that were as soft as the voice he used with almost every female customer that walked through the door. He had more marriage proposals than anyone could keep track of. If you were a single female in or near Indy and liked to hit a bar every now and again, you knew who Delroy was. He tipped his eyes up at the office area above the main stage. "Up with Becky." Becky Taylor was Murton's girlfriend and a contracted agent for the MCU. "It's quieted down a little. They might be between rounds."

"That bad?"

Before Delroy could answer the office door opened then slammed shut. Murton took the steps two at a time and walked past Virgil and Delroy without saying a word. He went through the kitchen and a few seconds later they heard the back door slam shut.

Delroy looked at Virgil. "What dat you just ask me, mon?"

"Would you go and check on Becky? See if she needs anything."

"Yeah, mon, but let me say this first: How many times dat man save your life, you?"

"Too many to count, Delroy. You know that."

"Maybe it not for me to say, but Murton and Becky, you and Sandy…and now your kids? All of you the only family me and Robert have left."

Virgil cocked his head. "What are you saying, Delroy?"

"I'm saying you've been so taken up with this new land of yours dat you don't see the ground you're standing on, mon. It shifting right beneath your feet."

"What?"

"Our family is coming apart a little bit every day. You don't see it because you're not looking."

Virgil bit the inside corner of his lip. "Delroy, I think you might be exaggerating a little."

Delroy shook his head and began wiping the bar, more out of frustration than anything else. "Tink what you want, mon. But I tell you this: Delroy not see a man hurt dat much since I watch you bury your father." Then he turned to go check on Becky. He stopped at the foot of the stairs and looked back at Virgil. "Dat your bredren just walk out dat door. It won't be long we'll never see him again." Delroy made a fist and tapped himself twice on his stomach. "It not simply a gut feeling. Hear me when I tell you this: Someting bad coming our way, Virgil Jones. Maybe it already here."

Virgil looked at his Jamaican friend for a moment and saw the fear in his eyes. He nodded and walked out back to find Murton, but he was already gone. When Virgil tried to call him, Murton's phone went straight to voice mail.

CHAPTER FIVE

The crew, together again. It happened only a few times a year, if that. Their last job was over eight months ago, and they were ready. Itchy. They didn't do side jobs on their own, and they stuck to every plan like it was their religion. So far it had kept them all safe...and made them not quite rich. The not-quite part kept them going.

They approached each job as if it were their last, they kept emergency bottom-level identification—passports, credit cards and ten thousand in cash—with them at all times in case things went south. They never had, at least not yet. But the crew was always ready. If someone walked through the door and looked at one of them crooked they'd drop everything and walk away. The passports, credit cards and cash could get them out of the country to destinations they shared with no one, and their numbered accounts in the off-shore banks ensured they could live in comfort until they met up again...or not.

They were building for the future. They were smart about it, and almost there.

They traveled in a different vehicle for each job, a dependable used car purchased with fake IDs and wads of cash. This time it was a ten-year-old SUV with over one hundred thousand on the odometer. They all lived within an hour of each other near Portland, Oregon, and this job would be their biggest yet. But they had to get there first and they had a long way to go. Flying was not an option, especially with the guns. Too much of a paper trail.

When the last of them was ready and their gear was stowed they headed east, all the way to Kentucky. If the drive didn't kill them, they'd already decided the job might. But if they pulled it off, they'd be set for life and out of the crosshairs for good. They all knew it going in, so there was no sense in talking about it.

They took I-80 to Cheyenne, dropped down to Denver on I-25 and picked up I-70 all the way to St. Louis, then I-64 into Louisville. They took turns driving, stayed in the right lane with the cruise control set no more than three miles an hour over the limit. Getting pulled over wouldn't have been the end of the world...for them, anyway. It'd be a different story for the cop.

But the cops left them alone and the entire trip took thirty-nine hours, the only stops along the way for food, gas, piss, and cigarettes. They checked into a motel that took cash and didn't ask bothersome questions about vehicle tags, place of origin, or the purpose of their visit. They had to meet the old man in twenty-four hours. They went to their separate rooms and slept for twelve hours straight, then, finally, got down to it.

And things went a little sideways right out of the gate.

THE LEADER OF THE CREW, ARMON REIF, WAS BORN IN Germany before the wall came down to parents who were laborers by day, and agents of change by night. Their night work got them killed by the Stasi—one of the most hated and feared institutions of the East German communist government—and Armon, their only child, got shipped off to an Aunt who considered her former brother-in-law a dissident pig. Over the years Reif pieced together that his Aunt was an informer for the Stasi, and later discovered it'd been her that whispered into someone's ear about his parents. He kept his mouth shut, mostly because he was still a kid, but the pig comments were unbearable. They ate away at him like a little worm, year after year, the Aunt growing crustier with time and age.

When the wall finally fell in '89, Reif, now a young man, decided he'd had enough. He walked up behind her one evening without much thought at all and put the business end of a meat cleaver through the top of her head as she sat at the kitchen table. She fell face-first into her bowl of soup, the cleaver sticking out of her head like an ax from the chopping block out back. She blew one fat bubble in her creamy potato soup that sounded, Reif thought, a little like a wet fart. Then…nothing. She was gone.

With the chaos of the wall coming down and the demands placed on the authorities over the reunification process, nobody really gave two shits about an old lady who turned out to be a Stasi informant. Someone said it looked like she got what she deserved. Someone else thought she might have had a relative living with her…a young man, maybe? Then someone with some authority who was short on both manpower and patience said to hell with it and they buried her, then forgot about her. By that time Reif was halfway across the ocean, headed for North America.

And in the clear.

HE LANDED IN CANADA, STAYED LONG ENOUGH TO become an official Canuck, then emigrated to the U.S. and settled in the Northwest with dual citizenship. He spent a few years doing odd jobs, and stayed out of trouble. Feeling safe on the other side of the world, he worked on his language skills by telling stories of the old country, the work and subsequent death of his parents, and one night over too many drinks, the death of his Aunt. The next day he was introduced to a guy who knew a guy who had a small problem. Reif made the problem go away, collected a nice fat envelope for a few hours of work, and didn't give it a second thought.

Reif didn't know it, but he'd made an impression.

The guy, it turned out, not only had the occasional problem, he had associates who had problems from time to time as well. Reif put a crew together and over the years they handled them all. The jobs got bigger and the envelopes became briefcases, then eventually duffel bags, fatter and heavier every time.

They piled into the SUV, Reif at the wheel, and made their way back west on 64 out to a dry quarry set deep in the hills of southern Indiana. They were rested, but not quite fresh. Reif parked the SUV nose-first near the lip of the quarry and they all got out, hovering near the front of the vehicle. The other four, Paul Fischer, Eric Chase, Randy Stone, and Evan Reed had been with Reif for years. Reif had found Chase on his own, and later Chase had recommended Stone, and so on, all the way down to Fischer, who'd been brought in on Reed's say so.

With the exception of Reif, each of them had a specialty, all thanks to the generosity of the United States military. They each had something else in common, something Reif appreciated and could work with. They'd all been dishonorably discharged from various branches of the United States military. There was, Reif thought, nothing better than a well-trained rule bender.

The quarry was shaped like a lopsided bowl, cliff-steep all the way around, not quite a mile across, with a shallow-banked access area at the end of a wide dirt path, the same path where Reif had parked the SUV. He wanted to site the long guns, and take care of a problem that'd popped up unexpectedly. The problem had been discovered by Chase and passed quietly to Reif a week ago.

"Let's get the guns set up," Reif said.

Reed, Fischer, Chase, and Stone moved to the back of the SUV and got the guns and ammunition. The rifles were all the same…Heckler & Koch MSG90's chambered for standard 7.62 NATO rounds, and scoped with the Hensoldt ZF 6×42. Their accuracy was good up to about eight hundred meters with a competent trigger man. They brought the guns around to the front of the truck and got them loaded and ready.

"Gonna make some noise," Stone said to no one in particular.

"Take a look around, dude," Chase said. "We're all alone." He slapped a loaded magazine into the rifle, pulled back the charging handle to seat a round, pointed the rifle at nothing down in the bowl, and popped off three rounds in a row. "Welcome to Indiana."

Reif put his arm around Chase's shoulders, then took

the gun from his hands. "Let's not make any more noise than we have to." He put the gun to his shoulder and looked out at the quarry through the scope for a few seconds, then gave the rifle back to Chase. "Not much down there. We're going to need something to aim at. Wait here for a minute."

He went back to the SUV and looked for something they could use as a target. A hubcap would have been ideal, but the SUV didn't have any. He dug around in the back and finding nothing suitable, he moved to the front and pulled the headrest from the passenger seat. He tossed it to Fischer. "Count out three hundred yards and plant this in the dirt." Then, before Fischer could say anything, Reif took the rifle from Chase, turned to the others and said, "Okay, safety first. Get those mags out and clear the chambers. No one touches anything until Fischer is clear."

The others unloaded the guns and set them back in their cases. Fischer headed down into the bowl, counting his steps as he went. The others stood silently and watched him and when he was about a hundred yards out, Reif lit a cigarette and locked eyes with Reed and held his stare until the other man looked away.

Fischer stopped about halfway out and looked back over his shoulder. He had a funny feeling, but no one was moving. They weren't even looking at him. He turned around and kept going.

"What'd he do?" Stone asked.

Reif took a long drag on his cigarette, dropped it in the

dirt and snuffed it out with the toe of his boot. "Broke the main rule." He looked at Reed. "Took a side job, didn't he, Evan? That smash and grab in Northern Cali last month? How many guns did he pull out? He could have brought us all down."

"Still might," Stone said. "Now that the ATF is looking."

"He got out clean. And even if he hadn't, he wouldn't have given us up."

"Bullshit," Reif said. "He's got enough on all of us that he'd be out walking and talking like a free man while the rest of us sit in solitary. That what you want?"

Reed tipped his head to the side and tried a brotherly grin. "C'mon, Reif. Fisch is solid. I brought him in."

Reif picked up the rifle Chase had fired earlier and handed it to him. "I know. That's why you're going to take him out."

"No way, Reif. I served with him. He's like a brother to me, man."

Reif pulled a Beretta M9 from the back of his belt and pointed it at Reed. "Get down on the ground and get to it."

Reed looked at Fischer off in the distance as he kicked at the dirt, trying to push the rods of the headrest into the ground. Reed looked back at his boss, a little sorrow in his voice now. "Reif…"

Reif clicked the safety off and pointed the gun at Reed's face. "Him or you. No, wait a minute, that's not quite right. Definitely him. You're still a maybe."

Reed looked at the others, but they were no help. He got down in the dirt, rested the barrel on the bi-pod and took aim. Reif walked over and squatted down next to him, the Beretta resting casually across his knee, pointed directly at the side of Reed's head.

"Hey, Reed?"

Reed had his eye to the scope and kept it there. "What?"

"If you miss, you're a dead man."

Reed was already a dead man. He simply didn't know it. He took a deep breath and slipped his finger into the trigger guard. He exhaled slowly until almost all the air was out of his lungs. When his heart was between beats, he pulled the trigger smoothly, the way they'd taught him in the army.

The standard NATO 7.62x51 mm round travels almost three thousand feet per second. Fischer was three hundred yards away. He was dead before the ejected shell casing hit the dirt. Reed was still looking through the scope when Reif fired the Beretta. It took the side of his head off.

Stone jumped when Reif pulled the trigger. He quietly slipped his hand behind his back. Reif knew what he was doing without even looking at him.

"Relax Randy. Two steps up the ladder should do it, don't you think?" He put the gun back in his belt and remained facing away from Randy Stone. The message was twofold and clear: I trust you, and we're done.

Stone left his gun in his belt. "I should hope so, you crazy bastard."

Reif turned and smiled at him. "We never could have trusted either of them again. You know that."

Stone nodded. "I do. But now we're going to be shorthanded."

"We can handle it," Reif said. "And now the split is better for all of us."

"What about Gus?"

Gus was their current boss, and he was no more than a voice on the other end of the phone. None of them had ever met Gus. He was simply a voice that told them where to go and when. He was polite, soft-spoken, and a complete mystery to Reif. Gus wasn't even his real name…it was simply a name they'd given him because they didn't know his real name and he reminded them of Gustavo Fring from the television show, Breaking Bad. And because the money had never failed to show up when the voice said it would, they did what they were told.

Chase looked at the two dead men. "What about them?"

Reif tipped his head toward the SUV. "You'll find shovels and a pick in the back, under the gear. Drag Fischer up here. The ground's softer. They don't have to go in too deep, but we've got to cover them up. We're going to be around for a while."

The burial process took a little longer than any of them thought it would, the ground only slightly softer at the top of the bowl. Reif, being the good leader he was, did his share of the digging. When they were finished they loaded the shovels and the guns back into the SUV, turned around and headed back to the motel. Reif was in the passenger seat, sweating and breathing hard. No one said a word on the way back, but Chase and Stone touched eyes a few times in the rear-view mirror.

CHAPTER SIX

Patty Doyle's abductors took her to an abandoned house out in the country, the long gravel drive pitted and overgrown with weeds, the yard unkempt with grass that was so clumped and tall it looked like sagebrush blown in from the northwestern part of the country. A portion of the roof was missing, its rafters laid bare to the elements. Most of the windows had either been removed or had been broken out by vandals. A large Maple tree stood so close to one corner of the structure its giant limbs not only touched the roof, they crawled across its surface before elbowing upward across the peak. Nail holes on the siding wept rust-colored stains that looked like blood vessels under the pellucid skin of a neglected comatose patient in a long-term care facility.

The men parked their vehicles close to the house then pulled back the tarpaulin that covered Doyle. Her eyes were unblinking, wide with fear and thoughts of what the men had planned for her. When she tried to speak the sounds that came from her throat were muffled and unintelligible. A gag was tight around her mouth, her cheeks pulled back, her teeth exposed in panic and fear, a sharp contrast to her pitiful cries that were no louder than the breeze that whistled through the broken hull of the house. When they dragged her from the bed of the truck she fell flat on her back, the restraints preventing her from protecting herself. A sharp pain screwed itself through her side and made her eyes water. Neither of the men seemed to take notice, their thoughts elsewhere, their task at hand defined by something she couldn't imagine.

The driver of the truck pulled the keys from the ignition and jangled them merrily in his hand as he walked toward the house, the way someone might if they'd recently returned home from a day at the ballpark or an afternoon movie. The other man picked up Patty and hefted her across a shoulder as though she were a roll of carpet, then followed his partner.

He carried her feet first, her abdomen pressed tight across the top of his shoulder. He had one arm over the backs of her thighs, the other resting on the thin fabric that covered her ass.

Patty's head hung down close to his back and she smelled an odor she'd normally associate with an unsanitary highway rest stop. She'd been to Egypt two summers in a row, participating in school-sponsored archaeology digs. For months she'd labor in the hot sun uncovering tiny pieces of the past. She'd once found a tibia, and then, after days of careful digging, a human skull. She wondered about the skull for months. Who had that person been? What had their life been like? Did they know they were about to die? Had it been sickness that killed them, or violence?

She thought of her childhood and her mother, almost as if she were safe and warm, held in the light of her own past, her mother's indiscretions and cavalier attitude toward the sanctity of marriage suddenly forgiven. Then another thought, a strange one out of nowhere. Her mother's favorite song had always been Don McLean's *American Pie*, and when that thought hit her the lyrics of the song began to run through her head:

'This'll be the day that I die, this'll be the day that I die…'

EVEN THROUGH HER FEAR—OR PERHAPS BECAUSE OF IT— Patty knew she was in real trouble because the men hadn't bothered to disguise themselves in any way. That meant only one thing. They wouldn't have to worry about Patty providing the authorities with information of the vehicle that stopped or the physical descriptions of the men who'd presented themselves as kind and decent strangers, helpful in her time of need, men who had suddenly and viciously turned to monsters. They'd do what they were going to do, then kill her and bury her. She wouldn't be the first I.U. student to disappear without a trace. She probably wouldn't be the last.

She tilted her head away from the man who carried her and tried to get a look at her surroundings. The man felt her move and let his thumb slide underneath the fabric of her shorts, right at the bottom of her ass. When Patty tried to wiggle away from his touch he slid his hand deeper under the fabric. Patty choked back the bile at the base of her throat and stopped wiggling. The man took his hand away. Mostly.

The inside of the house smelled of mold and animal droppings. The floorboards creaked when the men walked across the bare planks. They moved through the house and into the kitchen. The smell was so bad Patty thought she might die right then and there. If she vomited from the smell, she'd choke to death because of the gag. She had to force herself to breathe through her mouth, her breath whistling through her teeth.

She heard the keys again and for a brief moment, as if he wanted her to see, the man who held her turned around and Patty watched as the other man unlocked a large padlock and swung the hasp away from the frame of the door. When he opened the door and turned on the light she saw a set of stairs that descended into a basement. The back side of the door and the walls on either side of the steps were covered with a dark-colored foam that looked like it had been constructed by placing small pyramids next to each other. Though she'd never actually seen it before, Patty immediately knew what it was.

Sound insulating foam. She knew if she ended up in that basement, she'd never see the light of day again. She started to moan and wiggle. That got her the hand again.

The fingers inside her shorts caused something inside her to shift. Panic and fear were replaced with rage. The new and improved Patty, the Patty who could turn your head wasn't the type of girl to mess with. Not when she was pissed. So Patty did the only thing she could do in the moment. It wasn't much, but it was all she had.

She pissed.

THE MAN WHO HELD HER ACROSS HIS SHOULDER LIKE A roll of carpet felt the wetness flow across his hand and for an instant—no more than a fraction of a second, really—had the thought that the presence of his hand inside her shorts was a source of sexual arousal for the woman. Then the reality of the event took over and he realized not only was he being urinated on, he'd deluded himself into thinking his touch had been a wellspring of desire no matter the circumstances, in effect making him a willing participant of his own humiliation.

He rolled Patty off his shoulder and she fell to the floor with a thud, the pain in her side flaring once again, but when she saw the look on the man's face she knew she'd scored a victory, no matter how minor.

The other man turned around at the sound of the thud. "What the hell are you doing?"

"The bitch took a piss on me. I'm covered in it." He wiped his hand against his pants and tried to brush the moisture away from the side of his shirt.

"That don't matter now. Let's get her downstairs. Grab her feet. I'll take her arms. We don't want any of the sound barrier ripped away." He bent down and grabbed Patty's arms. "Let's go."

The pee-soaked man grabbed Patty's feet and together they hoisted her into the air. "You got no idea what's happening here, sweet cheeks. But pull a stunt like that again and see what happens."

Patty pulled her lips back and exposed as much of her teeth as possible. Then she opened her eyes as wide as she could and stared at the man until he looked away.

Patty Doyle…still turning heads, anyway she could.

When they had her in the air, she let her body go as limp as possible, her ass low to the ground, effectively making the men work much harder to pick her up. They had to raise their arms higher than normal because they had her taped at the wrists, thighs and ankles, which meant their hands were close together as well. When they got her up both men ended up with their hands almost all the way up to their own faces. Patty, who'd taken two years to get herself in the best shape of her life, gave it everything she had.

When the men began moving toward the basement stairs she started pushing against the man who held her arms, which caused him to be out of sync with his partner. That gave her enough leverage to straighten her body and like a shot, she kicked as hard as she could, her feet connecting with the piss-covered man's face.

But he'd managed to turn his head at the last second, the blow catching him mostly on the brow and the side of his head. He dropped her feet and brought his hands up to his face. When he did, Patty used her core strength again. With her butt on the ground, she used both legs and kicked him in the groin as hard as she could. This time it wasn't a glancing blow. The man fell to his knees, the blood draining away from his face like someone had turned his faucet wide open. She yanked her hands free from the other man, rolled, and during the commotion managed to struggle to her feet. Her back was only inches from the basement door, but what was she going to do? Hop away?

That's when she heard the man who'd held her by her wrists say 'to hell with it.' He took two steps forward and pushed Patty down the stairs. She knew she was in for a ride, so she let her body go limp. In all likelihood the sound-proof foam saved her life. But when she peed again, this time it wasn't on purpose.

WITH THE WOMAN TUCKED SAFELY AWAY IN THE basement, the men moved her car behind the house and covered it with brush from the overgrown yard. Then they got in their truck and headed down the long drive to the road. Neither of them had done anything like this before. They were skittish…and a little surprised by the amount of fight the young woman had put up.

The passenger held his stomach. "It feels like my balls are floating around next to my liver."

The driver of the truck glanced at his partner and laughed as he turned out on the road, almost clipping a mail delivery truck in the process. The road was gravel and the mail truck swerved hard and for a moment they thought it might roll. But the driver managed to get it straightened out. It was a good effort on the driver's part, except the stress of the over-correction was too much for one of the front tires. When it blew, the mail truck veered to the side and nosed into the ditch, steam pouring out of the radiator from the impact with the embankment. The two men turned in the opposite direction and when they glanced in the rearview mirrors they saw the mail delivery driver stick his arm out the window and shoot them the bone.

"What a punk," the passenger said. "Remember when mailmen wore uniforms and were considerate and kind? Now they've got ponytails like a girl, barbed wire tats, and hoops coming out of their noses."

The driver hit the gas and accelerated away. "Don't know nothing about tats. Nose hoops either. I'll tell you what I do know. You almost got your ass kicked by a girl. A girl who was practically hog-tied. And you smell like piss. Maybe you ought to ride in back until you air out a little."

CHAPTER SEVEN

When it was time to go meet the old man they drove north out of Louisville on 65 and had a moment of slight panic as they approached the Ohio river. They'd been back and forth across the river twice since they'd arrived, but only on 64, traveling East and West, crossing over the Sherman Minton bridge each time, which was un-tolled. No one had bothered to check the map to cross north into Indiana on 65. The meeting was set right across the state river boundary in Jeffersonville. When they got to the bridge, traffic was backed up and while waiting in line they discovered it was a toll bridge and immediately knew they couldn't cross. Didn't want their faces on the cameras.

It took a little careful maneuvering to get out of line. Once free of the tangle they then had to backtrack the way they'd come in on 64 and cross the Sherman Minton again. They ended up following both sides of the same river in two different states. By the time they arrived, they were almost two hours late.

The old man wasn't pleased.

Of course he hardly ever was. Gus had told them that much and it was one of the main reasons they were there to begin with.

THE MEETING WITH THE OLD MAN WAS IN A TRAILER PARK a few miles northeast of Jeffersonville. They drove through the town and Reif thought if towns could cry, this one had been shedding tears for a long time. The trailer park was no different…pretty much what you'd expect as Southern Indiana trailer parks went. It was shaped like a horseshoe, the trailers angled in and packed tight. They made a slow pass through to take in their surroundings then turned around at the far end of the park and made their way back to the old man's place, which sat near the top of the curve, close to the toe of the shoe.

Most of the trailers looked to be decades old, any number of them wind-beaten and listing to either port or starboard, depending on where you stood in the giant hoof print. They were packed so close together you could stand on the porch steps of one and reach out and touch the unit next door. Empty beer cans, plastic pop bottles and fast-food paper bags were everywhere. If a weed was less than two inches tall it was considered part of the lawn... anything taller was probably thought of as a landscaping bush. The trailer next to the old man's sported a blue plastic tarp that covered most of the roof. It would have fit the entire roof except it had slipped its moorings and hung lopsided across the front quarter of the trailer.

The park was called Indian Village. If they were going to use Indian names, Reif thought Ass of Buffalo might have been a little more appropriate.

Stone, still thinking of Fischer and Reed, felt like he might be on thin ice, so he kept his mouth shut. Chase, however, knew the ice was a little thicker for him, though with Reif, you could never be too sure. He said it for him. "What a dump. The guy that's going to make us rich lives in this shit hole?"

Armon Reif laughed out loud. "Relax boys. Two things: One, he doesn't live here...this place is for meetings, and two, the old man isn't the one who's going to make us rich. Gus is, once the job is done. This guy's a small part of the bigger picture."

Chase looked out the car window and watched a young boy pedal toward them. He was riding a red and yellow plastic trike of some kind. What were they called? A Big Wheel? Chase thought it was something like that. He'd never had kids—in fact, never felt like he'd been a kid himself—so he wasn't sure, but he thought it sounded right. The pedals were connected directly to a large plastic front wheel. The wheel was cracked all along its circumference like it was ready to split in half. It wobbled side to side when the kid pedaled and was out of round, like maybe he'd made too many emergency stops. When they got out of the car the kid cranked the handlebars to one side, locked the pedals and skidded to a stop. He gave them a blank stare.

Stone tried on a smile and waved at the kid.

The kid looked at the three men for a moment, then shot them the bird and pedaled away.

"That right there is the epitome of trailer trash," Stone said. "The whole damn country's going to hell. How old was that little shit? Seven? Who teaches their kid that kind of thing?" He was getting hot. "I ought to go down there and show that pup the other end of his finger."

"Don't let it get you down," Reif said. "In a few months if the wind is right that kid will be dead."

"That's bullshit. We're too far south and you know it."

"So…what? You going to go terrorize a kid? When did you get so sensitive?" Then, "C'mon. Let's get to it."

THE OLD MAN WENT BY THE NAME OF RON WELLER, AND his anger was apparent as soon as they were through the door. "The hell you've been? You think I don't have better things to do than sit around here waiting on you? You're so late I thought you'd been pinched already. Timing is going to be everything on this job and you can't even show up on time for a meeting? I was told they were sending me the best of the northwest. It's already starting to look like I'm getting the least of the southeast."

Reif let the old man ramble…mostly because that's what old men liked to do. He wasn't really listening. He was looking around the inside of the trailer. Not that there was much to see. The interior walls had been removed and with the exception of a single notched-out bathroom at the rear and a small kitchen counter, the trailer was one big long narrow empty room. Skinny horizontal blinds covered all the windows, the only light coming from a single row of overhead fluorescents that hung low on thin galvanized chains. The lights made a faint humming noise that made Reif's teeth itch.

On the other side of the kitchen counter were a few six-foot collapsible tables. Next to the tables sat maybe twenty folding chairs leaning neatly against the wall. Weller had placed six of the chairs in a semicircle in the middle of the room. The trailer smelled of cigarettes, flat beer, and well-aged pizza, but it was surprisingly clean. Reif suspected the trailer was used as a meeting place for modern Nazis or the Klan. Something like that, anyway. It sure as hell wasn't for the book of the month club.

When Weller felt he'd made his point, or perhaps when he'd run out of gas—Reif wasn't quite sure—he sat down on one of the chairs and waited for the others to do the same. Once the four of them were seated, it became obvious they were two men short.

"Where's the rest of your crew? Wait, don't tell me. They overslept and are going to be here any minute."

Weller's grey hair was cut in a fifties-style flat-top, one that was starting to go a little round on top. He wore grease-stained blue coveralls and steel-toed work boots. Reif noticed that the laces of his boots didn't match. Something about that bothered him. It was…sloppy.

"You've got some smart ass in you, old man," Reif said. "I sort of like it. Just don't take it too far. I had an Auntie one time—she raised me up, you know—and she had some smart ass in her too. Her problem was she couldn't find her off switch. Know what I did?"

The old man grinned at him, his teeth dark with nicotine stains. "Helped her find it, did ya?"

Reif bit into his lower lip and nodded. "That I did. You want to know where the rest of the crew are? They didn't oversleep. I *put them* to sleep. If you want to go for a ride out to the quarry I'll show you where we buried them."

Weller's grin stayed on his face, but the light in his eyes went dark. When he spoke his voice was flat. "I don't need to know anything about that."

"Good." Reif stood from his chair and got right in the old man's face. "We're here and we're ready. Quit trying to get on top of me because no one has ever been able to do that. I doubt very much that you'd be the one to finally pull it off."

Weller held his stare. "All right. They said you were a tough guy. So let's get on with it, tough guy."

Reif continued to stare at him, waiting for the old man to look away. But the old man was a little tougher than Reif thought, so he finally sat back down, crossed his legs, then raised his eyebrows at him. "Where's the rest of *your* people? I thought we were all going to meet at once."

The old man shook his head. "My people are on another job. You'll meet them when it's time."

"What kind of job?" Reif wanted to know.

"The kind that ain't your business. Don't worry about things that don't concern you."

"Everything concerns me, old man. The sooner you understand that, the sooner you and I are going to be friends."

The old man barked out a laugh. He pulled a pack of Lucky Strikes from his pocket and lit up. He blew the smoke right at Reif. "This ain't no social gathering and I'm not interested in making friends. I'm interested in making money. So how about we get to it?" He replaced the pack of cigarettes and pulled out a slip of paper. "Here's the address where you'll be staying. Nice little house in a quiet neighborhood west of Louisville. Make sure you wipe down your hotel rooms before you leave. Move into the new place, keep the noise down and you'll be fine. I'd tell you to take the Sherman Minton bridge and allow for the time you need to backtrack, but I guess you already know that, don't you?"

Reif made a circular 'get on with it' motion with his hand.

"Report to the Jeffersonville Rail maintenance shop two weeks from Monday morning. That should give you plenty of time to settle in at the safe house. I've got the paperwork all set up under the identities you gave me. I run the shop so no one should give you any truck about anything. You won't be there long enough for the union to bother you, but if you have any problems I want you to walk away and come directly to me. Let me handle my people. Everyone understand that?"

They all nodded. Listening closely now. It was starting to get real.

"Everything is locked up tight," Weller said. "The car itself is locked, the container inside the car is locked, and the material crates inside the container are locked as well. I don't know which one of you is the cutter, but you've got some work ahead of you and it won't be easy. And you're going to have to be quick."

"We'll get it done," Reif said. "It's really only two cuts. We can cut the material crates later."

"Yes, but it's two cuts in a row, not at the same time. That means it's a lot of cutting, over a pretty short timeline."

"Anyway…" Reif said.

"Anyway, the stuff is manufactured right across the river in Kentucky. The shipment is headed to Purdue University for their research departments. The rail line handles the transportation of the material from Kentucky. The shipments are always guarded, but there's only one guard on the train and he rides up front with the engineer."

"Shouldn't be a problem, then," Stone said.

"How are you going to handle the tracers?" Weller asked.

They were getting into things Reif didn't want to discuss. "That's our problem. Don't worry about it."

"This is all happening in my yard. I am worried about it. When the Feds come knocking, they're not going to accept a shoulder shrug for an answer. This is DHS we're talking about. Those Homeland boys can lock you in a hole and toss the keys in a smelter. So it's a simple question, Mr. Reif. How are you going to handle the tracers?"

Reif looked away for a moment before answering. "The tracers aren't live. It's not like a GPS system. They're end-to-end. Scanned when they go out, and scanned when they arrive. What happens in between is off the grid."

"They'll be rethinking that pretty soon," Chase said.

"That they may," Reif said.

"How are we going to get them to divert to the maintenance yard?" Stone asked.

"There's a switch in the line south of the yard. If

there's a problem on the northbound main—and that happens time to time—they switch the track and run the line that passes right by the maintenance shop. If we disable an engine on the main line, they won't have a choice."

"So they go by the yard," Chase said. "Big deal. How does that help us?"

"It is a big deal," Weller said. "When they go by the yard they have to reduce their speed to a crawl. We can cut a brake line on one of the cars and that'll throw a warning at the engineer. Since he's right there at the maintenance yard, we'll be the ones in control of everything." He stood from his chair and retrieved a package from the table then pulled out a diagram…it was something of a flow chart that showed the sequence of events.

Reif thought it was a little crude, but had to admit it was a decent representation of what they were planning to do. The dollar value of the material wasn't very high, unless you had the right buyers. And their boss, Gus, assured Reif they did.

According to Gus, the buyers were Russians who claimed to be backed by ISIS, though Reif had his doubts. On the other hand, he didn't care either. Gus had told them they were hooked up with a terrorist group who'd never set foot in the states, but wanted to move up the radical ladder by doing something none of their fellow jihadists had ever done…

Set off a dirty bomb in the U.S.

They discovered making the bomb wasn't hard… they'd been doing that for years in Iraq. Even getting their hands on the nuclear material—though much harder—was still doable. But they'd never figured out a way to get one past the sniffers at any of the state-side docks. Sure, you could make a statement by taking out an embassy somewhere, but that sort of thing had a news cycle of about a week.

With Reif and his crew, the terrorists were now one step ahead of the game. They'd take the nuclear material already in the country and make a dirty bomb out of that. The bomb wouldn't do much physical damage…a building, maybe two depending on where it was set off. Gus hadn't told them that part yet. Even the material they were using wouldn't have long-term physical effects on a great number of people. Yes, a few hundred might die…maybe as many as a thousand. Reif thought that would be on the upper end of things, but the real damage would be the fear. It would rip the country apart. A small explosion with a few rads of radiation in a major metropolitan area would bring the country to its knees. The people would panic, the stock markets would crash, and anyone who knew that in advance would be in a perfect position to reap the benefits. The best part, Reif thought, is that the media would do most of the work for them.

He could already envision the headlines:

Terrorists Set Off Nuclear Bomb In U.S.

And why should he care? He wasn't a terrorist. He was a quiet, semi-wealthy Canadian, an orphan of agents of change, one who liked to dabble in the stock market. He'd short the market right before the blast and when it was all said and done, Reif and his crew would be worth hundreds of millions.

And they'd be gone.

CHAPTER EIGHT

When Patty Doyle regained consciousness she did so similar to someone who wakes from a dream and doesn't immediately remember where they are or the circumstances that brought them to a particular point in time. Her head and body ached from...what?

Then it all came flooding back in an instant and her eyes popped open. She'd been pushed down the basement stairs. The first thing she saw was a single light fixture above her head, well out of reach, surrounded by a protective cage of some sort. The light was on and it lit up her surroundings but it may as well have been a blanket that covered her spirit and soul.

She looked around the entire basement. Her captors were nowhere in sight. She was alone, the men either upstairs waiting for her to cry out, or gone. She held her breath and listened carefully for any sound from above, but it was of no use. The walls, ceiling, and virtually every single inch of the entire basement were covered with sound-proof foam. Any cries for help probably couldn't be heard if her rescuers stood at the top of the steps and listened with a stethoscope pressed against the door.

She was on her back on a simple canvas cot. The tape that had held her hands and legs and ankles was gone, her skin red and sore from the adhesive. Her jaw ached from the gag, the same type of feeling she used to get from smiling too much at charity fundraisers to finance the school's next expedition. A thick steel band was wrapped around her left wrist, the band shackled to a log chain that was looped around and locked to a metal post in the center of the room. A small, pale-green chemical toilet, the kind a camper might use, sat near the end of the cot. Two cases of bottled water were under the cot, along with a box of foodstuffs—tuna in stay-fresh foil packages, crackers, chips, beefy jerky, and vanilla-flavored protein bars.

When Patty Doyle stood a wave of nausea flooded her system and it took everything she had to make it to the chemical toilet. She vomited, then spat, thankful she saw no blood.

The chain was just long enough for her to reach the cot. Even when she laid down on the floor and stretched as far as she could she discovered she was at least ten feet away from any of the walls.

A single roll of toilet paper sat on the floor next to the

chemical toilet. It was the saddest site Patty had ever seen. She sat down on the cot and screamed. If someone had been standing on the other side of the basement door at the top of the steps, if they heard anything at all they might have thought it a bird screeching from very far away.

Patty screamed until her voice was used up and then fell into a restless sleep for an indeterminate amount of time. When she woke again, this time it was with the knowledge that she was a prisoner. But why?

The men had her and she'd been unconscious for long enough they could have done whatever they wanted, but they hadn't. Her initial fears of being sexually abused and then discarded were still present, but clearly the men had put some thought into what they were doing. Why go to all the trouble of setting up their little prison and then disappear? Wouldn't they try to rape her as soon as possible? She had given one of them a reason to wait, that was for sure, but what about the other? Maybe they were at a bar getting liquored up and ready for the big event. Patty hoped so. She'd be ready. She took the cot apart and ended up with a light-weight aluminum rod. She smacked it in the palm of her hand. If they wanted a fight, she'd give them one. Short of killing her, she'd figure out a way to escape. She was certain of it.

When Virgil turned into the bar's back lot the next day he found Murton sitting on top of a lopsided picnic table, one they all jokingly referred to as the 'Employee Lounge.' He sat down next to him, put his arm around his shoulder and gave him a squeeze. Then he waited.

He waited so long he thought perhaps his efforts; maybe even his very presence was going unnoticed. After a while, Vigil slapped both his knees and moved to stand but Murton clamped his hand on Virgil's shoulder and held him in place. Another full minute passed before he spoke.

"Something's wrong."

Virgil turned his head slowly and looked at Murton. "Really? I hadn't noticed. I'm not sure anyone has. Especially Becky, which sort of surprises me because she usually picks up on this sort of thing before any—"

"Would you please shut up?"

Virgil wasn't offended. He knew Murton was hurting, and more importantly, he heard kindness in his voice no matter the words he used.

"What is it, Murt? How can I help?"

Murton shook his head. "That's just it. I don't know that you can."

"I tried to call Gibson."

"I wish you wouldn't have done that. You're going to get tangled up in something that's not your business."

Virgil stood and faced him. "Not my business? Who do you think you're talking to? I'm your—"

Murton pointed a finger at him, little heat in his voice. "Boss? You can stop right there. I'll tell you who you are, Jonesy, and don't you ever forget it because things are changing and I don't know that they'll ever be the same."

"The hell are you talking about?"

"I'm talking about you're Small's husband. I'm talking about you're Jonas and Wyatt's father. That's who you are now and I couldn't be happier for you. But what's headed my way…I can't let you get wrapped up in it. I can't let that happen because when it goes to shit, and make no mistake, it's going to, I don't want to be the one who has to look at your family and tell them it's my fault that you're gone." Then he softened his voice. "My God, what about Jonas? Could you imagine what it'd do to him to lose another father?"

"No, Murt, I can't. I don't want to even think about it. But why do I have the feeling that you do?"

Murton looked up, a sad smile on his face. "You're smarter than you look."

Virgil sat back down on the bench. "Delroy said it feels to him like something bad is coming down the line."

Murton chuffed. "Sometimes I think that man has some sort of Jamaican juju or something."

"*Sometimes?*"

Murton stared off into the distance at nothing. "Do you know what I most admire about you, Jonesy?"

"What's that?"

"You never asked. Not once. Almost forty years now and not one single time have you ever tried to crack the door. That is some top-notch, grade-A love, brother."

Virgil knew what Murton meant. "I'll tell you something, Murt. There hasn't been hardly one single day I didn't want to ask. I simply figured you'd tell me when you were ready…when you wanted to."

"I know that. But it's not a question of want. Not anymore."

Virgil had been waiting most of his life to hear what Murton was about to tell him. He knew the story, the meat of it, anyway. What he didn't know were the details, the missing pieces that in all likelihood helped shape the man Murton had become.

Murton stood up. "C'mon. Let's go."

Virgil frowned a question at him. "Where?"

"Upstairs. If I'm going to tell it, Becky should hear it too. That's what we were fighting about. She's been leaning on me about the rest of the story for a long time."

"Maybe you should go talk with her first. I can wait. She's your—"

"Jonesy?"

"What?"

"Let's go."

They walked back inside and went upstairs to the

office over the bar. Murton looked, Virgil thought, like a man who knew he was headed for his own end. It wasn't staring him right in the face, but like a death row con, he knew it was there and all it took was a palm-size mirror stuck through the bars where he'd have an unobstructed view of what waited at the end of the line.

CHAPTER NINE

THEY ENTERED THE OFFICE AND FOUND DELROY AND Becky sitting quietly on the sofa. Delroy was either trying to help Becky simply by being present, or more likely, the conversation had stopped when they heard Virgil and Murton coming up the steps. The looks on their faces suggested the latter. Delroy stood when they walked in.

"Maybe I go back to work now, me."

Murton closed the door. "Delroy, I'd like you to stay. You don't have to, but I'd like you to."

Delroy looked at Virgil, who gave him a slight nod. He sat back down. "Yeah, mon. Whatever you tink."

Becky stood and Murton walked over and put his arms around his girlfriend. "I'm sorry," he said. "This isn't easy."

"Being downwind of history rarely is," Becky said.

Virgil thought her statement might have been one of

the most profound things he'd ever heard her say. He turned away and looked through the one-way glass window that gave out over the bar and listened as Murton took them back almost forty years to the night he joined Virgil's family.

THEY WERE BOYS, ONLY SEVEN YEARS OLD, AND HAD BEEN friends for about a year. After Murton's mother died, more than a month passed before Murton would speak to Virgil and even then it took yet another tragedy before the foundation of their friendship began to solidify, able to carry the weight of what the decades would bring their way.

Murton's father was something of an enigma. Like many men of his generation, Ralph Wheeler wasn't able to shake the standard of his era or the expectations placed upon him that in many ways amounted to nothing more than the social discord of his time. He had neither the fortitude nor the desire to change. And why should he? In his day, men were men. Ralph Wheeler's definition of a man was someone who was hard, mean, distant, able to hold his liquor, and unafraid to knock his wife around if she failed to meet his demands. Often those demands were ones set purposefully out of reach as justification for his own actions.

The night of the soccer game all those years ago changed everything. As difficult as it had been for

Murton, Virgil wouldn't have had it any other way. But decades later the night remained one of mystery, not only for what happened, but for what was said and never told.

Murton's father, for all his faults, knew how to keep up appearances. One way he accomplished this was by coaching his son's soccer team. There had been plenty of speculation and quiet whisperings that perhaps a month wasn't nearly long enough to wait before returning to the field. But Ralph Wheeler wasn't the type of man who listened to those who held no authority over him, so when he said it was time for Murton to take the field, that's what he intended to accomplish.

The problem was, Murton wasn't ready. When his father tried to force the issue things got out of hand. Ralph Wheeler first pushed his son out on the field in an attempt to make him play. When that didn't work, he pushed him further and harder. When he finally discovered it wasn't going to happen, he grabbed his son by the back of his neck and dragged him like a dog over to the bench then forcefully sat him down.

As he turned to walk away something else happened that would be a catalyst of change and alter not only Murton's life, but Virgil's as well. No one heard what it was, but whatever Murton said to his father upset him enough that Virgil's dad, the sheriff of Marion County at the time, quickly moved in to prevent any violence against Murton's person.

Virgil caught Murton's reflection in the glass and turned to face him. "Just say it, Murt. They're only words. Words from forty years ago. You couldn't be any safer than you are right this very moment."

The room was quiet for a long time. When Murton finally let go of his secret, the one he'd carried with him for decades, Virgil noticed a softness in him, one that he'd never witnessed in all their years together. There was something else in his voice too, though Virgil could hardly believe it. It was fear.

Murton looked at everyone in the room for a long time before he spoke. When he did, his jaw quivered and his voice sounded as distant as the memory of his past. "I killed my mom."

When Becky heard the words, her eyes got wide and she slowly backed away and sat down on the sofa.

Murton saw the look on her face and held up his hands. He shook his head and tried again. "I mean…that's not right. I didn't kill her, but I'm responsible for her death."

Virgil put his hand on his brother's shoulder. "Murt, I don't know what happened…not yet, but I do know this: whatever it was, you're not responsible."

Murton gently stepped away from Virgil's grasp and looked down at the floor. When he looked back at Virgil he said something completely unexpected. "Remember when we were racing back to your place? When Small was bleeding out after Decker attacked her?"

Virgil looked away for a moment, suddenly lost in his own thoughts. "Yeah. What about it?"

"You were scared. I could hear it over the phone. I think you were as scared as I've ever known you to be. More scared than when we were in Iraq, or when Mason died, or even when Pate and his boys had you strung up on that beam."

"You're probably right. What of it, Murt?"

"When we were on the phone I gave you some bad advice. I told you to bury it. I told you to push it down and get those thoughts out of your head. That was a mistake."

"Why? It helped me…in the moment anyway."

"It was a mistake because it doesn't work," Murton said.

Virgil was confused. He could tell that Delroy and Becky were too. "Murt—"

Murton shook his head and waved a hand, asking for silence. "About a year before you and I became friends my mom took me to the movies on a Saturday afternoon. Just me and her. Things were already bad at our house, my old man was drunk all the time and she wanted to get me out of there, if only for a couple of hours. Right before the movie started I told her I had to go to the bathroom. I was too old to go with her into the ladies' room, and she couldn't go with me into the men's room. So I went in by myself.

"The urinals were too high so I had to use one of the stalls. They didn't have doors on them back then, but hey, men were men, right? Who cared? So I dropped my pants and hopped up on the seat, peed and hopped back down. I was getting ready to pull up my pants when someone came out of the stall a few spaces down."

Murton stopped for a beat, his eyes closed, reliving the moment. When he spoke again his voice sounded almost robotic as he described the lewd things the man said and worst of all, how he…touched him.

Becky rushed over and threw her arms around him and held him for a long time. Virgil and Delroy looked at each other without speaking. When Becky finally let go, Murton finished his story.

"I tried to bury it. I pushed it down and pretended like it never happened. But it didn't work. I started acting out. Didn't even realize I was. One morning almost a year later it was so bad my mom took me out back and told me she knew something was wrong. She also told me that we were going to sit out there until I told her, even if it took all day and all night.

"I was only a boy. I was trying to protect her. I knew she'd tell my old man, and I knew he'd take it out on both of us, especially her for letting it happen to me. I did the best I could, but I couldn't keep it in any longer, so I told her the whole story. When I did she comforted me for hours. We talked about it, we went for a long walk together, and she promised me I would never be hurt again. I was so relieved I actually managed to fool myself into believing everything was going to be okay. But when we came home she asked me to wait out back. Then she went in the house and told my old man." He looked at Virgil. "It wasn't long before I heard them screaming at each other and then I heard him start to beat her. When I couldn't take it anymore I ran down to your place. That was the day we started working on the lawn with Mason."

"I remember," Virgil said.

"He killed her, Jonesy. My dad killed my mom that day because of what happened to me. And you know what I did? I ran away. He was killing her and I ran. He made it look like an accident, and he got away with it, but he killed her. I spent a month with that man after she died. I listened to his alcohol-induced ramblings. I saw the rage. He didn't speak to me for the entire month. Sometimes I'd wake in the night and find him standing at the foot of my bed holding a hammer.

"He didn't even feed me. He'd get up in the morning, throw back a few shots, head to work then come home and drink until he passed out. We didn't have any food. Nothing. Every dime went to the booze. By the time the night of the soccer game rolled around they'd already cut off our power and water. You know how I survived? How I ate?"

Virgil suddenly did and was surprised it took him so long to figure it out. "My mom?"

"Yep. She packed me a lunch every day and brought me a plate every night. Sometimes it wasn't much, but God bless her Jonesy, every day it was something. I wouldn't have made it without her."

Virgil nodded and turned away. When he looked back, Murton continued. "That night…at the game? I told him I knew what he did and the next time he passed out drunk I was going to kill him with that hammer he'd been too afraid to use on me. That's what set him off."

Virgil rubbed his face with both hands. "Listen, Murt, you were a kid. You were scared and all alone. Besides, when you showed up at our house that night, you never had to go back. You said something you didn't mean in anger. It happens. Maybe it's time to let it go."

Murton laughed without humor. "Something I didn't mean? You know me better than that, Jonesy. I not only meant it, *I tried to do it.* My mistake was not letting him get drunk enough. I thought he was passed out but he wasn't. He was waiting for me. I swung that hammer like I was swinging for my life. But he was ready. He grabbed it from my hands and threw it across the room. Then he started hitting me. Not too hard at first. He was pulling his punches. I could tell. He wanted to make it last. But I fought back. I got lucky, really. I kicked him in the groin as hard as I could and he went down. He fell over and rolled into a ball. When he could finally speak he told me if he ever saw me again he was going to kill me. That's when I ran to your house. You know the rest of it. Mason ran him out of town and here we are. I haven't seen him since."

Murton walked over and looked through the glass, out at the bar. Virgil turned as well and couldn't quite believe who he saw headed their way.

It was their boss, Cora LaRue, and Agent Gibson.

Virgil looked at Murton. "What the heck are they doing here?"

Murton gave Virgil a sad stare. "It's all connected, brother." Then, to Delroy. "I think it's getting a little backed up down there."

Delroy stood and looked down at the bar. It was still early and the place was mostly empty. "Yeah, mon. I see dat." He looked at Virgil. "You remember what I say about family." It wasn't a question.

Virgil nodded and Delroy walked out the door.

"You want to tell me what's going on, Murt?"

"Mac has asked me to do something that only I can do. Cora is here for my answer. I'm going to say yes. What I need from you is to let me."

"Let you? Murt, what the hell is it?"

"I'm afraid I can't say."

"Why not?"

Becky didn't like the direction of the conversation any more than Virgil did. "Murton Wheeler, you are going to tell us what this is about right now." It was almost a shout.

The door opened and Cora walked in, followed by Agent Paul Gibson. "Don't be too hard on him, Becky," Gibson said. He wore dusty jeans, a blue work shirt, and steel-toed boots. His hair was uncut and it looked like his last shave might have been a month ago. "He can't say any more because he's under orders not to."

Virgil looked at Cora. "Whose orders?"

She shook her head. "Not mine. How are you, Jonesy? Getting settled in with the new family and all?"

Cora was clearly trying to lower the tension, but it was neither the time nor the place, especially after the story Murton had just told. Oddly, Virgil answered her anyway. "I'm well. We're all fine, Cora. The kids are great. Things have never been better."

"I'll bet," she said. "Two thousand acres. I still don't believe it."

"Can we get back to the matter at hand?" Becky said. "Murt, what's going on here?"

"How about we all sit down," Gibson said. "I'll tell you what I can."

CHAPTER TEN

Reif, Chase, Stone, and Weller met one final time before they were scheduled to report to the rail yard. Weller wanted to go over the plan again. It might not have been completely necessary, but there was little room for error. Weller told Reif that he'd let him know when his men were back in town. "They'll be staying at the safe house with you. There's plenty of room."

"Putting all our eggs in one basket doesn't seem too smart," Reif said.

"Never been a problem before. The neighbors think it's a corporate rental, which is exactly what it is. Nothing is going to happen if you do what I say and keep your heads down and your mouths shut. Besides, they won't be showing up until there are only a few days left to go."

"I'll tell you something I don't like," Chase said. "We've never had to blend in like this. Every other time we've practiced off-site then went in, did the job and got out. This is a whole other animal."

"Don't have a choice on this one," Reif said. "We can't be lurking around in the dark the night before trying to figure everything out, and we can't practice off-site. We've got to go in, get established, figure out the yard, the equipment, all of it."

"Still don't like it."

"Relax, Chase. It's two weeks. We've got good IDs, and we'll do like the old man says. We'll keep our heads down, and when we disappear they'll be looking for guys who don't even exist."

Weller was nodding. "He's right, you know. There really isn't any other way to do it. If there was, I'd be all over it. But since there isn't, I need you boys to understand something: This is your job, so I'll leave you to it. But remember, when you're in my yard, I'm the boss. You'll do what I say, when I say it. Everybody got that?"

They all nodded at him…even Reif. Ego aside, he thought, the old man was right. They couldn't go in there and start throwing their weight around. Like it or not, they had to be regular workers for a while. Heads down, mouths shut, and all that.

"We get it," Reif said. "Let me know when your people are going to show up."

"Do that," Weller said.

They stood to leave. "Let me ask you something,"

Reif said to the old man. "What brought you into this? What's in it for you?"

"Doubting me already, boy?"

"Call me boy one more time and see what happens. When someone answers a question with one of their own it's usually an indication that they're stalling for time to think up a proper response. I've already given you plenty."

"I'm not stalling for nothing. Your people vouched for me, didn't they?"

They had, Reif thought, but he wanted to hear it for himself. "Yes, they did. They told me you had some problems a ways back. Said you could be trusted."

"I did, and I can," Weller said. He scratched the back of his head then shoved his hands into the pockets of his coveralls. "There's a debt that needs paid. It's big and it's old…damned near as old as I am. At least that's what it feels like anyway. The way I see it, this will get it squared."

Reif didn't like that answer at all. "Why is this the first time I'm hearing about this?"

"Beats me," Weller said. "Ask your people. They brokered the job, not me."

"Who comes calling if this debt doesn't get paid?"

"None of your business."

Reif was on him like a cat. The barrel of the Beretta was against the side of the old man's head before he knew what was happening. "You don't get it, do you? I'm making it my business." He pressed the gun hard into the side of Weller's head. "Now answer the question. What happens if this debt doesn't get paid?"

Weller leaned into the pressure of the gun and turned until the barrel was pressed against his forehead. "Your gun don't scare me. Neither do you. Pull the trigger and walk away. It'll save me a mess of grief down the road. The debt is personal."

Reif looked straight at the old man and knew he wasn't going to answer. He could see it in his eyes. He put the gun away. "Somebody who's not afraid to die is a dangerous man to work with."

"You got it backward. You assume the debt is mine to pay. I never said I wasn't afraid to die. I'm afraid to keep living. Why do you think I took this job?"

Reif shook his head, put his gun away and walked out the door, taking Stone and Chase with him.

When they were gone the old man walked over and sat down on one of the chairs. He listened to the car doors shut, then heard the ping of gravel as the three men drove away. He waited ten minutes before he stood and put the chairs back with the others in the kitchen area of the trailer.

He took a quick peek through the blinds to make sure he was alone. If they came back now they *would* pull the trigger. Maybe that'd be for the best, he thought. He let go of the window blind, took out his phone and made a call.

The call was answered on the other end with a single word. "Yes?"

The old man hesitated, but he didn't know why. Or perhaps he did and simply didn't want to admit it to himself.

"Hello?"

"You're all set. I told them I'd let them know before you arrive. I hope that's all right. When exactly are you going to get here?"

"I'll let you know," the other man said. Then he was gone.

CHAPTER ELEVEN

Gibson looked at Becky, then Virgil. "I want the two of you to understand something. I'm allowing you to hear this. Do you follow what I'm saying?"

"No, I don't," Virgil said. "How about you dumb it down for us a little."

Cora jumped in. "He's saying this is a federal matter, and DHS has the point. The state is using limited resources to back him up. I guess I should say states, because Kentucky is in on it too. Virgil, you know Jack Grady." It wasn't a question.

"Yes, I do." He looked at Becky. "Jack Grady is the lead detective of Kentucky's Criminal Apprehension Bureau…part of their state police force. CAB is Kentucky's version of our MCU."

"I know CAB," Becky said. "I've got access to their —" She stopped herself and glanced at Gibson.

There was a moment of silence, then Gibson said, "You're in CAB's database?" He had a muddled look on his face.

Becky looked at Cora, who was pretending she hadn't heard her last statement.

"No…I was going to say I have access to their phone directory," Becky said.

Gibson visibly rolled his eyes. "Right. Anyway, Grady is working with us, and Murton will be handling things on this end for the State of Indiana. As I was saying before, I'm allowing you and Jonesy in on this meeting because federal regulations aside, I have no doubt whatsoever that you'd end up with the information anyway."

"In on what, exactly?" Virgil said.

"We'll get to that in a moment," Cora said. "Right now I want to make something clear to everyone in this room. As of this moment, assuming he agrees to it, under orders from the governor, Murton Wheeler is on temporary assignment to the federal government as an undercover agent. That means he no longer answers to me, or the governor." She glanced at Virgil. "You either."

Virgil ignored her. "Murt, what's going on? Last time you went under for the feds we didn't see or speak with each other for twenty years."

"You think I don't remember that?" Murton said. "Pate was a suspected pedophile. Why do you think I took the job?" He was looking at Gibson when he said it. Gibson was about to say something when his phone buzzed at him. He looked at the screen and tried to keep the expression from his face. He held up a finger to the others, a 'just a moment' gesture, and punched the answer button.

"Yes?" He listened for a few seconds, frowned, then said, "Hello?" After a few moments: "I'll let you know."

"Who was that?" Murton asked.

Gibson looked at Murton for a moment, as if he was considering how to answer the question. He let it go and so did Murton. Then to everyone, "There's a company in Kentucky called Radiology, Inc. They manufacture—"

Virgil was losing patience. "Yes, yes. They manufacture nuclear pharmaceuticals. Everyone in the room knows this, Agent Gibson. In case you've forgotten, I wasted almost an entire month chasing a paper trail across the state that turned out to be a clerical error on Radiology's end."

"Was it?" Gibson asked.

"What's that supposed to mean?"

Gibson seemed to consider his answer carefully before he spoke. "We have logical, credible intelligence that suggests the clerical error on Radiology's end wasn't actually an error."

Virgil shook his head. "Yes, it was. I documented everything in my report. Your department was copied."

"I know. I read your report. And you're right. There was a clerical error."

"Yet you just said there wasn't. So which is it?"

"It was an error on paper. An error we believe they placed there on purpose."

"To what end?"

"We think it was a test."

"A test? What kind of test?" Virgil asked.

"One that would allow them to observe our response," Gibson said. "The whole thing was a set-up. They inserted an error into their logs to see what would happen if any of their product turned up missing."

Virgil was confused. "Why?"

"Listen, I don't want to get into all the details here. No disrespect, but this isn't exactly a secure environment."

Cora stood and looked at Murton. "Mac needs an answer, Murt. You're in or you're out."

"How about we can the skit, Cora. He knows I'm in." Murton looked at Gibson. "Just like he does. They've known for months."

"Then we'll get everyone briefed on their duties and specific assignments first thing tomorrow morning down at the MCU," Cora said. "That's all for now."

Gibson stood and moved to the door, but Virgil wasn't having it.

"Cora?"

Cora was positioned next to and slightly in front of Gibson, which meant he couldn't see the look on her face or the direction of her eyes when she spoke. "I said we'll get up to speed tomorrow morning. Is that clear, Detective?" A little gravel in her voice.

Virgil saw her move her eyes back and forth between himself and Gibson. Message received.

"Yeah, I guess so. See you tomorrow."

Virgil stood near the window and looked out over the bar until he saw Cora and Gibson walk out the front door. He turned around. "Murt?"

Becky walked over and put her hand on Virgil's arm. "I love you, Virgil. You know I do. But I need a few minutes with my man."

"Wait for me downstairs?" Murton said to him.

Virgil walked out the door and wondered if maybe Delroy was right. Had the ground beneath his feet been shifting and he hadn't noticed? And why did an agent for Homeland Security look like he'd just stepped off a factory floor? Virgil didn't know the answer to the first question. That one would take some thought. But the answer to the second one was obvious: Gibson was working an undercover op, and he was about to pull Murton in with him.

Virgil sat at one of the four-tops, his eyes glued to the office window above the stage. He couldn't see anything other than his own reflection because the glass was mirrored. It was also angled outward at the top which gave Virgil a perfectly good view of himself staring at himself. He wondered what Murton might be telling Becky. Would he tell her the truth? Or would he tell her what she wanted to hear? Maybe it would be some reasonably balanced combination of both, if such a thing were possible.

Delroy came to the table with two cups of Jamaican Blue and sat down beside him. "What is it, mon?"

"I wish I knew, Delroy."

"You smarter than dat. You know someting."

Virgil looked away from the window and at his friend. "I really don't know much more than you do. Gibson wants Murt to work an undercover op for the feds, but neither he nor Murt have said what it's really about. Cora said they'd brief us tomorrow morning."

Delroy took a sip of his coffee then puffed out his cheeks and sat back in his chair. "He been runnin' back and forth to dat address in Kentucky almost everyday. Sometimes he stay all night. When he get home, Becky say he showers, then go right back. What he looking for, him?"

"You'll have to ask Murton that question, Delroy."

"I have. He won't say. So now I'm asking you."

"I think he's looking for his father."

Delroy shook his head. "We buried his father. His name was Mason Jones."

"His real father, Delroy. The biological one."

"What I say still true."

Delroy was right, of course. Mason had raised Murton as his own son. From that night over forty years ago, until the day he died, Mason had loved Murton with his whole heart.

"I don't tink he looking for his father, me. I tink he's looking for something he thought he'd never get."

"What's that," Virgil said.

"Retribution." Delroy stood and slid his chair back in place. "But what he end up with is regret. Or maybe someting worse. You wait, you see. It on you to make tings right, Virgil Jones."

"Why?" Virgil felt himself getting irritated. "When exactly did I become the arbiter of another man's life?"

Delroy was irritated now as well, something Virgil rarely witnessed. "Yeah, mon. You keep asking yourself dat. It all right with me." He turned to walk away, then stopped and placed his hands on the back of the chair. "Delroy would never accuse you of being small-minded. But sometimes you a little short-sighted."

"What would you have me do, Delroy?"

"Maybe you go ask Jonas. It practically staring you in the face, mon."

"Jonas? What in the world does he—"

Delroy didn't let him finish. He still had his hands on the back of the chair. He picked it up and slammed it down on the floor, effectively silencing Virgil in the process. But when he spoke his voice was sincere, his question almost sad. "You ever heard of the Lethe? It from a river in Hades whose water when drunk make the souls of the dead forget their life on earth."

"What's that supposed to mean?"

"It mean dat boy given to you…he not only a gift. He's a reminder of who you are, *whose you are*, and what you're supposed to do. The question is, are you man enough to do it?"

Man enough? Virgil was so angry and confused by the words his friend spoke he stood and walked out of the bar. Had he known what was going to happen he would have stayed.

An entire month would pass before he saw or spoke with Murton again. And when that day finally came, Virgil, gun in hand, wouldn't drink from a river where Greek mythology promised forgetfulness, though he would, in many ways, feel as though he'd lost a part of his soul.

CHAPTER TWELVE

After his conversation with Becky, Murton went downstairs to speak with Virgil, but discovered he'd already left. When he asked Delroy about it, the answer he received wasn't exactly what he expected.

"How should I know dat, me?"

"Did he say where he was going?"

Delroy pointed to a booth. When Murton looked that way he saw it was empty. "There's no one over there, Delroy."

"Yeah, mon. But not for long. Follow me." There was no mistaking his tone.

They walked over and took a seat. Murton had been friends with Delroy for a few years now and knew better than to try to steer the conversation. He simply waited for him to speak.

"It not where Virgil go that concern me. It where you about to."

"Why are you so worried about this?" When Murton saw the look on Delroy's face he instantly regretted the question.

"Now maybe I understand where Virgil gets it. Da both of you run around sometimes like what you do have no effect on the other people in your lives."

Murton looked at his friend for a moment, then stood up.

"Where you going, you?"

When Murton spoke he discovered it wasn't nearly as easy to deceive his Jamaican friend as he thought it might be. "It's work, Delroy. I can't talk about it. I'm under orders not to." They both waited a beat, neither willing to acknowledge what they knew was about to happen.

Murton took the lead, mostly because he knew Delroy wouldn't. "Besides, I'm kind of hungry. I think I'll step into the kitchen and see what Robert's got cooking. You want anything?"

"What I want can't be found in dat kitchen. I tink you know dat."

"Look, Delroy, I…"

Delroy waved him off, the fear and frustration riding like a carrier wave embedded on the back of his words. "What about Becky? Dat woman love you with her whole self. You two remind me of Virgil and Sandy. You on your way. You going to tell me I'm wrong?"

Murton shook his head. "No, I'm not."

He pointed a finger at him. It shook when he spoke. "Then you tell Delroy this: Who going to look after her when you go through dat door over there because we both know you're not hungry and there's a good chance you won't be back, don't we?"

Murton laughed, but there was little joy in the sound that came from his mouth. "Delroy, I think that Jamaican imagination is getting the better of you. How about you grab us a couple of Red Stripes and I'll get some of that shrimp Robert's cooking. There's nothing to worry about."

"We going to start lying to each other now, mon?"

"Delroy—"

"You one of the best friends I ever had, me. The tings we done together for each other, for Virgil and Sandy, they some of the best parts of my whole life. I know it feel like you maybe only have one way to go, but dat just not true, mon."

Murton laughed again, but it was forced and sounded false. He started to say something, except Delroy wasn't done. "How do you expect me to do it, mon? Huh? You tell me how."

"Tell you what, Delroy? I don't even know what you're talking about."

Delroy stood so fast he knocked his chair over. He got right in Murton's face. Murton let him. "Dat boyish grin you always flashing around don't fool me, no. You tell me how I supposed to let you go. You tell me how to say goodbye to one of the best men I've ever known because I don't know how to do dat. Neither do Virgil, or he'd still be here. You can pretend all you want, but you can't run away from your past, Murton Wheeler. It faster than you."

Murton placed his hands on Delroy's shoulders. "You're the best, Delroy. Relax. I'll get some grub and be right back."

Delroy nodded at him, a small tear slipping out of the corner of one eye. "Yeah, mon. We do it your way then. Two beers coming right up."

Murton walked over to the kitchen entrance and looked back over his shoulder. He wanted to burn the image of Delroy, the bar, everything into his mind because he knew, on some level his friend was right. He might never see any of it again. But Delroy was wrong about one thing: Murton wasn't running away from his past. He was running toward it. He pushed through the swinging door, went through the kitchen and out the back.

Delroy pulled two Red Stripes from the cooler, popped their tops and carried them back to the booth. He took a sip of his beer and stared at the kitchen entrance, willing the door to swing back open, hoping to see Murton's smiling face, his hands full with a plate of food.

By the time he finished the first beer, he knew Murton was gone. Becky walked down the stairs and slipped into the booth next to him. Delroy put his arm around her shoulders and when he did, she placed her elbows on the table and buried her face in her hands.

When Virgil left the bar he didn't have a destination in mind, so he simply drove. He needed to cool off and try to wrap his head around something he knew little about. He wasn't mad at Delroy for what he'd said. He wasn't even mad at Murton. He was mad at the situation…mad that he didn't have the information he needed to help his best friend. He drove out of the downtown traffic and approached 465, the loop that circled the city.

What was the message Delroy was trying to send? Virgil would do anything to help or protect Murton. Delroy knew that. Was he trying to push him out to protect him, or pull him closer to help Murton? He understood the similarities between his life and his father's. Mason had taken Murton in when he had nowhere else to go. Virgil and Sandy had done the same for Jonas. Delroy said he felt something bad was coming their way…and now Murton was about to take an assignment with the feds. And even though Virgil knew the situation was different this time, he couldn't help but wonder if Murton might be getting in over his head, or worse, be left to fend for himself if Gibson's op went bad.

He'd get as much information as possible out of

Gibson tomorrow at the meeting. But right now, it was time to put his own feelings aside and talk to Murton.

He turned the truck around and headed back to the bar.

He'd only been gone a half-hour, and when he walked in he found Robert behind the bar, something which rarely happened. Known far and wide for his authentic Jamaican cuisine, Robert was one of the most respected chefs in the city. He regularly received offers from restaurants all across the Midwest. As a Jamaican chef he had no equal.

His bartending skills were another matter altogether. In short, he knew how to make two different kinds of drinks: Rum in a shot glass, or draft beer in a mug.

"Hey, Robert. Practicing for the mixology exam?"

"Yeah, mon. You a laugh a minute. Anyone ever tell you dat?"

"All the time. Have you seen Delroy? Actually, never mind. It's Murton I really want to talk to."

"Delroy upstairs with Becky. Maybe you should go up, but I tell you dis, mon: Delroy not too happy with you today, no."

"Believe it or not, I've already managed to piece that together. The problem is, I'm not quite sure why."

"That's because he wants you to do someting you unwilling to do."

"What's that?"

Robert shrugged. "I don't know, me. Dat man works out of his own zip code. Half the time I don't know what he talking about and I grew up with him. I always listen though, me. Maybe you should too, mon."

"I will. I am. You didn't answer me though. I need to speak with Murt. Where is he?"

"Dat seem to be the question of the day, no?"

When Virgil entered the office he felt like his day was going in circles. Delroy and Becky were sitting on the sofa again and the conversation stopped when he walked in, as it had before. Becky's eyes were red, and the table that fronted the sofa was covered with crumpled tissues.

Virgil pulled a chair over and sat down. He leaned forward, his forearms resting on his thighs. He chose his words carefully. "Becky, I don't have all the facts yet but here's what I know for sure: Whatever Murt is involved in, he's not alone. I'm going to back him up all the way. I promise. Nothing is going to happen to him."

Delroy dropped his head and stared at the floor. When Becky spoke, her voice sounded distant and dull, like she was speaking to him from the other side of a wall. "Don't make promises you can't keep, Jonesy."

"I don't."

"You just did."

Virgil took a breath. "What did Murt tell you? And where is he, by the way?"

"He wouldn't tell me where he was going…not exactly. But he told me where he'd end up. When he'll be back is anybody's guess. Let me ask you something, Jonesy." Becky's voice suddenly didn't sound distant anymore. "Did you know about what happened with him and Decker?"

"Of course. Didn't you?"

"Yes, but I can tell by the sound of your voice that you didn't get the entire story. Don't feel bad. I didn't either until a little while ago."

"What do you mean? What's the rest of the story?"

"Why did you leave earlier?"

The question caught Virgil off guard. "Well, I needed to clear my head a little, which I did. I'm fine now."

The sarcasm in Becky's voice couldn't have been any thicker. "Oh, thank God. You have no idea how worried we all were regarding your state of mind."

"Hey, Becks, c'mon. I'm trying to help here."

"If you were trying to help you wouldn't have left because you're probably the only person in the world that could have stopped him. But you didn't and now he's gone."

Delroy placed his palm on Becky's thigh. "Don't be too hard on him. It my fault he leave. I was trying to help, but I only made tings worse."

"Delroy, thank you. But I didn't leave because of what

you said. I left so I could think about it for a few minutes. Everything seems to be happening all at once." Then, to Becky: "Tell me what I'm missing, Becks. What did Murt say to you? Tell me all of it."

Becky took another tissue from the box and very unselfconsciously blew her nose. She tossed the used tissue on the table, looked Virgil in the eye and told him everything Murton had said to her before he left.

By the time she was done, Virgil was sick with fear, and outside of his family and the people in the room with him, wasn't sure who he could trust.

CHAPTER THIRTEEN

AFTER HIS LAST CASE, WHEN DECKER HAD ALMOST KILLED his wife and unborn son, Virgil and Sandy made a promise to each other. There'd be no secrets or withholding of information between them, no matter the circumstances. It was Sandy's idea, one that Virgil readily agreed to. And why not? Other than his venture into the arena of mind-altering chemicals a couple of years ago, he'd never kept anything of substance from her. So the promise was an easy one. Except…

They'd agreed that anything that could be even remotely dangerous to them or their children would be talked about immediately, and if possible, in person. After what Becky had told him, Virgil didn't feel like he had the time, much less the patience to drive all the way home and have a sit-down with Sandy.

But then he thought back to a few months ago and

the image of his dying wife, the blood on the floor, her lips turning blue, the backdoor thrown open by the powerful beat of the helicopter's rotor blades, Bell cutting into her abdomen, the blood pouring out of her, how he'd almost lost her and what that would have done to him. It all came flooding in at once…a flashback that made him sweat with fear and anxiety every time it happened.

He kissed Becky on the forehead, then told her and Delroy good-bye.

When he got in his truck, he said to hell with the rules, hit his lights and siren, and headed for home. He was running hard.

So was Murton.

Virgil tried to call Murton and got a robotic-sounding voice telling him the number he'd dialed was no longer in service. He drove on, the siren wailing away, becoming more frustrated with each passing mile. The frustration came from a sense of paralysis. In the moment, there was nothing he could do.

He killed the siren a half-mile out and turned the flashers off as he entered his drive. By the time he arrived he'd managed to take all the disparate worlds of thought —what he'd been told by Becky, what he knew about Murton, Delroy's intuition—and piece them together in a way that he hoped would make him sound almost like he'd not quite lost his mind.

After Decker tried to kill Sandy, he'd gone on the run. Virgil stayed by his wife's side throughout the entire ordeal, which left Murton the task of finding Decker and bringing him in. Or so most everyone thought.

Except Murton didn't plan to bring him in. He planned to do what he considered the only logical thing when it came to guys like Decker. He planned to take him off the board. What he didn't know at the time was Agent Paul Gibson of Homeland Security had also been tracking the case, working it from a different angle and with an entirely different agenda. So when Murton caught up with Decker and killed him, Gibson was ready and waiting with a cleaning crew to dispose of the body, and more importantly, a long-term plan. Since Murton and Gibson had worked together in the FBI, Murton hardly gave it a second thought.

But Gibson had been two steps ahead of the entire operation the whole way. He could have prevented Decker's death, but he hadn't, for reasons no one really wanted to scrutinize. Everyone knew—though no one said it out loud—if they started asking those types of questions Murton could be in more than a bit of trouble. So everyone kept their mouths shut, a killer was off the streets, and Sandy, Wyatt, and Decker's biological son, Jonas were all safe.

They sat on the back deck, looking out at the pond. "I

know all of that, Virgil," Sandy said. "What I don't understand is why Murton agreed to take the assignment."

The assignment was to go undercover for the DHS and work his way into the Russian operation that had backed the fracking play in Shelby County. He'd start with a month in lock-up at a federal holding facility in Oregon.

"When he was undercover with the FBI and inside Pate's organization, they made him look attractive by creating a false record of conviction. Murt's got a rap sheet that's longer than my—"

She held up her hands. "Please don't say it. I get it. A couple of minor offenses."

"This is serious," Virgil said, though he couldn't help smiling. "The story is, he's being sent to Oregon to await trial on charges of racketeering, extortion, bribery, murder, and money laundering. Gibson says there are a few guards inside the facility who'll take the occasional envelope if it's fat enough. They're hoping the guards will notice his record and make contact with the people they work for."

"Who's that?"

Virgil looked out at the pond and didn't answer right away.

"Virgil?"

He turned and faced his wife. "You know I have to help him, don't you?"

"Of course I do. He's your brother. I'd be worried if you said you wouldn't. What does worry me is the fact that you're not answering my question."

"Delroy thinks I have to choose."

Sandy let a question form on her face. "Choose? Choose what?"

"Between Murton and my family. He didn't come right out and say it but the message was clear. He feels like something bad is coming down the line…that it might already be here. I'm starting to believe him."

"There is no choice, Virgil. Murton *is* your family."

"I know that." He snapped it at her. Then immediately, "I'm sorry. He meant I'd have to choose between helping Murton and being here for you guys. You and the kids."

Sandy didn't get it. "Why? Where do you have to go?"

"I don't know. Wherever it leads."

"You didn't tell me who the guards are working for."

It's the same people who backed the deal in Shelby County. The same people Decker ultimately worked for. The Russians."

Sandy was completely recovered from her injuries. She was strong and didn't suffer any lingering aftereffects, no PTSD, no emotional issues. It happened, she survived, and she was past it. She slapped him on the thigh. "Good. I say go get 'em, cowboy."

"You might not think that in about two seconds."

"Why?"

"Because the Russians are fronting the money to an ISIS splinter group. Murt told all this to Becky. That's how I found out about it. Their plan is to set off a dirty bomb in the U.S."

The color drained from Sandy's face. "Where, exactly, in the U.S.?"

"Here. In Indiana. They want to hit us right in the heartland."

It took Sandy a minute to absorb everything. Her next question got right to the core of the matter. "Why Murt?"

"He's being leveraged. It's how the feds operate. I think Gibson saw an opportunity with Murt and took it. His history of undercover work with the FBI, his ready-made rap sheet, his connection to Decker…it all fit his model of the perfect operative."

"I can see that," Sandy said. "But you and I both know that there must be dozens of undercover operatives, maybe even hundreds who could handle this type of thing who are already working for either DHS or the FBI. The only thing that sets Murt apart is his connection to Decker. And if that's true, then it sounds like he's being used, or set up, or whatever."

"That's all true, except Decker isn't the only connection."

Sandy cocked her head. "What?"

"Murt isn't the only Wheeler with a rap sheet. According to Gibson, Murt's father, Ralph did some time too. He was released years ago, but the people who were protecting him on the inside aren't the types who forget much. They're looking for payback, and Murt's father is involved."

"And you think Murt has his own agenda, one where he not only takes care of Gibson's problems, but his own?"

"That's what I'm afraid of. Why else would he take the assignment?"

Sandy thought about it. "It's been a long time, Virgil. He was only a kid. I can't believe that Murton is the kind of man who would hold a grudge for forty years then go to such extreme measures to…" She let her statement hang.

Virgil finished her thought. "Kill his own father?"

She nodded at him. "Is that possible? Is he capable of that?"

"I don't know. If you'd have asked me a month or two ago…before he started looking for him, I'd have said no. Now? I'm not sure."

"What are you going to do?" Sandy said.

Virgil looked down at the pond in their backyard. "Same answer. I'm not sure."

CHAPTER FOURTEEN

They spent some time talking about the idea of Sandy, Huma, and the kids all going to Jamaica for a while. They lived close enough to the city that if a dirty bomb went off they could be in real danger...not from the explosion, but the subsequent fallout. Sandy dismissed the idea right away.

"That won't work, Virgil, and you know it. Suppose the worst happens, and these terrorists manage to set off the bomb. I can't be out of the country with the kids. Who knows how long it'd be before we could make it back? And what would we come back to? A place we could no longer live?"

"That's my point," Virgil said. "If the bomb goes off, I don't want you and the kids anywhere near here."

They went back and forth with it for a while the way

married couples do when discussing the ramifications of a possible nuclear attack, which is to say they got absolutely nowhere. In the end, Sandy said, "Besides, you promised me a honeymoon in Jamaica and until you make good on that, I'm staying right here. You'll simply have to do your job and catch these people."

Huma stuck her head out the door and said, "Hey guys, Jonas is getting hungry. Jonesy, are you going to fire up the grill and burn some chicken beyond recognition like you usually do, or should I nuke something for him?" Then, "What? What'd I say?"

Virgil decided to let the women handle dinner. He took a lawn chair and a bottle of Red Stripe down to the pond and sat next to his father's cross. He didn't have to wait long.

"Things aren't always as complicated as you seem to make them, Virg," Mason said. He picked up a small stone and skipped it across the pond. The water was still and smooth and when the stone bounced across the surface, the water remained undisturbed, as if the rock hadn't touched it. Mason clapped his hands together. "Bet you can't do that."

Virgil's father, Mason Jones, had died during a shootout at their bar a few years ago. The bullet was meant for Virgil, but hit Mason instead. After he died,

Sandy, Murton, and Delroy brought his bloodied shirt and a young willow tree out to his house. They put the shirt in the hole and planted the tree over it. A small tornado later destroyed the tree so Virgil cut what was left of its trunk into a small cross as a memorial to his father. Mason picked up another stone and bounced it in his hand. "Want to give it a go?"

He stood next to the cross, shirtless as always, the scars of the gunshot wound in his chest still visible. When he looked at his dad's skin, it reminded him of his newborn son's...pink and fresh.

Virgil heard some sort of racket behind him up at the house. When he turned in his chair he saw Huma lugging the grill into place on the deck. She smiled and waved at him. He waved back.

"I'm not keeping you, am I?" Mason asked.

Virgil squinted one eye at his father. "I was going to ask you the same thing."

"I'm not sure I take your meaning."

"I think you do," Virgil said. "Is my grief keeping you here?"

"Where, exactly, is 'here,' Virg?"

Virgil threw his hands up in the air and let them fall in his lap. "Here we go again."

The conversations Virgil had with his dead father were at once confusing and heartwarming. It sometimes reminded him of the ones he had with Delroy.

"I think you and Delroy need to take a communications class or something. Have you ever noticed that neither of you ever actually say what's on your mind? You sort of circle around it and expect me to fill in the gaps."

Mason put his hands in his pockets and leaned against the cross, a smile tugging at the corner of his mouth. "That's usually what happens when two people are talking about different things at the same time. Do you remember the night we moved back into the house, after the fire?"

It was the second question of the day that caught Virgil off guard, forcing him to change direction and alter his thought process. After a moment he said, "Of course I do. I was scared to death."

"Well, maybe not that scared," Mason said.

Virgil gave him a look.

"Okay, okay," Mason said. "Just making a point. Anyway, you were scared, and I knew it. So was I. That's why I slept on the floor by your bed that night. You remember our conversation the next morning?"

Virgil thought about it. "You said you'd never leave me. In fact, you promised me you'd never leave me."

Mason nodded. "That I did. And here I am."

"At what cost?"

"There is no cost, Virg. I've tried to tell you countless times…everything is exactly the way it should be."

"Delroy said something to me today. Have you ever heard of the Lethe?"

Mason waited a long time before he answered. "It's all Greek to me," he said, but the look on his face suggested otherwise. "I'll tell you something though, I learned a long time ago to listen very carefully to what that man says."

"It's not as easy as it sounds."

Mason nodded. "It does take some practice. I'm not quite sure how he does it, but he has a good sense of intuition."

Virgil thought for a moment and when he spoke he chose his words with care. "Murt's in trouble, Dad."

"You don't know the half of it, Bud."

"Care to fill me in?"

"I would—"

Virgil cut him off. "Wait, let me guess…you're not allowed to?"

"Well, there is some truth in that, except what I was going to say was I don't have time. Or, more to the point, you don't." Mason looked past Virgil. "I think Huma might need a little help."

Virgil turned and looked at the house. Huma was running across the yard, dragging the hose behind her. It looked like the entire grill was going up in flames. The whole unit was one big fireball and was threatening to take the deck with it.

Virgil ran to the house, grabbed the hose from Huma and began to spray down the grill. When the fire had been beaten back enough, he kicked the grill off the deck and into the yard.

"What the hell happened?" Part of Huma's hair had

been singed but other than that she seemed okay. "Are you hurt?"

She was shaking. Adrenaline. "Stop yelling at me, Jonesy."

Virgil lowered his voice. "Sorry."

"I'm fine. I don't know what happened. I turned the gas on and it wouldn't light. I thought maybe something was wrong with the sparkler thingy, or whatever it's called—"

"That'd be the igniter," Virgil said.

"Yeah, whatever, the igniter. So when I opened the lid to check…"

"You have to open the lid before you turn the gas on, Huma. Otherwise it could…ah, never mind. You're sure you're okay?"

"Yeah, but I think I ruined your grill."

Virgil didn't care about the grill. "Don't worry about it. I'm glad you're okay. Listen, how about we all go out to eat tonight?"

Huma pulled at the ends of her hair, inspecting the damage. "Let me clean up a little if that's okay. Maybe find a hat." Then, "By the way, were you talking to someone down by the pond? When I waved at you I didn't see anyone, but then when the grill went up I thought I saw someone through the smoke."

Virgil turned and looked at the cross. His father was gone, of course. "Must have had some smoke in your eyes or something."

Huma stared at him and didn't say anything. After a few moments Virgil put his arm around her and led her inside. "C'mon. I'm hungry. Let's go eat."

CHAPTER FIFTEEN

Ethan Sanders and Janie Cassidy were ready. They were high school seniors, had dated each other exclusively for almost an entire semester and both remained unfortunate virgins. That was about to change.

Ethan was a virgin because he wasn't a jock, didn't hang with the cool kids at the Jeffersonville high school, had a job as the assistant manager at the cineplex, and a two-year run of acne that would have left a leper feeling like he'd won a beauty contest. But he was kind, had good manners, a swift, if not somewhat wry wit—you learned to be funny in a hurry when your face looked like you were walking around with a permanent case of the measles—and the smartest kid in no one's favorite class, Calculus.

Janie remained a virgin for other reasons. She wasn't unattractive, she was simply plain, uninterested in cat-eye make-up, high heels, tight jeans, and three hundred dollar hairdos. She wore oversized glasses in an attempt to make her face appear smaller than it actually was and still carried a little baby fat that didn't want to go away. In short, there wasn't much about Janie that interested any of the boys in her class. And even if there had been, her mother had drilled into her over and over the dangers and pitfalls of teenage pregnancy. Like that was ever going to happen.

But when she started having trouble with Calculus, Ethan volunteered to help her through the difficult parts. They spent their afternoons together, their noses buried in the books and eventually young Ethan got her up to speed. Then one day out of nowhere, Janie leaned over and kissed Ethan right on the lips. She even slipped him a little tongue. That got Ethan up to speed as well.

"I had to do something," she told him. "I didn't think you'd ever make a move."

Ethan wiped a hand across his oily face, then down the side of his jeans. "I don't have any moves," he said. Pure honesty.

For months they didn't do anything except kiss and hold hands. Then one day in the back of Ethan's car—a genuine piece of shit Geo—Ethan got brave and ran his hand up inside of Janie's bra. When she let out a little moan he kept going. But then, she stopped him.

"I want to do it, Ethan, I really do. But not in the back seat of the car."

It was a problem for them. Both their mothers were always at home and they had nowhere to go. So Ethan got creative and bought an inflatable mattress, a cheap blanket, and a box of Trojans. When he told her his plan, Janie forgot all about the lectures her mother had given her, ready to let young Ethan help her learn something other than Calculus.

He parked the Geo around the corner from the opening of the quarry and removed the mattress from the box and let the air pump do its job. The sun was out, the day was warm, and when the mattress was ready, Janie was too. She'd stripped off her clothes, laid down on the cushion of air, covered herself with the blanket, conveniently leaving one bare breast exposed and patted the spot next to her. Ethan had his shirt off and was fumbling with his shoes. He was all the way down to his boxers when Janie sat up, made a face, and said, "What's that?"

"What's what?" Ethan asked.

"That odor. My god, don't you smell it?"

Suddenly Ethan did. He'd been so caught up with Janie's singularly exposed tit that he hadn't noticed, mostly because he'd been breathing through his mouth. But the breeze had shifted, and when he inhaled through his nostrils the offensive odor hit him like a slap in the face. "Whew, that's bad. It smells like a dead animal."

Janie wrapped the blanket around her body, stood and walked over to Ethan. "Must be a pretty big animal. Look." She pointed behind him, further down in the quarry. A flock of Turkey Vultures were picking at something. They were too far away to tell what it was.

"Wait here," Ethan said, a little wary. "I'm going to go check it out." He slipped his shoes back on and walked closer to the large birds. When he got within twenty feet or so, he stopped, picked up a few small rocks and chucked them at the birds to scare them away. When Janie saw his acne-covered back, it didn't bother her at all. But when he threw the rocks at the birds, she thought, hmm. He sort of throws like a girl. She put her clothes back on, the moment lost...not so much to Ethan's lack of athletic ability, but to the god-awful smell of death.

It took a number of throws, but Ethan finally managed to scare all the birds away. They took flight and circled the area, cawing away at the intrusion. When Ethan got close enough to see what the birds had been feeding on, he gagged twice, then vomited all over what would in a matter of days become a federal crime scene.

The Clark County deputy arrived much earlier than either Ethan or Janie would have predicted. They were still trying to stuff the mattress back into the box when he rolled up in his cruiser and burped his siren at them. He was a barrel-chested man, his brown uniform shirt strained at the buttonholes, his head shaved, his steel-toed boots polished and shiny. Without the uniform, he looked like he'd fit right in with the Klan or any other type of white supremacist group.

When the deputy walked up to them his mouth carried a crooked grin, as if a lewd joke played behind his eyes, one he had to work to keep in check. He was not, Ethan decided, someone he'd want to meet in a dark alley, badge or not. Maybe especially because of the badge.

"What are you kids doing out here?" he asked. "This area is off-limits to the public." He let his eyes roam over Janie's body from head to toe. Ethan saw him lick his lips, the crooked grin never leaving his face.

"We weren't doing anything wrong," Janie told him. "We're the ones who called."

"Uh-huh. I've managed to piece that together."

Ethan told him what they'd discovered. The deputy went and had a look, and seconds later the crime scene was contaminated a little more.

The sheriff of Clark County, a no-nonsense, lifelong cop from a long line of family cops showed up an hour later and took charge. By the end of the evening, the bodies had been bagged and tagged, and copies of fingerprints and dental molds had been sent to the NCIC to determine the identities of the two men. The prints would be a little iffy—this from the Clark County Coroner who thought the two men had probably been in the ground for the better part of a month. "Too much skin slippage. I'll get some fluids and run that through the DNA database though. What about the state?"

The sheriff pulled a toothpick from behind his ear and stuck it in the corner of his mouth. "What about them?"

"Do you want me to copy the reports to them as well?"

"That's standard procedure, as I understand it."

The coroner rolled his eyes.

The prints turned out to be a bust. But three days later the DNA came back with a hit on both of the men. Paul Fischer and Evan Reed. Fischer had been involved in a holdup at a gun shop in northern California, a smash and grab done in the middle of the night. He'd been masked and wearing gloves, but sometime between the smash part of the operation and the grab, he'd managed to cut himself and leave a nice little trail. Once the military turned over the proper records the California cops knew who he was. They discovered he lived across the line, up near Portland. They turned the matter over to the Oregon State Police, who promised to keep the California cops updated.

The Oregon cops went through Fischer's and Reed's residences and backtracked their history and known associates. Word eventually filtered out to the streets and when that happened, all the mainline hustlers, street dealers, bagmen, and grifters of every stripe looking to score some goodwill against future crimes got their motors running. Eventually, a two-time loser who was looking at life without parole on a bogus bust came forward to his probation officer and gave him a name.

Randy Stone.

The cops took Stone's place apart with the same efficiency they used to deconstruct the lives of Paul Fischer and Evan Reed. By the end of the next day, they had all the names…all the way up the chain to a guy with dual citizenship in both the U.S. and Canada. Someone named Armon Reif. Because Reif had dual citizenship, ICE got in on the action and it became a federal case. As a matter of procedure, DHS was pinged, and when that happened —for reasons neither the Oregon nor the California cops were ever told—the whole investigation seemed to grind to a halt.

Out of courtesy the lead investigator for Oregon called his counterpart in California and gave him the news. "It's a joke," the Oregon guy said. "Every single one of these guys is from my backyard."

"It's the feds," the California guy said. Being from California, he was a little more laid back than the Oregon guy. "What can you do?"

"Nothing, I guess. Still pisses me off. I've got their pictures plastered all across the state. They better think twice before they ever show up here again."

"Well, keep me up," California said. He didn't really care.

"Do that."

CHAPTER SIXTEEN

The next morning Virgil was up early...much earlier than he would have liked. He showered as quietly as possible and kissed Sandy good-bye. She mumbled something in return that was either 'love you,' or 'leave me alone.' Optimist that he was, Virgil whispered 'love you too,' tip-toed down the hallway and out the door. He hopped into his truck, jumped on the highway, and set the cruise control to five over the limit.

Heading South.

Down to Shelby County.

Last night over dinner they'd talked about the land, and couldn't quite come to an agreement over who should farm it for them this season. Sandy thought Sunnydale was the better choice, while Virgil leaned toward the remaining members of the Shelby County Co-op. Three mega-farms owned by Angus Mizner, Basil Graves, and Cal Lipkins ran the Co-op. It had been six members, but two of the six, Charlie Esser—whose land Virgil now owned—and Vernon Conrad, had been killed during Virgil's previous case. The remaining member, Hank Stutzman, had moved to Arizona after auctioning off his house and all his equipment.

"I think Sunnydale is more trustworthy," Sandy had said. "Mr. Johnson was completely honest and upfront about his operation and his intentions."

Virgil hadn't disagreed with her on the point. "That's true. I feel the same way. Carl Johnson is about as honest as they make them anymore. But when you look at the numbers we'll get a better deal from the Co-op members. They've got the advantage when it comes to covering their costs, and they've got the manpower to make sure everything gets done right, and on time."

"It isn't all about the numbers, Virgil."

"You're right, it's not. But it's mostly about the numbers."

Huma had been listening quietly, taking it all in. After a few more rounds of back and forth between Virgil and Sandy, she asked a question. "What happened with Stutzman? I don't quite understand that."

Virgil explained it to her. "When the lawyer presented the fracking deal to the group, they all wanted to go through with it, except for Charlie Esser. Stutzman jumped the gun a little and auctioned everything off, right down to the goddamned spoons—his words, not mine—and when the deal didn't go through he was stuck with no equipment, no place to live and no other choice. So he did what he'd intended to do all along. He and his wife moved to Arizona."

Huma thought about that for a minute. "So what happened to his land? Was that part of the auction?"

"No. He still owns it. The Co-op is farming it for him." He turned his attention back to Sandy. "That's another reason the Co-op would be better for us. They already know how to take care of someone else's land."

Sandy was about to reply but Huma wasn't done yet. "Jonesy, didn't you say that Sunnydale isn't in the Co-op because their operation isn't big enough?"

"Yeah."

"And you want to go with the Co-op because the numbers are better?"

"Yes, that's right."

She went back to her dinner without saying anything else. Sandy looked at Virgil. He shrugged and Huma caught it.

"Think it through, big guy. You'll get there. Pass the potatoes, will you please?"

He figured it out. When they got home from dinner, Virgil made the calls and set the meeting up. Now, at not quite five in the morning he turned his truck into the Co-op's lot. The others were already waiting for him. When he walked inside he found them seated at the table, each with a cup of coffee. They all looked like they'd been up for hours. They probably had, Virgil thought.

Lipkins got the first jab in. "That's a pretty fancy truck you got there, city-boy. I've got a load of manure that needs hauling. Think I could borrow it for a day or two? Get her nice and broke in for you."

Virgil had become friendly with the group over the past few months. They were all pretty good guys, Lipkins the possible exception. He wasn't exactly mean, but he did like to see how far he could push people. But Virgil wasn't afraid to push back. In fact, he thought if he didn't, Cal Lipkins was the type of guy who'd keep applying the pressure until something cracked. He'd seen it happen with Vernon Conrad.

"You could, Cal, except there are too many buttons on the dash. It'd take you too long to figure everything out. Besides, like goes with like. If you're hauling shit, you should do it with a piece of shit…sort of like the one you're driving. Did one of these other boys have to tow you here this morning, or did it actually start?"

Cal's face reddened, and they all laughed. Even Cal, though not nearly as much as the others. Virgil poured himself a cup of coffee and sat down. He nodded to Carl

Johnson, an acknowledgment of his presence as the other outsider, then got right to it.

"We've made our decision. I wanted to meet with all of you together because it's probably not something you're expecting. And in the spirit of full disclosure, I've already informed Carl, here, and he's agreed to it."

"Well, there you go then," Lipkins said. "Congratulations, Carl. Hope you've got the manpower. You're going to need it." He stood from the table and looked at Virgil. "Thanks for wasting my time." Then to the others: "Who wants breakfast? Angus? Basil?"

"Cal, sit down," Virgil said softly. "You don't know what I'm about to say."

Angus Mizner and Basil Graves remained seated. "Christ almighty, Cal," Graves said. "Do you have to be so dramatic about everything? Let the man say what he's gonna say."

"We already know what he's going to say."

"No we don't, Cal," Mizner said. "Now sit down."

Lipkins looked confused and a little angry, but he sat back down in his chair. He had big grey bushy eyebrows and he eventually raised them at Virgil.

"If everybody agrees to it, you're all going to get a piece of the deal. Here's what I'm thinking. I want you to tell me why it won't work."

None of them could. Virgil's plan—it was actually Huma's, though he'd never admit it to this group—was simple enough. Carl Johnson of Sunnydale Farms would handle the land for Virgil and Sandy this season on a trial basis, with an option to continue as needed, year-to-year. By taking on the land, it gave Johnson enough acreage that he was eligible to join the Co-op if he so desired.

Johnson so desired.

The Co-op would make Carl Johnson and Sunnydale Farms part of its operation, giving him full access to the manpower, equipment, and bulk purchasing agreements already in place. The addition of Virgil's land back into the fold would enable them to further leverage their positions with their suppliers, and allow Johnson to manage the land in ways he otherwise wouldn't have been able to accomplish. It was a win for everyone.

They all liked the idea, even Lipkins. And though he tried to find something wrong with it, he couldn't. They all shook on it, then got down to the nut-cutting.

The nut-cutting took the better part of three hours. All the minor details were ironed out and Virgil signed a stack of papers…purchase orders, maintenance approval forms, agreements to let the Co-op make decisions on his behalf, and on and on and on. With that done, everyone agreed that Virgil would keep his nose out of the business, especially Virgil. It was his idea.

"I trust you guys. I'll want to look at the books at the end of the season, of course, but I'll let you do your thing. Maybe bring my kid by once in a while…show him a tractor or something if I have the time, which I probably won't."

"The books won't be a problem," Mizner said. "They're handled by an outside firm. We'll make sure you get copies of everything."

Graves was nodding. "He's right. The books won't be an issue. We're all tighter'n a crab's ass at the waterin' hole. In this business you've got to be. But we're not out to screw anybody."

"Got any questions, just let us know," Lipkins said. "And bring your boy anytime. In fact, leave him with me for a week. I'll make a man out of him."

Everyone laughed, including Virgil, who would leave Jonas alone with Cal Lipkins as soon as pigs started taking flight. They all shook hands again and stood to leave. Time to get to work. Virgil hung back and made a phone call and when he finished he found Lipkins admiring his truck.

"It really is a pretty nice truck. Probably can't haul much, but I bet it hauls the mail, if you take my meaning."

Virgil smiled at him. "It sure does." He opened the door. "Here, let me start it up. Wait till you hear the engine. It sounds fantastic." He hopped inside and turned the key and when he did, all he heard was a faint clicking sound. He'd left his headlights on, and now the battery was dead.

He looked at Lipkins. "Uh, got any jumper cables?"

Lipkins bit into the side of his cheek. "Well, I'm pretty sure I do. Don't know if my piece of shit is up to the task or not, though. I wouldn't want to put a strain on the battery. Maybe you should call triple-A or something." He turned and walked away.

Virgil thought he heard him add, 'asshole' at the end of his statement. He spread his arms out and said, "Ah, Cal, I was giving you a little shit. Isn't that what you guys do? Cal? Hey, c'mon Cal."

Lipkins got in his truck and headed toward the road. When it was clear he wasn't coming back Virgil took out his phone and called Mizner, who was back at the co-op ten minutes later. "What is it with that guy?" Virgil asked after they got his truck started.

Mizner's eyes glazed over and he didn't look at Virgil when he spoke. "Cal's had a rough go of it over the years. Took some pretty heavy losses. Personal and professional. Never really got past them. He wasn't always like that. Now…" He let the statement hang.

Virgil did too. "Thanks for coming back." He got in

his truck and buzzed the window down. "Anything else I need to know about him?"

Mizner squinted at him. "Is this Virgil the cop or Virgil the farmer asking?"

Virgil thought about what Sandy had said to him. He looked at Mizner and said, "I'm not a farmer." When Mizner didn't answer he buzzed the window up and drove away.

CHAPTER SEVENTEEN

Despite his already long morning at the Co-op, Virgil was a little early for the meeting. When he got to the MCU's new facility—they were still finishing up some of the renovations—much of the parking lot was full of contractor vehicles and he discovered there was no place to park. He dumped his truck back out on the street and jogged to the entrance. Miles caught him at the door.

"Hey, Jonesy. Got a second?"

Virgil looked at his watch. "Hey, Ron. Not really," he lied. "I'm running late as it is. Maybe—"

Miles wasn't listening. Or maybe he was and simply tired of being dodged. "That seems to be the pattern with you, doesn't it? C'mon, follow me. This will only take a second." He turned and started down the hall. Virgil shook his head and followed him.

They ended up in Ron's office. As the actual head of

the MCU, Ron had taken the biggest office in the building. Virgil didn't care, as he was rarely there anyway. He still considered the office over the bar his main working space. He only showed up at the MCU headquarters when absolutely necessary. Two men waited inside and they both stood when Virgil and Ron walked in. Virgil knew one of them. The other was a stranger to him.

"Virgil, you know Andy Ross."

Ross had made a minor miscalculation on another case and Virgil chewed him out in a very public way. He apologized a short time afterward, as the chewing had been a little excessive. Ross desperately wanted to be a part of the MCU and Virgil had later cleared a path for him into the unit. Another thing that rubbed Miles the wrong way.

"Sure do. How's it going, kid?"

Ross was maybe fifteen years younger than Virgil and came highly recommended by the SWAT commander, Jon Mok. "It's going well, Sir. Happy to be here."

"Happy to have you. And save that 'sir' shit for guys wearing ties...like this one." He jerked his thumb at Miles. "Everyone calls me Jonesy."

Ross seemed to take a moment to inspect Virgil, who was dressed in a black t-shirt and blue jeans, over half-top boots. Proving he was up to the task, Ross asked, "What's that cologne you're wearing, Jonesy? It's sort of unusual."

"It's essence of cow shit No. 7. I was at a meeting down at the Shelby County Co-op. We had to figure out who...ah, never mind." He realized it would take too much explaining. He turned his attention to the other man and stuck out his hand. "Virgil Jones. Call me Jonesy. You're…?"

The other man shook his hand. "Birth Certificate says Christopher Patrick Lawless. My mom calls me C.P., but everyone else calls me Chip. Guess I'll be working with Mimi Phillips? I came from the St. Joe County Metro Homicide Unit. It's an honor to meet you, Sir…uh, Jonesy."

Virgil smiled. "A cop named Lawless, huh? That's perfect. Yeah, you'll be working with Mimi. Have you met her yet?" He was looking at Miles when he asked. Miles didn't try to hide his grin. Things had been tense between the two of them and they needed something to break the ice.

"No, I haven't. I think that's next on the agenda. Detective Miles wanted us to meet you first."

"Did he?" Virgil appreciated that and made a mental note to cut Ron some slack. His job was tough enough. "Well, welcome aboard guys. You'll see me around. Ron will get you up to speed. He's the boss. I'm a working grunt, same as you."

There was a moment of awkward silence, the kind you get when no one really knows who is supposed to step in and cover up the very obvious bullshit Virgil was spreading around.

Lawless took the lead. "I haven't met Mimi, but I have

spoken to her on the phone." Then, to ensure his point was made, he added, "My God."

That got them all going. It made Virgil feel a little like a pig, but when you're right, you're right. Mimi's voice was so hot it was possible she single-handedly contributed to global warming. Virgil clapped Lawless on the back. "You'll fit right in. Good to have you both. Ron? If there's nothing else? I really need to be on my way."

Miles seemed to soften. "Anything I need to know about?"

Virgil answered carefully. "Yes. But let's get to it later, okay?"

Miles nodded. "Sure."

Virgil thought it was the most neutral pronunciation he'd ever heard.

He took it.

Then Rosencrantz caught him in the hallway. "Jones-man. Got a second?"

"Ah, Rosie, I really don't." Then, like an idiot, "What's up?"

"You know that thing I'm working down in Bloomington?"

"I've had my ear on it," Virgil said, which wasn't a complete lie. He knew the basics, but little else, so Rosencrantz gave him the meat of it.

A female student at the university in her final year had recently disappeared. The MCU didn't normally handle missing person cases, but the Bloomington Chief of Police was married to a woman who sat on the board of directors of a company who'd contributed heavily to the governor's last campaign. The student had interned at the same company the previous summer as the chief's wife's assistant. By all accounts, her internship had gone well, and a job was waiting for her once she graduated. But now, in what was her final semester at I.U., she'd dropped off the map as if she'd never existed.

"It doesn't sound like there's been much progress," Virgil said.

Rosencrantz shook his head. "There hasn't. She lived off-campus with her boyfriend, a guy by the name of Nate Morgan. He's a student at the U, same as her. She's studying archaeology and he's in the school of medicine."

"You've eliminated him as a suspect?"

"Not officially, but if he's involved he's one hell of an actor. He admits that things were a little rough. They weren't together all that much, but he swears on his life he knows nothing about it. I tend to believe him. You ought to see this guy. He's about a foot shorter than you and weighs in at around one-twenty, tops. He's local, not one single person has had anything bad to say about him, other than the whining."

"Whining?"

"Yeah. I've never heard anything like it. It reminds me

of those parents who baby-talk to their kids, then end up baby-talking all the goddamned time, even to adults, know what I mean?" Then, with a look of skepticism, "Say, you're not doing that with Wyatt are you?"

"I'm not," Virgil said, annoyed with himself that he answered the question. "Being a whiner doesn't automatically get someone a pass or eliminate them as a suspect, Rosie."

Rosencrantz gave him a look. "Thanks for the update. He volunteered to take a lie detector test."

"So set it up. Let me know how it shakes out. Listen, I've got to run." Virgil said.

Rosencrantz wasn't finished. "I did. Not only that, I watched them administer the test. When they were finished the technician said if the boyfriend had anything to do with her disappearance she'd kiss me on the lips."

"Well, at least you've got something to look forward to."

Rosencrantz visibly shuddered. "Are you kidding? Margery would kill me. Besides, this is one of the scariest broads I've ever seen. I think she buys her makeup from an automotive paint supplier. Her B.O. smells like she's got a night gig as a pin-setter for the local bowling alley during league season. If the guy turns out to be guilty, which he's not, I'm going to change my name and disappear myself."

"So what's next?"

"That's just it…I don't know. There have been no

ransom demands. The family doesn't have any money anyway. Her old lady died a few years ago. Fun fact: she'd been married so many times she had a wedding officiant on speed dial."

"All the ex-husbands check out?"

"Yup. Solid, credible, and verified alibis on every last one of them."

"So what do you want from me?"

Rosencrantz puffed out his cheeks. "Look, I hope they find the kid, I really do. You know me, Jonesy, I've got a heart of gold. The whole thing is tearing me up. But maybe it's a case of 'like mother, like daughter.' She probably got tired of her whiny geek boyfriend, got a better offer from someone else, and split town."

"What about her bank and cell records?"

Rosencrantz scratched the back of his head. "Yeah, that is a problem. Both have been idle ever since she left. No signal on the phone and no money taken from her account."

"That's great information, Rosie. But I'll ask you again, what do you want from me?"

"I want off it, is what I want. Even the Bloomington fuzz thinks this one is going to end up like some of the others they've had down there. It's tragic, it really is, but how much time am I supposed to devote to it? We don't even have a crime scene to process. I was wondering if you could speak to Ron for me. I've tried, but—"

Virgil held up his hands. "Sorry, Rosie. No can do. I'm on thin ice with Ron. You know that."

Rosencrantz nodded. "I know." Then he leaned in closer and said, "But everyone around here knows you're really the boss. Can't you…I don't know, reassign me or something? I'm all for catching bad guys, but it's ninety-nine percent this chick is gone, like a paternity prank that went bad or something."

Virgil looked at him for a moment. "I think you mean fraternity."

Rosencrantz frowned at him. "Yeah…that's what I said."

Virgil shook his head. "Unless something big comes up, you're on it. Mac likes to keep his donors happy."

Rosencrantz didn't want to hear it. "You know those Bloomington dicks can't find their own asses without a guided tour. Their idea of a hot tip usually involves a college freshman in heels and a short skirt."

"So enjoy the view. I do have an idea though, if you're interested."

Rosencrantz looked relieved. "Yes. Please. Anything."

"Go back down there and figure it out. You'll be a hero and be able to move on to the next case."

He let his eyelids droop. "Gee, thanks, boss. That's a big help. I better not get any shit over my mileage reimbursement."

"Talk to Ron. I'm sure it'll all work out." He clapped him on the shoulder and walked away.

Rosencrantz wasn't finished though. "Maybe we ought to rename our squad. MCU could stand for Missing College Undergrad."

Virgil was already around the corner and gone, his mind on other things.

CHAPTER EIGHTEEN

HE DIDN'T GET FAR. CORA GRABBED HIM AS HE ROUNDED the corner. This, Virgil thought, is why he didn't spend more time at the office. "What's up?" he asked, a little more annoyance in his voice than he intended. "I'm going to be late for the meeting. And why aren't you there?"

Cora gave him a look. "Let's step into your office. And how about you ratchet it back a little? We've got a few minutes and I need to talk with you."

Virgil tugged at his earlobe and made an effort to slow down a bit. "Sure." He looked around for a moment and Cora caught it. They were new to the building and this was only the second time Virgil had been inside.

"You don't know where your office is, do you?" Cora said, a satisfied grin on her face.

Cora led him through the building, tugging at his elbow twice as he almost made a couple of wrong turns. Once there, they discovered his office hadn't been furnished yet. It was completely empty. "Maybe Ron is trying to send you a message," Cora said. "I guess we'll have to stand."

Virgil covered for him. "I told him I wanted to pick out my own stuff. I haven't gotten to it yet."

"Right. Listen, I spoke with Gibson earlier this morning. The meeting has been set back an hour. And we're having it over at the federal building instead of here."

"Why?"

Cora shrugged. "Who knows? It's probably a turf thing. I'm sure Gibson doesn't want to walk into our building and make a presentation. He wants us to come to him. Don't be so surprised."

"I'm not, really," Virgil said. He walked over to the window and raised the blinds to let some light in. "Did you tell Becky?"

"Everyone knows."

"What about the governor?"

"What about him," the governor said as he walked into the room. He looked around the empty office. "I came down to inspect the new digs. I guess they're saving your office for last. I love the natural light, though. It really sort of opens up the whole room." He smiled at his own joke, then said, "So, Jonesy, how's it feel to have fuck-you money?"

Virgil gave the governor a flat stare. "I wish everyone would stop saying that. I don't have *any* money, Mac. I have the land, that's all."

The governor shrugged his shoulders. "Same thing, really. If you're smart, that is." Then he raised his chin a fraction of an inch, an unmistakable whiff of authority in his voice. "I don't believe I've ever heard you call me that before."

Virgil felt his face redden. "Uh, sorry, Sir. That sort of slipped out."

The governor waved him off. "Let me know if you need any advice. Our family made its money in real estate."

"Yes Sir, I will."

"Jonesy, drop the 'sir,' will you? How long have we known each other? You're one of the few people I have in my life who tells me the truth whether I want to hear it or not. That matters to me more than anything. Mac is fine."

Virgil nodded. "You got it. Listen, about Murton…"

The governor held up his hands. "I'll let you and Cora handle the details." He paused in thought for a few seconds, then said, "However, I do think—"

"Mac." Cora snapped at him. "Let me."

Virgil knew what was happening. He'd seen it before with Pearson when he'd been the governor's chief of staff. Had to protect the boss.

The governor tipped his head and said, "Well, guess that's my cue." He looked directly at Virgil. "Anything you need, you'll have it."

"Thanks, Mac."

The governor walked out the door, then two seconds later stuck his head back in. "Listen, when we're in public though…"

Virgil got it. "Yes, Sir."

AFTER THE GOVERNOR WAS GONE: "IS HE BEING squeezed?"

Cora didn't hesitate. "No. And even if he was, he wouldn't let it get in the way, not on something like this."

Virgil thought she was probably right. Politics was one thing. A bomb laced with radioactive material was a whole other matter. "Murt told me he was there, the night Decker was…handled. Why?"

"Mac agreed to meet with Gibson and hear him out, that's all."

"With cleaners standing by? C'mon, Cora."

"Yeah, that was a little out of bounds."

"A little?"

Cora shrugged it off. "It's the big leagues, Jones-man. Their paths were bound to intersect anyway. The fracking deal in Shelby County was just the tip of the iceberg.

Gibson wanted Mac to release Murton so he could work the undercover part of his operation."

"Gibson looked like he was going to go under himself."

"I noticed that," Cora said. "How about we get Becky and head over to the federal building?"

"You bet."

The three of them arrived right on time at the federal building. They were delayed a few minutes while Virgil checked his weapons. With that done, they were all assigned visitor badges and led to a conference room on the third floor. Agent Gibson was already present, along with two other agents Virgil didn't recognize. When he tried to introduce himself, the agents gave him a blank stare.

"Don't mind them," Gibson said. "Have a seat, please."

"They all sat down and Virgil got right to it. "Where's Murton? Why isn't he here?"

Gibson sucked in his cheeks and looked at nothing. After a few seconds, he said, "Murton has already begun his portion of the operation. As such, he won't be joining us this morning."

Becky jumped up from her chair. "What?"

One of the two agents observing the meeting took a

step forward and Gibson caught it out of the corner of his eye. He held up a hand and the agent stopped, then returned to his place against the wall.

"Murton told me this morning that he was going to be here," Becky said. "He didn't say anything about starting right away."

Gibson held out his hands in a 'what can I say?' gesture. "An opportunity presented itself. When I informed Murton, we both agreed it would be in the best interest of the operation if he took every advantage."

Becky sat down in her seat. Virgil saw the look on her face and found himself relieved he wasn't on the receiving end of her glare. Gibson seemed unfazed.

"Then where, exactly, is he, Agent Gibson?" Virgil asked.

Gibson looked at his watch. "I'd say passing over central Iowa right about now. He's on a prison transport aircraft, headed to the federal pen in Sheridan, Oregon. Most people don't know this, but they really do call those flights Con-Air."

Becky pointed her finger at Gibson, about to say something. She was hot. Whatever it was wouldn't be helpful, Virgil was certain. He put his hand on her arm and looked at her. She lowered her arm and placed it on the table, both her hands now clenched into fists.

"Walk us through your thought process, Agent Gibson," Cora said. The tone of her voice suggested it wasn't a request.

Gibson paused, an effort to show who was in charge. "Murton is on his way to Sheridan. Given the length of the flight and then the ground transportation to the facility itself he should arrive in about six hours. After that, he'll be processed and put into protective custody for a few days. That will create a level of...mmm...curiosity, among both the other inmates and the guards. He's perfectly safe."

"How so?" Virgil said.

"Jack Grady is with him. In case you hadn't noticed, Detective Grady isn't here this morning either. He's on the plane with Murton, acting as a corrections officer. When they get to the facility, Grady will stay on as a guard." Gibson looked at Becky. "He's not alone. We've thought this through."

"You better have," Becky said. She said it through her teeth.

Gibson went on to tell them the entirety of the plan. "After a few days in protective custody, he'll be released into the general population. We expect someone will make contact with him and offer a way out in exchange for his unique abilities."

Virgil was starting to put it together. Murton had been an explosives demolition expert during his time in the service. With his military background and his criminal record, he'd be the ideal candidate to get inside a terrorist cell planning to detonate a dirty bomb in Indianapolis.

"What's your plan if no one makes contact?" Virgil wanted to know.

"We're confident they will," Gibson said.

"How about you answer the question?"

Gibson sighed, as if he were explaining the situation to a group of middle-school students. "We have valuable, credible sources already inside the facility. We are completely confident this will play out the way we anticipate."

Now it was Virgil's turn to point a finger, and he did. "Bullshit. You might have people already inside, but you and I both know that no plan ever executes without something going sideways, even if it's only a minor diversion. So answer the question, Paul. What if no contact is made? What happens then?"

"Then we pull him out, simple as that. He'll return to duty for the state and we'll have to reassess our options."

"And what are those options?" Cora asked.

"I'm afraid I can't say. That's classified information."

Virgil laughed without humor. "Of course it is. No different than any other federal operation, is it? The state does all the work, takes all the blame when things go to shit, all while the feds sit on their collective asses and watch from computer screens."

"That is not what is happening here, Detective," Gibson said, a little hot now.

"Isn't it?"

"No, it's not." He paused for a moment to collect his

thoughts, but when he spoke, his words came out quickly, as if he didn't want to address what Virgil had said. "There's more at play here than you realize."

"I think everyone understands the stakes, Agent Gibson," Cora said.

"Especially me," Becky added.

Gibson tried some diplomacy. "Murton is the perfect candidate for the job. That's why we're using him."

"That's not the entire reason, though, is it, Paul?" Virgil said.

Gibson turned and looked at the other two federal agents. "Could we have the room, please?"

The agents looked first at Gibson, then each other. After a moment one of them shrugged, opened the door and they both stepped out.

Gibson waited until they were gone. "No, it's not the entire reason. When Murton found out about the operation, he volunteered. It seems he has some unfinished business with his father…a father who happens to be one of our confidential informants on this case."

"You know what the problem with all of this is, Gibson?" Becky said. "You couldn't let the sleeping dog lie. Murton hadn't seen or spoken with his father in decades. He wasn't even looking for him until you showed up one night with a cleaning crew, along with a carrot and a stick. He considers you a friend."

Gibson was getting annoyed. "It's a damned good

thing I did show up, otherwise your beloved Murton would be sitting on death row for Decker's murder."

Virgil barked out a laugh. "That's one way to view it. Here's another: You were there before Murt was. You had cleaners in place, ready and waiting. Murt might have gone down for taking Decker out, but chances are when it all came out in the open, you'd be right there with him." Virgil leaned into his statement. "And it would have come out, Paul. I guarantee it."

Gibson chuffed. "Would it?" He turned his attention to Cora. "What's your take on the matter, Ms. LaRue? Better yet, what say the governor? What's his level of culpability in the matter regarding Decker's death? He was there too, you know." He looked at Virgil. "By the way, how is your son, Jonas, Detective? Everything seems to have worked out well with your family, hasn't it?"

Virgil jumped out of his chair and was across the table before Gibson knew what was happening. He grabbed Gibson by his tie and yanked him forward, their faces inches apart. "Bring my son into this mess you've created and I will personally make sure they never find *your* body. Am I making myself clear? A cleaning crew won't be necessary."

"Jonesy," Becky yelled. "Let him go. Jonesy…"

Virgil pushed Gibson away so hard he stumbled and fell to the floor on his butt.

"I could charge you with assault on a federal officer," Gibson said as he stood. "That's mandatory jail time,

Jones. Touch me again and see what happens." He straightened his tie and jacket.

"Mention my son again," Virgil said. He wasn't backing down.

Cora took over. "That's enough. Both of you. Sit down." She looked at Virgil. "I mean it."

Virgil was breathing through his mouth. He finally nodded at her and took a seat. She turned her attention to Gibson. "As for you, Agent Gibson, let me make something perfectly clear. The governor brought me on to his team to get his house in order. I've done exactly that. It was no easy task, believe me. But done is done. You think we didn't take certain precautions before your little meeting a few months ago? Bring whatever you've got to the table and we'll let the public decide who's culpable. I promise you this: It won't be Murton Wheeler." She shook her head and let out a little chuckle. "And it sure as hell won't be Mac."

Gibson suddenly didn't look so smug.

"Now," Cora continued, "how about we all start over?"

Gibson chewed on the inside corner of his lip. "This meeting was held as a courtesy. It's now over." He looked at the three of them. "Stay out of our way. It's not a request." He opened the door and the two agents stepped back into the room. "These gentlemen will show you out.

Once they were back in Virgil's office at the MCU, he thought for a moment, then pulled out his phone.

"Who are you calling?"

"Jack Grady."

"Don't bother," Cora said. "I already tried."

Virgil let the phone ring anyway. When he was connected he got the same 'no longer in service' message. He wanted to throw the phone against the wall, but managed not to. "So all of our connections to Murt and the entire operation have vanished."

"That about says it." Cora walked over and looked out the window. When she turned back, her face was cast in shadow. "Gibson pulled Murton into his operation by dangling the only carrot he had. Murt's father. Maybe that part doesn't matter now that he's in. I don't know because we don't know how Ralph Wheeler fits in with all of this. What I do know is if you and Becky are going to help him, you're going to be operating without the assistance of the federal government."

Virgil—now glad he hadn't destroyed his phone—called Ron Miles. "Are you still in the building? Good. Would you come down to my office? I'm here with Cora and I need to ask you something." He listened for a moment, then said, "I don't know. Hold on." He gave the phone to Cora. "Would you tell Ron where my office is, please?"

Miles walked in thirty seconds later and stopped right inside the doorway. The corner of his mouth twitched upward. "Where's all your stuff?"

Virgil ignored the question. "I need a favor."

If Miles was surprised, he didn't show it. "I'm sure it was a simple mix-up. I'll make sure you get some furniture as soon as possible."

"Ron, I don't care about that. I need something else."

Miles gave him a suspicious look. "What?"

"Rosencrantz is tied up with the missing I.U. student. I need Ross."

"What for?"

Virgil glanced at Cora. She raised her eyebrows, let the corners of her mouth turn down, and nodded. Virgil spent ten minutes and laid it out for him. When he finished the look on Ron's face was similar to that of a person sitting in the front seat of a small passenger plane as the unmistakable odor of an electrical fire assaulted their nostrils.

"Ron?"

Miles nodded, took out his phone, and called Ross. "Get up to Virgil's office right now." There was a pause, then Miles turned his back and lowered his voice. Second floor. It's the only one with no furniture."

Virgil heard him. Cora did too. When he turned back

around they both stared at him. "Really, your stuff is on the way. I swear."

Ross showed up two minutes later. "You're assigned to Virgil until further notice," Miles said. "You'll report to him and he'll fill me in as needed. That clear?"

Ross looked around the room. "Yes, Sir."

Miles looked at Virgil. "Good luck." He walked out before Virgil could respond.

Virgil looked at Ross. "Let's go, kid."

When they turned to leave the room Cora called out to him. "Jonesy?"

He thought she was going to try to stop him, but she surprised him instead. She walked over and placed her hand on his chest. "Be careful."

Virgil told her he would. He didn't know exactly what he was going to do, but he knew with every fiber of his being he would not stand idly by while Murton went off to slay the dragons of his past. Like it or not, he planned to stand shoulder to shoulder with his brother to the bitter end.

Of course, that was four weeks ago.

CHAPTER NINETEEN

FOUR DAYS AGO

Almost four weeks passed in agonizing slowness. Virgil, Becky, and Ross worked every angle they could think of to help Murton and Grady. Since they knew where both men were—Murton was in lock-up at Sheridan, with Grady there as his backup, most of their efforts went into researching two disparate things: missing or stolen explosives was one. Ralph Wheeler was the other. The ATF cooperated with them regarding the explosives, but mostly, Virgil thought, because there was nothing to cooperate on. There'd been no unsolved thefts of any explosive material large enough to cause any real concern. Would that change when and if Murton got out of prison as planned? Virgil didn't know. He also didn't say anything to the ATF about it.

Ralph Wheeler was a ghost. Becky, with all her research skills and backdoor entries into almost every usable database that mattered turned up exactly nothing on him from the time he'd been released from Sheridan over ten years ago. She'd spent weeks looking and still had feelers and traps out, but they'd now reached the point where no one had their hopes set very high.

They also went back to Radiology, Inc., the nuclear pharmaceutical manufacturer in Louisville, and met with the CEO, Rick Said. While he wasn't happy to see Virgil and Ross, he assured them he'd cooperate with their investigation.

"I simply don't see it," Said said. He didn't look much like a nuclear pharmaceutical company CEO. He looked, Virgil thought, more like a writer, or maybe an anthropologist, though Virgil would have been the first to admit he didn't know what an anthropologist looked like and probably wouldn't even if one walked up and slapped him. He was dressed in blue jeans that sat high on his waist and wore a tan shirt with too many pockets. His white hair was combed neatly to the side. They were seated in his office and Said pulled out a bottom desk drawer and propped a boot on top of the corner. "All of our people are vetted ten ways from Sunday."

"Looks like you're going to have to re-examine your procedures then," Virgil said. "Somebody slipped through. Our researcher says your logs were tampered with and since all of the actual material has been accounted for, we have to believe she's right. Unless you have a different idea, that is."

Said locked his fingers together in a steeple, the way CEOs do, and thought about it. "I don't," he eventually said. "But when I think about it, I can't put my finger on who it might be. We run a pretty tight ship. I know every single person who works here. To think that one of them…" He shook his head and let the thought finish itself. "Anyway, I meant what I said. I'll help in any way I can. If word of this got out, we'd be finished. No one is more interested in catching these guys than I am."

"There's more at stake than your company's reputation here, Mr. Said. If enough of your material gets packed into a bomb, we're talking about the loss of an entire city."

Said put his feet on the floor. "Yes, yes, of course. I know what's at stake. I didn't mean to imply that I'm unsympathetic to the situation. I've got family in Indy."

"So do we," Ross said with a little bite. He might be new to the unit, but it wasn't his first day as a cop working a civilian.

Said raised his hands, palms out. "Guys, really, I get it. Our next big shipment goes out in four days. Tell me what to do."

"We've got an idea," Virgil said. "But we're going to have to be careful."

After he told him what he wanted, Said was a little reluctant. "It's a fine idea, except I don't know who to pick."

Virgil's plan was simple enough. They'd take one of Said's employees, someone he trusted, and temporarily remove them from their position. They'd fabricate a story…death in the family, a serious illness, something, and replace that person with one of their own. Once they had that person inside, they'd watch for indicators that someone was doctoring the records.

"You won't have to pick one person," Virgil said. "In fact, we'd like you to pick a handful of people. People you'd trust with your life…your family's life. Then give the list to us and our researcher will do a deep dive into their history. It's what she does, and she'll pick the one who's the cleanest. Then they'll get a nice long vacation out of the country, all expenses paid, and our guy will be brought in to take their place."

Said frowned. "I guess I don't have to ask who's paying for this vacation, do I?"

"You can ask," Virgil said.

"But you already have the answer," Ross finished the thought for him.

"Okay, okay," Said said. "But let me ask you something. "If this researcher of yours is so good, why not do the opposite? Why not look at everyone and figure out who's in a position to be compromised?"

"We already have," Virgil said. "Everyone came back

clean on a basic check. We can't go any deeper because there are too many people. Going that deep on everyone would take weeks and we don't have that kind of time."

Said didn't like it much, but he went along with it.

Virgil wanted to talk about the shipment. "How big is it?"

"It's a big one," Said said. "An entire container is being sent up to Purdue University. They'll use most of it for research, and periodically distribute the rest to hospitals and other medical facilities as needed. Most people don't know that…that the universities handle secondary distribution."

"I take it this shipment is big enough to be cause for concern if it ended up in a bomb," Ross said.

Said visibly swallowed, then nodded. "I'll be making arrangements for my family to leave the area until that shipment arrives safely at Purdue, if that tells you anything."

Virgil shook his head. "I can't legally tell you not to do that, Mr. Said, but I'm going to anyway. If word of this gets out, the entire state…maybe even the entire Midwest is going to panic. You could start something that might do more damage than the bomb."

Said pointed a finger at them, his voice tense. "That's bullshit, and you know it."

"It isn't," Virgil said. "People would die. They'd panic and they'd run. There'd be violence, suicides, accidents, everything." He walked over and got in Said's face. He'd been prepared for this type of reaction and knew how to bring Said back to earth. "And that's the human cost. Think about the financial costs. Your company is publicly traded, isn't it?"

Said didn't answer. He didn't have to. Virgil could see his wheels turning. He knew if he leaked the information and it got out of control, the value of his company would be reduced to nothing. When he finally did speak, his tone was resigned, the fear in his voice real.

"Catch these bastards then. I'll do what I can. You'll have the names later today."

Virgil said they'd be in touch.

Later that afternoon Said sent them the names of five people he said were beyond reproach. Virgil called Becky into his office, gave her the names, and told her to get started. She took the list and turned to leave just as Cora walked in, a binder tucked under her arm.

Virgil caught the look in her eye. "What?"

"Mac wants you in Bloomington. The Doyle case."

"Rosie's on that."

"Not anymore. Ron pulled him off. A couple of kids found two decomposed bodies in a quarry down in the southern part of the state, so that's his. Besides, we need fresh eyes on Doyle. This is a big priority with Mac."

Becky walked over and stood next to Virgil. "What about Murton?"

Cora chose her words carefully. "He's operating outside the scope of our department, Becky. It's been almost a month and not only haven't we heard from him or agent Gibson, we've gathered no logical or credible intel that helps him or us."

"We have to keep trying," Becky said, a touch of panic riding in her voice.

Cora looked at Virgil. "We can't let our personal lives dictate how we do our jobs." She turned and fixed her gaze on Becky. "Virgil works for me. You're a contracted agent hired by him. How he allocates his resources outside of this office is not my concern." She handed the binder to Virgil. "Here's everything on the Doyle case. This one doesn't slip through the cracks, understood?"

Virgil said he did.

"Get it figured out. And good luck. I think you're going to need it." She was looking at Becky when she said it.

VIRGIL AND BECKY WERE STILL PROCESSING WHAT CORA had told them when she popped back into Virgil's office and turned on the television.

"What is it, Cora?" Becky said.

She looked at Becky then pointed at the TV. "There's

a riot in progress at Sheridan. So far two inmates have been killed, a guard is in critical condition, half of an entire cell block is on fire and one inmate is missing."

"Who's missing, Cora? What's the inmate's name?" Virgil asked.

Cora flipped through the channels until she got one of the cable news networks. The network showed an aerial view of the prison facility. The shot was high enough they saw other helicopters circling below. Though no actual flames were visible, smoke was pouring out of the doorways and narrow windows at one end of the facility. A line of fire trucks was positioned outside the perimeter of the grounds. The firemen wouldn't be able to fight the fire until the prison was properly locked down.

Virgil stood and moved closer to the TV. "Cora, answer me. Who's missing?"

Cora didn't have to. The aerial shot on the screen was replaced with a picture of Murton. His head had been shaved and he was dressed in an orange jumpsuit. The caption on the screen identified him as Michael Weller.

Virgil looked at his boss. "Cora?"

Cora turned up the volume on the television and said, "Look."

A reporter was standing outside the fence, his hair and jacket and tie blown sideways by the wind. He was in mid-sentence when Cora raised the volume.

"…have learned the corrections officer who was injured during the escape has died. The officer, Jack

Grady, was a rookie at the facility, originally from Louisville, Kentucky. Doctors have told us he died only moments ago from what they're calling a TBI—a traumatic brain injury. We're also being told that while heroic efforts were taken by the surgeons to reduce the swelling of his brain, their efforts were unsuccessful and officer Grady died on the operating table. No other information is available regarding the escaped felon, Michael Weller, however authorities have informed us that when captured, Weller will face additional charges of first-degree murder of a law enforcement officer, which carries a mandatory death sentence if convicted on those charges."

Becky looked at the TV for a long moment before turning to Virgil. She moved her lips, but no words came out of her mouth. Virgil stood and moved toward her, but she shook her head and walked out of the room.

Because Becky worked as a contracted agent for the MCU, she didn't have an office at the new building. When Virgil went looking for her he wasn't surprised to discover she was no longer there. He made it back to his office where he tried to concentrate on the information contained in the Doyle binder, but no matter the speech Cora had given him, he found he wasn't up to the task. He took out his phone and called Delroy.

"Yeah, mon. Just a little while ago. She seemed upset too. What you do now, you?"

"I'll be there as soon as I can. Don't let her leave."

"How I do that, me?"

"Probably by not telling her I'm on my way."

"Yeah, mon. Dat might be the first good idea you've had lately."

Thirty minutes later Virgil was at the bar. He spoke with Delroy for a few minutes, then went up to the office. "It could be part of the plan, Becks. The escape. He was sent out there to get the attention of the right people. It looks like he may have done exactly that."

Becky was sitting on the edge of her desk. "At what cost, Jonesy? You heard what they said. Jack Grady is dead. It doesn't matter what they were doing or how they planned to do it. Murton is going to be on the hook for the murder of a police officer. Even if it all comes out that the whole thing was an undercover operation, which you and I both know it won't, he'll still be charged and convicted of murder."

Virgil leaned against the desk and put his arm around her, but she pushed him away. "This is your fault, Jonesy."

"Me? How is this my fault?"

She punched him in the chest with the sides of her

fists. "You're his brother. You promised me nothing was going to happen to him, remember?" She punched him again. "I told you not to make promises you couldn't keep, but you wouldn't listen. You could have stopped him from getting involved in all this but you didn't, and now not only is he gone, he's being hunted for the murder of Jack Grady." She punched him some more until Virgil wrapped her up in his arms and held her tight.

He didn't know what else to do.

CHAPTER TWENTY

VIRGIL WAS UP EARLY THE NEXT MORNING, SLEEPY-EYED after a long night of reviewing the Doyle book. He was making a fast run to Bloomington in hopes that he might be able to break something loose. He wasn't hopeful, but he had to try. Since he lived close to highway 37, the main stretch from Indy to Bloomington, the trip wasn't that bad. He used his flashers and siren when the traffic was heavy and made the trip in thirty minutes.

Rosencrantz had been working alone in his search for Patty Doyle, running his investigation apart from the Bloomington Police Department. Despite what Rosie'd told him a few weeks ago, Virgil thought the Bloomington guys had and still were doing everything they could to find the missing woman. Rosencrantz had made the hot tip remark out of pure frustration. The truth of it was,

Virgil thought, the detectives assigned to the case were doing every single thing there was to do. In addition, they freely shared every scrap of information with Rosencrantz. When Virgil went over those scraps as a whole, he couldn't figure out what they might be missing. He'd have to start over. Look for something out of the ordinary if he was going to find her.

Then he revised his own thought process. Given the amount of time that had passed, he was all but certain his efforts wouldn't end up with Patty Doyle returning safe and sound, back to her young life and normal routine. In all probability the work would amount to the recovery of a body and prosecution of a suspect should one be captured and charged.

He hung his head and massaged the bridge of his nose with his thumb and forefinger, the grimace on his face a stark contrast to what he hoped to find, measured against the hard reality of what he thought he probably would.

HE WAS AT HER APARTMENT. IT WAS A SMALL, TWO-bedroom unit less than a half-mile from campus. Though it was the last place she'd been seen, the Bloomington Crime Scene technicians had long ago ruled out the apartment itself as the scene of the crime.

Virgil knew the history of the university and missing young women was not a good one. The university, and by extension, the city of Bloomington had something of a problem with young women falling prey to kidnapping and murder. Spend any amount of time in the cold case files of the Bloomington Police Department and all the information is readily available. The cases, both cold and solved added up to a grisly array of murder, mayhem, and tragic mystery.

A young college student goes for a bike ride and never returns. Three years later her remains were discovered in a swampy thicket in nearby Morgan County. An evening stroll through downtown Bloomington takes you past several well-known places—a popular bar, an upscale apartment building, a row of townhouses—all of which happened to be the last stops of another young female college student. When she turned the corner behind the row of townhouses she disappeared forever, never to be seen or heard from again. Her body was never recovered. A national campaign was mounted, her story appearing on the national news and prominent television programs like *America's Most Wanted*. But the case was never solved and few legitimate tips ever materialized. Or what about the hotel in Bloomington where yet another young female student partied with her friends the night she died? At some point the party ended and she left for home. Her body was later found near a narrow country lane right outside the city limits.

Drive around long enough and you'll find memorials marking the spots where young female victims have been found. Flowers, cards, hand-made crosses, and withered balloons in ditches, faded and deflated, much like the people they attempt to honor and memorialize. Those were the thoughts running through Virgil's mind as he looked around the apartment. He opened the binder, found the number he needed, and pulled out his phone. When the whiny voice of Nate Morgan answered the call, Virgil told him where he was and what he wanted.

"I can't right now," Morgan whined. "I'm about to walk into class."

"Which class?"

"Biology. I've got an exam we're prepping for."

"Thanks for the info. Here are your choices: Get over to Patty's apartment right now, or I'll personally come over there and drag your sorry ass out of class in handcuffs."

"What? What? You can't do that. I didn't do anything. I'm not guilty of any wrongdoing. Nobody wants to find her more than I do."

"Just as soon as you're all prepped for your test, though, right?"

"Hey, that's not fair."

"Yeah, it sucks to be you, Nate. You know who else it sucks for right now? Patty Doyle. And I didn't say you were guilty. I simply said get over here." He put some gravel in his voice. "And I mean right now. If I don't see you inside of thirty minutes, I will personally make your last semester of college a genuine shit show. Are you hearing me on this, Nate?"

NATE MORGAN DIDN'T LIKE IT, BUT HE SHOWED UP. He brought some attitude with him and Virgil had to hand it to the kid, whiner or not, at least he had his balls out.

"This is bullshit, man. I don't know what college was like for you, but for me, it's a job. I've got to keep my grades up or I'll lose my scholarship. If that happens, I'll never get accepted into med school. Do you know what that would do to me?"

"No, I don't. And guess what? I don't care. I didn't go to college. I served in the military. Stop making assumptions with people you know nothing about. And lose the attitude because if you don't, here's how this is going to go: You were the last person we know of that saw Patty Doyle prior to her disappearance. No, no, let me finish my thought here because you see, Nate, I don't think you're guilty. But it doesn't matter what I think. What matters is what the public thinks. If I don't get some cooperation from you starting right now, you won't be prosecuted in a court of law, but you will be convicted in the court of public opinion. How do you think that might look if you get through med school? Think anyone will want to hire a doc with a questionable history regarding another missing female I.U. student? I doubt it, but then again, I could be wrong. It's happened before."

Nate Morgan sat down on the sofa. "What do you want from me? I already told the campus cops, the Bloomington police and that other state guy, Rosepetals or whatever his name is—"

"That'd be Detective Rosencrantz."

Morgan waved it off. "Yeah, yeah, whatever. I told Rosencrantz, the Bloomington cops, and the lie detector woman everything I know. I passed the lie detector by the way. With flying colors. Those are the words she used."

"Yeah, I see that. It's right here in the binder."

"I know," Morgan said, a little annoyed now. "That's my point. I don't have anything else to offer."

Virgil didn't say anything. He simply stared at him.

After a full minute, Morgan said something that surprised him. "We were about finished anyway."

"Finished? What do you mean, finished? With school?"

Morgan shook his head. "No. Well, yes…with school, but that's not what I'm talking about. She and I were about finished with our relationship. She was starting to get a little bored. I could tell. She was getting a lot of looks ever since she got in shape and I think she sort of enjoyed it or something. I mean look at me. I'm no prize and she turned out to be pretty hot. It was only a matter of time before she sent me on my way."

"That make you jealous? Maybe a little angry?"

Morgan turned the corners of his mouth down and let his head rock back and forth. "Nah. I liked her better when she needed me. Who wouldn't? No one wants to be around someone who doesn't want or need them, am I right?"

Morgan's denial of anger and jealousy was so matter of fact, Virgil believed him. "Was she seeing anyone else that you know of?"

Morgan was emphatic in his response. "No, absolutely not. She wouldn't do that. Not to me or to herself. She simply wasn't like that."

Virgil rubbed the bottom of his nostrils with his index finger. "So what was she like? What was she passionate about?" Morgan took so long to answer Virgil thought, *no wonder she was going to break it off with him. He doesn't know.*

When Morgan finally did answer, the information was basic. "She liked two things, man. Her work—the study of archeology—and running. She ran five miles every day, rain or shine."

Virgil made a mental note that Nate had referred to Patty in the past tense. He turned to a particular page in the binder. "If she loved her work…her studies so much, why did she skip a three-hour lecture on the day she went missing?"

Morgan shrugged. "The class was a drag. Some sort of ethical bullshit. She wasn't in to it. It was the first time she skipped one of her core classes though. I don't know if that matters or not."

"Probably doesn't," Virgil said. He wrote it down in his notebook anyway. "So if she skipped her class that day, she…" he let it hang.

Another shrug. "She said she had something she had to get at the post office. And I know she would have gone for a run."

"Where did she usually run?"

Morgan pinched an eye shut. "Different places. Sometimes through campus. Sometimes around town. Every once in a while she'd drive out to the Yellowwood State forest and hit the trails. She didn't have a particular route. She just ran. Had one of those apps on her phone that tracked how far she'd gone. Some sort of GPS thing or something like that. So about the time she hit the two or three-mile mark, she'd swing around and head back home."

Virgil had been writing everything down and suddenly stopped. He thought for a few seconds, then took out his phone and made a call. "Hey Becks, it's me. Yeah, I'm good. Anything? Well, keep after it." Then, "Hey, hold on a second." He took the phone away from his ear and looked at Morgan. Do you know the app? It's name?"

Morgan shook his head.

"iPhone, though, right?"

Morgan nodded at him.

"Listen, don't take this the wrong way, but I need you

to go wait outside for a few minutes. Don't go anywhere. Just wait."

Morgan rolled his eyes and walked out the apartment door.

To Becky: "Sorry, Becks. Listen, I need two things: Tell Ron...wait, scratch that...*ask* Ron to get the paperwork in order for a subpoena on Doyle's iCloud account. She had some sort of GPS jogging app on her phone. There's a possibility she went missing while doing her daily run. If we can get those records, we might have our first solid lead in this case."

"I can do that," Becky said. Virgil thought she sounded awfully tired. "And I will. But if you can get me her username, I've got a program that can—well, never mind. Can you get her username?"

"Good question. Hold on." Then, "Morgan." He shouted it at the apartment door.

The door popped open. "What was Patty's iCloud username?"

Morgan smiled in a sad, wistful way. It was 'SheDigsItIU.' Capital letters on the S, D, both I's and the U."

"Thanks. Don't happen to know the password, do you?"

"What do you think?"

"Yeah, yeah." He pointed at the door. "Back outside." Once the door was closed: "You get that, Becky?"

"Yeah, I got it. Might take a while."

"Call me if you get something, otherwise I'll get with you tonight or tomorrow."

Becky promised she would.

CHAPTER TWENTY-ONE

That night a Department of Homeland Security Gulfstream G-5 taxied across the tarmac at the Louisville airport and parked near an obscure hangar at the far end of the field. A nondescript sedan with Agent Paul Gibson at the wheel pulled up to the jet as the air-stair door lowered into position. The pilots kept the engines running as the lone figure exited the aircraft. He got into the sedan and the jet taxied back out to the runway, powered up, and began its takeoff roll. A few seconds later it disappeared into the night sky.

Gibson drove through the city and a half-hour later parked at the address where Reif and his crew were staying. The men walked up to the house and Gibson used a key on the front door. When they were inside with the door closed behind them, the lights came on and Paul

Gibson and Murton Wheeler found themselves surrounded by Reif and his men, each with a shotgun leveled at them and ready to fire.

Wheeler and Gibson were unfazed. Murton took the lead. "They said you'd be expecting us. How about you throttle it back to idle and lose the hardware?"

Reif looked them over for a moment. "How do we know you're who you say you are?"

The old man they all knew as Ron Weller came around the corner. "Put them guns away. I ought to know who they are." He pointed at Gibson. "The one that looks like he's been out in the woods is with me." Then he jerked his thumb at Murton. "The one with the bald head there… that's my boy, Michael." Ralph Wheeler looked at Murton. It was the first time they'd seen each other in almost forty years.

Murton, who spent almost half his adult life working undercover, who was trained not to show surprise of any kind when placed in a compromising position, simply couldn't help himself. He shot Gibson a quick look. He'd known at some point during the operation he'd be in contact with his father, except not quite so quick…and not now.

He turned his attention back to the other men, then singled out his father. "How's it going, Pops?"

Ralph Wheeler didn't answer. Murton could tell by the look on his face they were both thinking the same thing…

the words they'd last said to each other the night Murton joined Virgil's family.

Chase broke the silence. "Hey, I saw you on TV. You're the one busted out of the joint back in Oregon." He lowered his gun.

Stone did the same. "Yep, that's him alright. They're saying you're the one who killed the guard."

"I don't give two shits what's on TV," Murton said. "I didn't kill any guard."

Reif shrugged, like it made no difference to him. "They'll still hang it on you if you're caught." He turned his attention to the old man. "This was the job? Busting your boy out of the can?"

Ralph Wheeler nodded at him. "Yup. Looks like they did it too." He shook hands with Gibson, then quick as a cat, even as he still held Gibson's hand in his own, he turned to Murton and threw a left-handed punch that caught him square on the jaw. Murton staggered back a step and dropped to one knee. He spat blood on the floor and wiped the corner of his mouth with his sleeve. When he stood, his father was right in his face.

"That's for getting caught. I ought to take you out back and give you a proper welcome."

Gibson got right between them and pushed the old man back. "That's enough. No one is going to do anything. He's out and we're here. Let's all settle down. We've got work to do."

Murton looked at Gibson. "Fuck you and your work. I'm out of here. Thanks for the ride." Then to his father: "And fuck you too, old man. The first one was free, mostly because you're right. I shouldn't have been caught. Try it again though and see what happens. Should have used that hammer when you had the chance."

"You sure know how to hold a grudge, don't you, boy?" When Murton didn't answer Ralph Wheeler laughed, then lunged forward and wrapped Murton up in a hug. When he released him he grabbed his son's face and kissed him on the forehead. "Goddamn me to hell, it's good to see you."

Murton turned his head and spat more blood on the carpet. "Yeah. Whatever you say, Pops." He looked at Gibson. "I'm not screwing around. I meant what I said. I'm out of here." He moved toward the front door. As soon as he did Gibson had his weapon out. The sound of the slide ratcheting into place stopped Murton in his tracks.

"You're not going anywhere. You knew the cost of busting you out. It's time to earn your keep."

Murton turned back and looked at Gibson. "Pull the trigger. See if I care."

Reif laughed. "You sound like your old man."

Murton slowly turned his head and looked at Reif. "Insult me again and I'll rip your wiring out." Then, after a few seconds, he took a deep breath and let his body relax. "Where's my room?"

Reif tipped his head. "Right down the hall. C'mon, I'll show you." He looked at both of the men he thought were named Weller. "Families…never had any use for them myself."

Ralph Wheeler gave Murton a hard look, then left the house.

Reif followed Murton into the bedroom and closed the door. Murton unzipped a duffel and ignored him. He went through the contents of the bag Gibson had prepared for him. He saw the guns at the bottom of the duffel and moved them to the top.

"What's the story between you and your old man?" Reif asked him.

Murton was ready for the question. Gibson had briefed him on Reif…and the fact that Ralph Wheeler was working as a confidential informant for DHS under the name of Ron Weller. "It's long and it's sad and I'm tired. Ask me some other time."

Reif stepped closer. "I'm asking you now."

Murton turned and faced the other man. "They told me you're the type who likes to think he's in charge of everything. I get it. I've spent my entire life around assholes like you."

Reif took another step toward Murton, a Beretta now

in his hand, resting against his thigh. "What'd you call me?"

Murton shook his head. "Great. An asshole who's hard of hearing to boot. Look—"

Reif brought the Beretta up and pointed it at him, exactly as Murton expected he would. Reif had been so offended by the remarks he hadn't noticed Murton moving into a fighter's stance, his body turned slightly sideways, his feet spread, his weight perfectly balanced.

When Reif brought the gun up, Murton was in a perfect position to use Reif's momentum against him. He wrapped his left arm inside Reif's and put a hold on the barrel of the gun, twisting it back toward the other man, his wrist collapsing against the pressure. He put his other hand inside the crook of Reif's elbow and pushed. Reif ended up against the wall with his own gun pointed at his chest, his wrist about to break against the pressure Murton applied.

"Don't ever point a gun at me again," Murton said. He put more pressure against the wrist and when he did, Reif winced in pain. Murton released the magazine from the gun and clicked the safety to the on position. He then jacked the slide, ejected the round from the chamber and caught it, all with his free hand. When he let go and stepped back, Reif was holding an empty gun. The entire encounter lasted about three seconds.

"I used to do this shit for a living," Murton said. "I've got a resume that'd make a Navy Seal look like a schoolgirl at the prom." He picked up the magazine and sat down on the bed and stared at Reif, who was sweating and massaging his wrist.

"They told me you were good," Reif said, some color coming back into his face. "I was testing you, is all."

Reif was trying to save some face, so Murton let him. He nodded. "I figured as much. I'd have done the same thing," he lied. He looked at the magazine he was holding. He needed to let Reif have his dignity back or they'd have an ongoing problem. "So, we good?" Murton asked. The question gave Reif what he needed—the allusion of power and control.

Reif nodded at him. "Yeah, I'm good."

Murton tossed him the magazine and laid back on the bed, put his hands behind his head and used the duffel as a pillow. He had one hand wrapped around the butt of a handgun inside the bag in case Reif wanted to test him a little more.

But Reif was done. He slapped the magazine in the gun and slid it back in his belt. "I really would like to know about you and your old man." He said it in such a matter-of-fact way that Murton almost answered him.

"I'm tired, I just busted out of the joint and flew more than halfway across the country. We're all on the same team here. They said you needed a demolitions guy so here I am. I'll tell you the story when I get it straight in my own damned head. Close the door on your way out."

After a few nights on the hard surface of the floor, Patty put the cot back together. The days crept on and eventually turned into weeks. The chemical toilet was approaching the limits of its capacity. The toilet paper was almost gone. She'd been rationing her food supply, but she was dangerously low. Empty water bottles were everywhere. If the men didn't come back soon, she'd die a slow death, not from sexual abuse as she initially feared, but from starvation and dehydration. She almost wished they'd return. Maybe they'd bring her more supplies.

Her thoughts kept returning to one single issue: Why? Why had she been taken? She was nobody. Her mother and her real father were both dead, and the pitiful excuses for step-fathers her mother had chosen had all abandoned her. None of them had money. Every last one of them were alcoholic, low-rent losers. Why? Why? Why? She couldn't get the thought out of her head. She'd thought about it for weeks.

Then suddenly one day she did know. Knew like she'd been slapped in the face with it. It *was* a ransom demand. She knew who was on the hook, and she even thought she knew why. Not exactly why, but close enough, given the nature of what was at stake. But even if the demands were met, the men would never give up her location. Why would they? She'd seen their faces.

Patty wondered which would go first…her mind, or her body. Now that she had an idea of what was happening and why, she was betting on her mind. She was down to a dozen packages of tuna and a few bottles of water. Like that mattered anymore.

CHAPTER TWENTY-TWO

That night Huma got the kids fed and in bed, then decided to take some time for herself. She'd yet to experience Jonesy's bar and informed Virgil and Sandy it was high time she did. Virgil told her to enjoy herself and gave Delroy a quick call to let him know she was on her way.

"Yeah, mon. Send her down. About time she have a little fun, no?"

"You bet. And listen, her money stays in her pocket, okay?"

"Of course. Respect, mon."

With that done, Virgil and Sandy were alone on their back deck, sitting next to each other on a love seat. They were quiet for a beat, comfortable in the silence the way happily married couples often are. Then Sandy said something and it didn't really surprise Virgil. "It feels like we're moving in different directions lately."

Virgil looked at her. "You're beautiful."

"Thank you. So are you, boyfriend, but don't try to misdirect the conversation."

He grinned at her. "I'm not. I promise. I simply needed to say it out loud." Then, "What's on your mind?"

"I think I already told you."

Virgil thought about it for a moment. "I understand. If I'm being honest with you, I sort of feel the same way."

"You haven't said anything about it."

Virgil massaged his forehead with the flat of his palm. "It's not as easy as it sounds. You know that. I'm back at work, doing my thing, doing what I love and you've not only survived a horrific incident, but our lives have been completely turned around. We went from a financially stable working couple with no children, to a family of four with a live-in nanny, and two thousand acres that could bleed us dry. If we don't get a good season out of that land, we'll be in a real bind."

"That's all true," Sandy said. "But you're sort of doing what you accuse others of."

"What's that?"

"You're circling the main issue and expecting me to fill in the gaps. The real issue isn't the land, or our finances. The real issue is us, and how we're parenting our children."

"I think we're doing okay. It's on-the-job training."

"That's true. What's also true is you're missing a lot of class time. You're hardly ever here, Virgil. Half the time you're gone when I get up in the morning and the other half you're home after the kids are asleep. I know Wyatt's just a baby, but he still needs his father. He needs your touch. And in case you haven't noticed, Jonas is practically begging for it. I love Huma, and quite frankly, I don't know what I'd do without her right now. It feels like she's already a part of our family. But she's not a substitute for you…for your presence here, as the man of our house."

Virgil looked out toward the pond. Sandy was right, of course. She usually was. "I'm sorry. I'm trying to help Murton in any way I can and I'm failing at every turn. We have absolutely no information to work with. None. And this young woman in Bloomington? It's been weeks. If she's not dead yet she will be soon, I just know it. She didn't take off. Somebody grabbed her and that's that. Another young female I.U. student is gone and she'll never be back. A year from now she'll be a footnote in the local historical records…a file in the cold case drawer that no one wants to think about, much less look at. And this is someone's child, Sandy. It's tearing me up.

"Delroy told me our family is coming apart at the seams. He indicated that I'd be put in a position where I'd have to choose. I'm starting to believe he's right. So…I'm sorry. I'll try to do better. Nothing is more important to me than you and the kids. You know that, don't you?"

Sandy took his hand and held it tightly. "Virgil, I'm not questioning you or your loyalties to your family or your job. I know you're doing the best you can right now. And I know how hard it is. Murton is a part of our family too. Don't lose sight of what matters. Try to find a way to make room for us. And by us, I mean you and me. I know our family is changing…has changed, but at the core of it there has to be room for what got us here, otherwise what's the point?"

Virgil felt himself start to relax, like a knot inside his being was beginning to unwind. He put his arm around his wife, took a deep breath and let his head tip back. He closed his eyes and said, "I don't know what to do next. I can't even think." He was talking about his work.

Sandy knew he was, but she wasn't having it. She threw a leg over and straddled his lap. "I could think of a thing or two."

Then his phone rang.

THEY IGNORED THE PHONE AND LET IT GO TO VOICE MAIL. As it turned out, Sandy was quite the thinker.

AFTERWARD, WITH ALL THE HEAVY THINKING COMPLETE, they showered together and that got them thinking again. When the water started to run cold, they hurried out and got dressed. Sandy went to check on the boys and Virgil went to check on his phone. When he brought up the recent call list he saw it'd been Becky who tried to reach him. He punched in her number.

"What's up, Becks?"

"I tried to call you an hour ago."

"Sorry. I was taking care of something."

"How *is* Sandy?"

Virgil thought it must have been something in his voice. "She's great, Becky." He stepped off the deck and began to wander down toward the pond. "What do you have? Something on Murt?"

There was a pause before she answered. "I'm losing my mind here, Jonesy. How could he do this to me...to us?"

Virgil sat down in the chair next to his father's cross. "I don't think he's doing anyting to you, Becks. I think he's doing something for you, no matter how hard it might seem right now, in the moment."

Her voice took on a lighter tone. "Did you hear yourself?" Then, as if her question was rhetorical in nature she spoke without waiting for an answer. "You said 'anyting.' For a second there you sounded almost exactly like Delroy."

But Virgil didn't want to let the moment go. "Becky, I promise you, I'm going to take care of Murton. I'll figure it out." When she didn't respond, he asked her about the subpoena for Doyle's iCloud account. "Ron sign off on it?"

Their connection cut out for a moment and Becky said something that could have been either a yes or no, Virgil wasn't sure which. "Becks? I lost you for a second. What'd you say?"

"He said he'd get the paper going, but I haven't seen anything yet. Meanwhile, I've got everything I need set-up and ready to go. I'm waiting to pull the trigger. That's why I called you earlier."

"What, exactly, does pulling the trigger entail?"

Becky told him.

Virgil didn't hesitate. "Do it."

"Ron likes his i's dotted and all that."

"I'll take care of it. Besides, you work for me, remember? Ron doesn't like the arrangement, but that's his problem, not ours."

"You got it, Jonesy."

Virgil heard an unusual background noise over the phone followed by a rapid set of keystrokes. "What are you doing?"

"Pulling the trigger, Sherlock."

"Let me know."

Becky said she would. Then she said something that made Virgil feel as if he alone had the power to determine Murton's fate. "I don't know how I know this, only that I do. I think he's out there and he needs your help, Jonesy. In fact, I think he's counting on it."

How do you respond to that? Virgil thought.

He sat by the cross for a while and thought about what Becky had said to him. Virgil believed that the women of the world who love their men have connections to them beyond the boundaries of normal time and space. He'd seen it too often to think otherwise. His mother and father had it, Sandy could practically read his mind, and Murton and Becky seemed to have it as well. If Becky thought Murton was out there and counting on him to help, Virgil was ready and willing. The problem wasn't one of want; it was one of how. He thought back to the beginning and how everything had started and decided that protecting the boss was one thing. Doing it at the expense of others, especially people Virgil loved and cared about was another. In short, it was time to get some answers, straight from the horse's mouth. In this case, a horse named Mac. He took his phone out and punched in the number. Right before he hit send he saw his father.

"You sure that's a call you want to make?" Mason asked.

"What, you can read my mind now?"

"Not exactly. But I know how you think." Then Mason smiled and pointed with his chin. "Besides, I can see the screen on your phone."

Virgil cleared the screen and stuck the phone back in his pocket. "I work for the man. Why shouldn't I call him?"

"You report to him, Virg. You work for the state."

"Are we going to argue semantics, now?"

"Who says we're arguing?"

Virgil took a deep breath and started over. "Why shouldn't I call him?"

"I never said you shouldn't. I asked if you were sure about it."

"The other day I told you Murt is in trouble. Then you said, 'You don't know the half of it.' What did you mean?"

Mason was leaning against the cross, his arms folded over his bare chest. He waited a long time before he said anything. Virgil let him.

"Murton told you something the last time the two of you spoke."

Virgil nodded at his father. "He sure did. Did you or mom know about any of that?"

Mason shook his head. "No. But that's not what I'm referring to. He made a simple statement right when Cora and Gibson showed up. Gibson's not the enemy, by the way, no matter how this shakes out. Neither is Mac."

Mac? What the hell? "I don't care about Gibson. What was the statement?"

"It'll come to you," Mason said. "Right now there are other things to consider."

"Such as?"

"You've kicked the hornets' nest this time, Bud, and good."

"Meaning?"

"Meaning they aim to destroy you if you keep pushing an issue that's outside the boundaries of their agenda."

"Let them try."

"Don't deceive yourself, Son. They won't do it with force. Their kind never do. They'll come at you from outside the lines. They'll use lawyers and the courts and even the Patriot Act if they have to. They'll whittle away at you until there's nothing left to give."

"What are you telling me?"

"I'm telling you that your thinking on this entire affair is a little one-dimensional. I think that's the message Delroy has been trying to send you as well."

"I don't even know what their agenda is. How am I supposed to do anything about it if I don't know what I'm up against?"

"Remember how mad you were that day when Cora and Pearson showed up and fired you? Whew, I don't think I've ever seen you so cranked up. Skipped your badge right into the pond."

Suddenly Virgil's mind was racing. He was learning to listen to how his father expressed himself...not only the statements he made. When he answered, he was cautious with his words. "I might not have been thinking clearly. I remember, though. I appreciate you fishing it out for me."

"Believe it or not, it took me a while to find it." Mason smiled as he spoke, not because of his words, but because he knew Virgil was finally starting to understand.

"Everything is exactly the way it should be. Wasn't that essentially what you told Becky?"

"I guess it was, although I didn't use those exact words."

"You might think this subjective, but I promise you, it's not. You're one of the smartest people I've ever known. You'll figure it out and when that happens, you'll know what you have to do, whether you want to or not."

Want to or not? Virgil felt an odd sensation pass through his stomach. "That's your gut talking to you, Virg. I hope you're listening. Anyhow, I guess I'll be on my way. Keep your phone in your pocket until you've got all the facts, Son."

Virgil looked away from the cross. He did so with purpose. It was hard sometimes to watch his father disappear. When he was sure he was alone he looked back and despite the fact he now considered conversations with his dead father a normal part of everyday life, he couldn't quite believe what he saw sitting on the edge of the cross.

CHAPTER TWENTY-THREE

LONG BEFORE CORA BECAME THE GOVERNOR'S CHIEF OF staff, the position was held by Bradley Pearson. Pearson believed he was untouchable; a political operative of the highest order. He had dirt on everyone and anyone that mattered and he wasn't afraid to let them know he'd use it to his advantage if need be. Virgil never knew if it was the power of the position, the lure of easy under-the-table money, or a guttural rapacity that caused him to cut corners, skirt the edges, and in general live his professional political life as if the rules applied to others, not him. But when you stray across the double yellow line without knowing what's around the corner, you often end up a victim of your own making. Virgil hadn't been present when Pearson was killed, but he suspected when the moment arrived it came with an array of conflicted emotions, among them, fear, surprise, and a sense of how deeply he'd been deceived. Perhaps not, though. Who could really say? What he knew for sure was Pearson had been the alchemist of his own destruction.

But there was someone who knew full well the depths of Pearson's malfeasance: Nicole Pope. Nicole and her twin brother Nicholas had amassed volumes of information on Pearson in an effort to systematically dismantle his life. They succeeded in grand fashion, but like narcissists everywhere, it hadn't been enough. Why? Because the ego is literally insatiable. It is a beast that devours everything in its path. The Pope twins had to prove what they'd done, and more importantly why. When Nichole Pope showed up at the bar two years ago and gave Virgil a thumb drive with everything Pearson had done over the course of his political career, Virgil didn't want to look at it. Why would he? Why feed the beast when its victims were all dead?

He remembered setting the thumb drive on the cross, reasoning he'd destroy it and leave Pearson to rot in hell and let the Pope twins deal with their own demons any way they could. He was, in fact, thinking it from the very spot where he now stood. He could picture the entire scene like it was only yesterday…he turned to grab the thumb drive from the top of the cross, ready to crush it under his boot. But when he looked at the cross, the thumb drive was gone and his badge—the badge he'd thrown into the pond—sat there in its place.

Virgil walked over to the cross and picked up the

drive. He still didn't know what it contained or how it could help him find and protect Murton, or if it even could.

Only one way to find out, he thought. Had he known what would transpire, that Delroy had been right all along, he would have done what he had intended to do two years ago. He would have crushed the damn thing under his boot.

But that didn't happen. He walked the drive up to the house and fired up his computer.

When Virgil plugged the drive into his laptop he had a little trouble getting his machine to recognize the device. Then he realized his security settings were blocking the recognition process. He fiddled around with the settings, ignoring the warning boxes that kept popping up asking him if he was sure he wanted to continue. When the computer finally decided that Virgil wasn't going to be dissuaded it showed him an icon of the drive. Virgil double-clicked it.

Nothing happened.

He double-clicked again and still nothing. He thought for a moment, single-clicked to highlight the drive, then selected file, open, from the menu. Another warning box popped up asking him if he was sure he wanted to continue. He swore under his breath, clicked yes to make the box go away and when he did, he was presented with another box, this one asking him for a password.

Christ.

He typed in the name 'Pearson' and clicked the continue button. The box appeared to vibrate rapidly on the screen but nothing else happened. Then, thinking he was being clever, he typed BPCoS. The letters stood for *Bradley Pearson, Chief of Staff*, and had been a vital clue in the Pope case and the death of Pearson. The box vibrated at him again. He leaned back in his chair and placed his hands behind his head, and thought about the Pope twins. He pulled out his notebook and began making a list. He spent twenty minutes thinking of various words and phrases connected to the case and wrote them down. Ten minutes later he'd tried them one by one until he'd crossed them all off the list.

Now what?

Then he laughed at himself and picked up the phone. He'd been so amped up regarding the contents of the drive he'd momentarily forgotten that he had in his personal employ one of the best computer people he'd ever known. "Hey Becks, where are you right now?"

"Can't you tell?"

Virgil listened for a moment and knew. She was at the bar. "How long are you going to be there?"

"Why do I have the feeling no matter how I respond, you're going to say something that will change my answer."

Couldn't argue that, Virgil thought. "I'm at home. I'll be there in about thirty minutes."

"What do you have?" Becky asked.

"I was hoping you could tell me. See you in thirty."

But Becky wasn't done. "Huma and Delroy seem to be hitting it off."

Virgil grinned into the phone. "That's great."

"Yeah, except half the women in here want to tear her hair out. I think she's the new teacher's pet."

"See you soon," Virgil said. He hung up and went to tell Sandy he was leaving. When he walked into the boys' bedroom she was asleep next to Jonas. He covered her with a blanket, made sure Wyatt was breathing…he was—that still scared the bejesus out of him—and left her a note saying he was at the bar and he'd be back as soon as he could.

He grabbed his laptop and the list of failed passwords and headed into the city.

WHEN HE WALKED IN HE FOUND HUMA SITTING AT THE end of the bar chatting up Delroy, who appeared to be hanging on her every word. He stood and watched them for a moment. Huma Moon looked lovely, Virgil thought. There simply wasn't another word for it. Most of the interactions he'd had with her so far had been at the house and this was the first time he'd seen her outside of her work environment on her own, having a good time. Her blond-white dreads were tied back and covered with a scarf, the ends poking out the back. She wore a floor-length flower print dress with sandals, a multitude of bracelets on each wrist, and giant silver hoop earrings. The look fit both her personality and her name.

He walked up, put his arm around her shoulder and gave her a squeeze. "You look lovely, Huma."

"Dat she do," Delroy said. He never even looked at Virgil.

Huma gave him a toothy grin, then turned back to Delroy. "Maybe it's the company I keep."

Delroy laughed his big Jamaican laugh. Virgil noticed Becky had been right. Huma was getting the evil eye from a few of the female customers who wanted Delroy's natural affections on them, not some hippy chick with white Rastafari hair who'd never been in before. Who did she think she was?

Delroy may have had his attention on Huma, but he didn't let it get in the way of his job. He was mixing drinks, pulling draft beer, washing glasses, swaying and singing along with the music all at the same time.

"How's business tonight?" Virgil asked.

"Shaking and baking, big mon." He looked at Huma. "The clientele seems to be on da uptick too."

Virgil was going to say something to Delroy about the other customers, but then thought, screw it. He knew when to butt out. "Becky upstairs?"

Just as he spoke the house band cranked it into overdrive and Virgil's words were lost to the rhythmic beat of their original Reggae music. Delroy leaned across the bar. "What's dat, mon?"

Virgil shook his head and moved behind the bar. He leaned into Delroy's ear. "Ask her to dance, Delroy. I've got the bar for a few minutes."

Delroy pulled his head back and tipped it to the side. "You a good mon, Virgil Jones. Anybody ever tell you dat?"

Am I? Virgil thought.

"What was dat?" Delroy said.

"Nothing. Go. I've got this." He set the laptop under the bar and watched as Delroy took Huma's hand and led her to the dance floor. When he asked the two women at the other end of the bar if they'd like another drink they gave him a dirty look, got up, then walked out without saying a word. Virgil laughed out loud, the sound lost to the music.

Delroy's work ethic brought him back to the bar after three songs. Huma's night out didn't appear to be over though. Virgil grabbed the laptop and headed upstairs to the office. He found Becky standing near the window that looked out over the bar. When he walked in she turned and gave him a hug.

"What was that for?"

"That was a good thing you did down there," Becky said.

Virgil let his eyes slide away from hers. "I think it was his break time anyway."

"Why do you do that?"

"Do what?" Virgil asked.

"Undervalue your generosity with others."

Maybe because I sometimes feel like I don't deserve what I've been given, Virgil thought. *Or worse, I do and I fail to reconcile the books often enough.*

"Yoo-hoo. Anybody home in there?"

Virgil held out the computer. "Here's my laptop."

Becky took it from him and laughed.

"What's so funny?"

"What do you have as a desktop model? A Commodore 64? Man, this thing is ancient. If it's broken I don't think I can help you."

"It's not broken. See that thumb drive?"

"What about it?"

Virgil filled her in on the basics, skimming over the details of how the drive ended up in his possession.

"So you plugged it in and started exploring, huh?"

Virgil turned his palms upward. "Yeah. I wanted to see what was on it. What's the harm?"

Becky removed the drive and placed the laptop in one of her desk drawers.

"I'm going to need that computer back."

She didn't appear to be listening. She opened a cabinet behind her desk and Virgil saw a rack of electronic equipment with various green and red lights flashing in and out of sequence. Becky flipped a few switches and Virgil watched the lights go away.

"What are you doing?"

"Killing the WIFI. Please tell me you did the same thing at your house before you plugged that drive into your laptop." The look on Virgil's face gave her the answer. "Yeah, I didn't think so."

"Isn't that a little over the top, Becks?"

"You tell me. This drive came from the sister of the guy who hacked his way into Pearson's personal and professional life without anyone ever knowing it happened. He also managed to write the code that scammed the lottery out of hundreds of millions of dollars, depending on which particular story you believe."

I still think maybe it's a little excessive."

"Think what you want. Her last name was Pope. Never mind the fact that she was the modern-day equivalent of Lucrezia Borgia, I'm erring on the side of caution. I'll be over at your place tomorrow to see how badly you've been compromised."

Virgil puffed out his cheeks. "Jeez, I didn't think about any of that. I thought it was probably a spreadsheet and some Word files or something."

Becky pulled out a laptop of her own. "Uh-huh."

"So why not use mine?"

"Two reasons: One, they don't update Windows XP anymore." She held up her computer. "And two, this little baby is air-gapped."

"I don't know what that means."

"Duh."

"Becky…"

"Okay, okay. Air-gapped is a network security measure that ensures a secure computer is physically isolated from unsecured networks…you know, like that little thing they call the internet. That's why I killed the WIFI. There's more to it than that, but you can Google it if you want the rest of the details."

Virgil shook his head. "I don't. But if that drive is compromised won't you ruin your computer too?"

She let her eyelids droop. "Do you have your gun with you?"

"Yeah. Why wouldn't I?"

"Is it loaded?"

"Of course."

"And you know how to use it, how to aim and shoot and reload and make sure it's safe when it's in your holster and all that jazz?"

Virgil held his hands up. "Okay, I get it…you know what you're doing. How long to crack the password?"

"Depends on how many characters. I've got a rainbow table that runs through a sequence—"

"A what?"

"It's called a rainbow table. Please don't make me

explain it. We're looking at anywhere from a couple of hours to a couple of days."

"A couple of days?"

"It is what it is, Jonesy."

Then Virgil had a thought. "Hey, wait. Maybe this will speed things up." He handed Becky the list of failed passwords he'd already tried.

Becky managed to say thank you, sucking on her cheeks the entire time.

"You have a bad tooth or something?"

"Nope. I'm good."

He went downstairs. Huma was still at the bar making eyes with Delroy.

Virgil went home.

CHAPTER TWENTY-FOUR

Virgil was back in Brown County again the next day. He had the last known whereabouts of Patty Doyle... the Yellowwood state forest, but if she was out in the hills, they'd need dogs and helicopters and hundreds of people searching. And they wouldn't be searching for a survivor. They'd be searching for a victim. He pulled up to the park ranger's gate and hung his state ID out the window. "Virgil Jones with the state's MCU. Where can I find whoever is in charge around here?"

The ranger at the gate was an overweight, jolly-looking man with a crew cut and a dark green uniform that made him look like a boy scout troop commander. A single button was missing on his uniform shirt. His pants were tucked into his black military-style boots. The boots themselves were scuffed and dusty.

"What's the MCU?"

"Major Crimes Unit. Part of the state police."

The ranger tucked a bubble of air inside a cheek, his head bobbing up and down. "Yeah, I've heard of you guys. You're looking for the park office," he said, his face open and honest. He pulled a park map from a clear plastic holder nailed to the side of the gatehouse, took a pen from his pocket and circled a spot on the map. He held it out for Virgil to see. "We're here," he said, pointing with the pen. "Follow this road straight ahead and it'll take you right to the office." He handed him the map. "Never been here before?" His question was friendly and sincere.

"Never had the pleasure," Virgil said. "Do you have a name for me?"

The ranger looked down at his chest and pointed to his name tag. "Jim. Says so right here. See?"

Virgil bit into his lower lip. "Sorry. That's not what I meant. I need the name of the person in charge of the park office. The head ranger? Is that what they're called?"

Jim nodded in an exaggerated manner, his face taking on a reddish tint. "Gotcha. That'd be Bill Moyer."

Virgil closed his ID and put it back in his pocket. He laid the map on the dash. "Thanks."

"Everything okay?" Jim the jolly green ranger asked.

Virgil stared straight ahead. The forest was deep green, the trees packed tight across the rolling hillside. A lone deer—a Buck—stood still at the edge of the tree line, his head turned toward the park entrance. "I doubt it," he said. "Sure is pretty out here, though." He took out his phone and brought up a picture of Doyle and showed it to Jim. "Ever see this woman before?"

Jim studied the picture for a few moments then shook his head. "I'm sorry, no."

When Virgil pulled away from the gate the deer took two quick strides and disappeared into the forest.

VIRGIL HAD NO EXPECTATIONS OF WHAT THE PARK OFFICE might look like, but if he had he probably would have been disappointed. The building wasn't much bigger than the gatehouse at the entrance; a small single-story affair with a single entry door and two small windows on either side. A large radio antenna bolted into a concrete base jutted skyward. He parked his car and went inside the office.

Moyer was waiting for him. Virgil introduced himself and the two men shook hands. Moyer's grip was strong. He was stocky and looked as solid as a slab of granite. His uniform was starched and creased to perfection. "Some sort of trouble?" he asked. Then without waiting for an answer, he added, "Jim said you needed to speak with me."

Virgil took out his phone and again pulled up a picture

of Patty Doyle. He handed his phone to Moyer. "Ever see this young lady before?"

Moyer didn't hesitate. "Sure have. She's the one gone missing, right?"

"When did you last see her?"

"Uh, maybe I better revise my last statement," Moyer said. "I've never actually seen her, seen her. In person, I mean. I've seen her on the news. That's how I recognized the picture." He handed the phone back.

"I was told she liked to run the trails out here. With some regularity as I understand it."

Moyer looked around the small office…like maybe he was expecting Patty Doyle to pop up behind him. "I wouldn't know, to tell you the truth. We get thousands of people through here every month. I've been here long enough that I know a few of the local regulars, but that's only a fraction of the whole."

"What about any of the other rangers or employees?"

Moyer shrugged. "I can't really speak for anyone else. You'd have to ask them. Not an easy task, either."

"Why not?"

"Because between the rangers, the groundskeepers, the guides, and the volunteers we've got over a hundred people here and most of them are on rotating shifts in different parts of the park. You want to talk to all of them, you're going to have your hands full for a while."

Virgil didn't want to hear that. He wanted to clear this case one way or another as quickly as possible. "I don't have a while, as you put it. Or more to the point, Patty Doyle doesn't."

They both stood with that sobering thought for a moment. Then Virgil asked a basic question. "Does everyone in the park report to you?"

Moyer gave him a half nod. "In a manner of speaking. I'm in charge of the entire park, so the rangers and some of the other staff report directly to me. But not everybody. For example, the guys who mow and take care of the trees and whatnot, they report to the head groundskeeper, and he reports to me, and so on and so forth."

That got Virgil thinking. "Tell me about it...the reporting process."

Moyer gave another little shrug. "Not much to tell, really. Most of the time the grounds keeping stuff is fuel and maintenance reports. Expense items, you know, like a new mower part or something. It makes my eyes bleed sometimes."

"What about the rangers? What sort of reporting do they do?"

"Depends on the day, really. I imagine it's a lot like your police work. If it's a busy day, there's lots of paperwork and reporting. If it's a slow day, there isn't any paperwork at all."

"We don't have any slow days."

"I suppose not," Moyer said. "But you take my meaning."

Virgil did. He gave Moyer a date and asked to see all the reports filed for that day.

Moyer turned to get the reports then stopped. "Uh, listen, I'm all for departmental cooperation and all that, but aren't you supposed to have a warrant or something?"

Virgil closed his eyes momentarily and rolled a kink out of his neck. "That'd be a subpoena, not a warrant. In any event, we both work for the state, Mr. Moyer. I'm trying to find a missing college student. How about we stay inside the boundaries of the state and not make a federal case out of procedural protocol."

Moyer thought about it for a few seconds. What was the harm? Besides, he had a daughter at I.U. "Wait here, I'll get the logs."

It took them all of two minutes to find what they were looking for. One of the rangers, a guy by the name of Chip Hamlin had a log entry that caught Virgil's eye. "Is he working today?"

Moyer turned and looked at the whiteboard behind his desk. "Sure is."

"Let's get him in here."

Moyer picked up the radio and made the call.

Hamlin turned into the lot ten minutes later and walked through the door. He was tall and narrowshouldered, with thick black hair turning grey at the temples. He had dark, deep-set eyes, and a hawkish nose. Virgil brought him up to speed and told him what they were after.

Hamlin started nodding right away. "Yup. I remember. I saw the girl too. Didn't know it was her though. In fact, now that I think about it, I've seen her out here quite a bit. She's sort of easy on the eyes, if you know what I mean." Then after realizing the possible implications of his own statement, he quickly added, "But that's only a middle-aged man's fantasy."

Virgil made a circular motion with his hand.

"Right. So anyway, I was up in the tower closest to the entrance. We let the visitors climb them for the view but we keep the lookout at the very top locked up. Had some problems with dope and sex over the years. Anyhow, I was in the lookout and I saw her standing next to her car outside the entrance."

"What kind of car?" Virgil asked. "What color?"

"Toyota Camry. Red. Older model, I'd say."

That's exactly right, Virgil thought.

Hamlin went on. "I used the field glasses we keep in the tower so I had a pretty good view. She had a flat and it looked like she was getting ready to change it out herself when a pickup pulled up and stopped."

"Tell me about the pickup."

"Not much to tell. Looked like a piece of shit. Couldn't tell the make. Might have been a Dodge, or an older GMC, but I can't say for certain. Didn't have any paint on it that I saw. Like it had faded away or something. Sort of a light gray color. Might have been primer, but I think it was just faded. Couple of old guys—way older'n me and I'm just past fifty—got out to help her. I watched for a few seconds to make sure everything was okay and it looked like it was. They started to change the tire, and I climbed down from the tower."

"Then what did you do?"

"I locked up the tower and made the climb down. That takes a few minutes, especially with these knees of mine." He looked down at his knees to emphasize the point. "Anyway, once I got down I hopped into the Gator and buzzed on out there. By the time I got there, everyone had gone. It's all in my report."

Virgil sucked on his cheek and looked down at the floor for a moment. Then he looked at Hamlin. "Let's take a little ride."

He followed Hamlin out of the park and they stopped near the area where he'd spotted Patty Doyle and the two men.

Hamlin pointed. "Right over there on the other side of

the drive." Virgil walked over and looked around. He didn't see anything. The drive was paved, the blacktop was free of blood or anything that could be of any evidentiary value. The grass along both sides of the drive was cut short in sections that extended about eight feet past the edge of the pavement. Beyond that, it had been allowed to grow wild and tall.

Virgil squatted down next to the edge of the grass and looked around. The area was completely free of debris of any kind. "They do a nice job of keeping this area clean."

Hamlin nodded. "They sure do. Gets mowed twice a week and we've got volunteers who come out every day and pick up the litter."

"Is that a big problem? The litter?"

"Not too bad," Hamlin said.

"It's a state park. You'd think people would have more respect for the land."

"Most people don't know the meaning of the word respect."

Virgil thought Hamlin's statement might have been a little extreme. When he stood and moved closer to the tall grass, Hamlin said, "Watch out for snakes."

"I will. How about you come help me?"

"Help you what?"

"Help me look for evidence…and snakes."

Hamlin joined him and together the two men walked back and forth through the tall grass covering an area roughly twenty yards in either direction from where

Doyle's car had been parked. It was slow going, the tall grass bending and obscuring the view of the ground with every step they took. "You think those two men I saw had anything to do with that young girl's disappearance?"

"No way to tell. If they did, your sighting of them could be significant. If they didn't, they were most likely among the last people who—"

"What is it?" Hamlin asked. They were about ten yards away from each other.

Virgil was balanced on one leg, his other stuck partway up in the air. "Two things. I've got what looks like a busted cell phone here."

Hamlin started to rush over.

"No, no, no. Stop," Virgil said. "Wait, forget I said that. Get over here, but slow down. I've got a snake wrapped around my ankle."

Hamlin crept close, inching his way over to where Virgil stood. When he finally got to him, he rolled his eyes, uncoiled the snake, and held it up in the air. "It's a Garter snake. They're harmless. Want to hold it?"

"No, I don't want to hold it. I want you to get it the hell away from me."

Hamlin shrugged and laid the snake back in the grass. "They don't even bite. Lots of people have them as pets."

"Snakes bother me. And I'm not lots of people. See that phone?"

"Yeah."

"Stay exactly where you are and don't take your eyes off it. Don't touch it either." Virgil high-stepped it out of the long grass and got a pair of latex gloves and an evidence bag from his truck. He put the gloves on and returned—with some reluctance—and picked up the phone by its edges. He dropped it into the bag and ran out of the tall grass.

Hamlin followed without running. He looked at the phone through the clear plastic bag. "Not going to call anyone with that." The phone was split almost completely in half, held together by only a few wires. "Must have been clipped by the mower."

"You sure this is the exact area where her car was parked?"

Hamlin nodded. "Yes. Absolutely. I had a perfect fix on it."

"Was it in the grass or on the pavement?"

"About half and half, I'd say."

Virgil could practically see it. The flat tire, the two men, a struggle, the phone getting lost under the car then struck by a mower and chucked into the snake-infested weeds.

"Think it belonged to her?"

"I'll know soon enough."

Hamlin gave him an odd look, and Virgil caught it.

"What?"

"Thought you'd be happier about it. Maybe it'll help you find her…get her back."

Virgil looked away, toward the forest. When he answered, his voice was heavy with regret. "She's been gone a long time."

CHAPTER TWENTY-FIVE

Virgil called Becky and read her the phone's serial number. She called back ten minutes later. The phone was hers. He thanked her and hung up. Okay, the phone was Doyle's, but that didn't tell him much…only that Doyle had been to the park. He already knew that.

Rosie had been right all along, Virgil thought. The case was dying a slow death. The only other thing to check was one final piece of information the boyfriend had told him about. Nate Morgan said on the day of her disappearance Patty Doyle had gone to the post office to pick up a package. He knew the post offices had security footage. If he could review that footage, maybe he'd see something that would help. It was a long shot at best, but one he had to follow through on.

The postmaster turned out to be a stickler for details. He wore the traditional blue post office uniform—apparently the only one in the building who did—and very unapologetically educated Virgil on the complexities of federal law with regard to the United States Postal Service. "I need a subpoena, plain and simple. My hands are tied." He said it with satisfaction, the corner of his mouth twitching upward.

"Look, I'm trying to find Patty Doyle, the missing I.U. student. She was in here a few weeks ago and I need to see if there's anything to see on those tapes. What's the harm? This isn't exactly Fort Knox."

The postmaster's left eye tended to wander, and Virgil found himself swaying back and forth in an attempt to remain within his field of vision.

"Bring me a subpoena and I'll show you whatever you need to see."

Great. Virgil had wasted a trip to Bloomington, time he felt he didn't have. He needed to wrap this thing up one way or another so he could get back to figuring out a way to help Murton. He was about to let the postmaster go, but took one final run at him. "What about the package?"

"What about it?" the postmaster said, his eye roaming around its socket like one of those magic eight balls.

"Apparently she was supposed to sign for it. Can you at least tell me if she picked it up or not?" They stood on the customer side of the counter, near a display of gift cards and specialty boxes. The postmaster had his back to the counter and Virgil noticed a young lady servicing the walk-in customers. The look on her face was undeniable.

"I'm sorry, Detective. Any packages that require a signature are followed through the system with a tracking number, not a name."

The postmaster disappeared into the back without another word, as if he could no longer be bothered by a law enforcement officer who was trying to skirt the rules. Virgil had a mental picture of him sitting on a throne made out of mailing tubes somewhere in the back of the building.

When he glanced at the counter girl, she stuck her neck out and opened her eyes as wide as she could. Virgil grabbed a gift box of some sort and got in line. When it was his turn at the counter he handed her the box and said, "You wanted to speak with me?"

The girl turned around to make sure no one was listening. "I go on break in ten minutes. Meet me on the east side of the building."

Virgil said he would.

TEN MINUTES LATER SHE POPPED OUT A SIDE DOOR ON THE east side and Virgil pulled his truck right up next to her. He buzzed the passenger side window down, but she climbed in and said, "Let's scoot. I don't want to be seen with you."

Virgil pulled out of the lot and parked around the corner along the side of the street. He threw the truck in park, killed the engine, turned in his seat, and raised an eyebrow at her.

"My name is Cassidy Bane. I'm a senior at I.U. like Patty Doyle was…is. I didn't know her, never met her or anything, but I'd like to help any way I can."

"Look, I don't want you to get in trouble or anything like that, and you really don't want to mess with federal law." Then, almost selfishly, "But if you have any information that could help me, I'll keep it to myself."

Bane checked her watch. "I've only got fifteen minutes, so there's not much I can tell you, but I do know this. I'll be graduating soon. This job is nothing more than a way to earn a little spending money. I'm not looking to make a career out of the post office. So what are they going to do? Fire me? Who cares? Anyway, Larry? The postmaster? He's got almost enough brains to sell the American flag at an Arab bazaar."

"So, not the brightest bulb in the lamp?"

"No. But bright enough to lie to you, and for you to believe him."

Virgil frowned. "Lying? About what?"

"Well, it wasn't a straight up lie. You can track those packages in any number of ways. By name, address of origin, a destination address, or the tracking number."

Virgil gave her a half-grin. He already knew that, but she was trying to help, and he appreciated it. He didn't press it with the postmaster because he knew it was a lost cause. He told Bane as much.

"Yeah, I guess that doesn't surprise me," Bane said. She took out her cell phone. "What's your number?"

"Why?"

She let her eyelids droop. "Because I'm going to send you a picture. C'mon, chop-chop. I'm on a schedule here."

Virgil gave her the number and two seconds later his phone dinged. "What's this?"

"It's a picture of the package. It's been sitting in the unclaimed pile so long it's starting to gather dust. Do you think it can help you?"

Virgil studied the picture and zoomed in on the return address. It was from someplace in Egypt that he'd never heard of. "I'm sorry to say, I don't see how, unless Patty Doyle was involved in some sort of international archeological smuggling operation."

"Well shoot," Bane said. "I thought it might be something."

"I appreciate it anyway," Virgil said. "Most people don't want to get involved. They look the other way, but you didn't. That matters." Then, "Want a ride back around the corner?"

"No, I'll walk. Can't be seen with the fuzz. It'd ruin my reputation as a bad girl."

"Can't have that," Virgil said.

Then Bane said something that surprised him. "Larry takes off in about an hour. You want to see the tapes, I can make that happen."

"Really?"

"Yeah. It'd be a piece of cake. The cameras are hooked into a single computer. It sits in a closet in the back all by itself. Nobody even looks at it. Never had to."

Virgil didn't want Bane to get in trouble with the law, especially federal law. "Look, I can't begin to tell you how much I appreciate what you're trying to do, but I can't let you jeopardize yourself over this."

"I don't intend to. I'll text you when Larry the loser is gone. The same door I came out of will be unlocked. It opens up into the sorting room. All the carriers are out so the room will be empty. The security computer is in the janitorial closet to the left of the entrance. You can't miss it. The door says 'janitorial supplies.' Nobody ever goes in there. If you don't believe me, check out the employee bathrooms. I walk across the street if I have to pee. Anyway, what you do is up to you." Then, as if the last part of the conversation hadn't happened, Bane added, "Good luck. I hope you find her. I really do."

"Me too," Virgil said. "I think I'll go get a cup of coffee or something."

"Sounds like a plan, Stan." Bane got out of the truck and walked away.

CHAPTER TWENTY-SIX

BANE'S ESTIMATE OF LARRY'S DEPARTURE WAS OFF BY thirty minutes, but when he finally left, Virgil got a text and headed back to the post office. He parked his truck next to the door and found it unlocked as Bane had promised. The security computer sat by itself on a plain gray institutional desk. The entire room smelled like Pine-Sol and urinal cakes. The computer was on, and Virgil noticed that the file he needed was already on the screen. *Bane really was a bad girl*, he thought.

The screen was split into four segments that gave simultaneous views of the front parking area, the lobby, the sorting room, and the counter area. Virgil hit the play button on the keyboard and watched the upper left-hand box as Patty Doyle turned her car into the parking lot. She entered the building and Virgil turned his attention to the lower right-hand box on the screen and watched as Doyle approached the counter. She was dressed in running shorts and a tank top with light-weight running shoes that looked like they'd been decorated by Jackson Pollock. Her hair was tucked back under a headband.

The security footage was video only. There was no audio, not that it was needed. Virgil could clearly see the interaction between Doyle and the counter person. Doyle said something, the counter person typed in a few keystrokes on the computer, then shook her head. Doyle crossed her arms for a moment, then turned around and left.

Nothing there, Virgil thought. He replayed the video and watched it again, first the upper left box, then the lower right. There was nothing to see, except, Virgil thought, one of the last few hours of Patty Doyle's life. He sat for a moment staring at the screen, thinking about what to do next when he noticed something.

He backed the video up and played it again. Patty Doyle had arrived at the post office during a slow time. She'd been the only retail customer in the building. But shortly after she'd pulled in, a pickup truck turned into the lot. When Doyle drove away, the pickup waited a few seconds and drove off as well. Whoever had been in the pickup hadn't entered the building.

Someone had been following Doyle.

He watched the video again, this time focusing on the truck. There was no chance to get a plate, the position of the exterior camera didn't allow for that. But the truck drove right past the camera and it was a perfect shot of the passenger side of the vehicle. Virgil paused the playback and looked at the truck. A male figure was sitting in the passenger seat, his features blurred from both the motion of the vehicle and the poor quality of the camera.

Virgil took out his phone and called Becky. "I need your help."

"Why are you whispering?"

"Because I'm breaking about ten different federal laws."

"Excellent," Becky said. "What do you need?"

"I'm looking at security footage on a computer at the post office. I need the footage but I don't know how to get it."

"Piece of cake. Maybe."

"C'mon, Becks. Time to shine here."

"Is it connected to their network?"

"I have no idea. How do I tell?"

"They wouldn't use WIFI. It'd be hard-wired into the wall. Is there a blue or yellow cord running from the computer to the wall? It'd look like a phone line, only fatter."

"Hold on." Virgil looked under the desk. "Yes. It's plugged into a wall jack."

"Which post office are you at?"

"The main one…in Bloomington."

"Okay, good. Now, look at the jack on the wall. Is it labeled? There should be a string of numbers on the jack."

Virgil told her to hold on again. He crawled under the desk and took a closer look. He was getting ready to read the numbers to Becky when his phone chirped at him. He pulled the phone away from his ear and looked at the screen. A text from Bane.

The text was in all caps. LTL IS BACK. GET OUT.

He fired off the numbers to Becky, including the file date he needed. He rapped the back of his head on the bottom of the desk when he stood up and had to put some effort into not swearing out loud.

"What was that?" Becky said. "Sounded like a big thump."

"It was. Listen, I'm in a hell of a rush here. What else do I have to do?"

"Nothing," Becky said, her voice calm. "Except get out. I'm already looking at the footage. "This the Doyle chick?"

"I'll call you back." Virgil ended the call and stood close to the closet door. He heard the exterior door open, then Larry as he called out.

"Hey, Bane, where are you? Whose truck is that out there? That's not a proper parking place."

Virgil cracked the door and watched Larry disappear through a hall that led to the front of the building. He stepped out of the closet, then ran outside, hopped into his truck, and drove away.

Unfortunately for Virgil, the security cameras caught the whole thing.

Once he was safely away from the post office, Virgil pulled over and parked. He called Becky again.

"You know," Becky said, "I think the Major Crimes Unit is supposed to fight and prevent crimes, not commit them."

"Says the girl who hacked the security footage."

"Hey, I do what I'm told. So now what?"

"You watch the footage?"

"Yeah, not much to see."

Virgil was about to correct her when she added, "Unless you count the weirdos in the pickup who were tagging her. Who cruises the post office? Am I right?"

And Virgil thought: *Oh Murton, I hope you know what you're doing.* "Is there any way to enhance that photo somehow? Maybe get a better look at who's in the passenger seat?"

"I'm working on that as we speak. But the truth is, we'll never get it clear enough to make a positive ID. There's only so much you can do."

Virgil didn't want to hear that. "Do the best you can, Becks. And send me a photo of that truck, will you?"

"Check your email, Jonesy. It's probably already waiting for you. I've got a great video by the way of you sneaking out of the post office. I can keep it and use it as leverage for a raise, or I can delete it from their system. Up to you."

"Very funny." Virgil thanked her and ended the call. When he checked his email, he saw the photo. *Fuck a bunch of federal law,* he thought.

He fired up his truck and headed back to the Yellowwood.

He also made a mental note to give Becky a raise.

HE FOUND HAMLIN OUTSIDE THE ENTRANCE, WALKING through the same tall grass where they'd found the phone. When Virgil pulled up, Hamlin walked over.

"I thought I'd keep looking. Who knows, right?"

Virgil bit into his lower lip and didn't speak. Hamlin filled the gap. "This part of the state? We're all sort of one big community. This girl gone missing? She's one of ours." He tapped his chest when he said it. "If I'd have known what was going on, I'd have jumped off that tower to get out there quicker."

"And killed yourself in the process," Virgil said. He brought up the picture and held his phone out the window. Hamlin took it. "That the truck?"

"If it ain't, it's an exact replica."

"Tell me more about the two men. Could you describe them?"

Hamlin looked away and didn't speak for a few moments. "I'm embarrassed to say I can't. I didn't get that good of a look. They were a couple of older guys." He wiggled the phone back and forth. "Although the profile of this one here looks like it could be one of them. I mean, it must be, right?"

"Probably. But without anything else to go on, it doesn't do us much good."

Hamlin gave Virgil his phone back. "You think I'm wasting my time walking through this tall grass?"

It probably was a waste of time. Based on Hamlin's description of events and the way they played out, unless they found a wallet with the driver's license of one of the men, they had all the evidence they were going to get. "I think if more people cared the way you do we'd all be a little better off." He dropped the truck in gear. "Take care."

Virgil headed back to Indy.

CHAPTER TWENTY-SEVEN

Ralph Wheeler had assigned Reif and his crew the most basic jobs he could think of. They were simple laborers, moving parts and equipment around the yard. They answered to no one except him, and despite his original assessment that they might be trouble, they did exactly as they were told. They kept their heads down and their mouths shut.

Over the last two weeks, they'd completed three practice runs of sorts. Ralph Wheeler had managed to create a problem on the main line, diverting the freight trains past the maintenance shop. On two of those occasions, they found reasons to delay the trains for a few precious minutes. When that happened, Reif and his crew moved into position and practiced their entry. They didn't practice on the trains that'd been delayed. That would have been far too risky…and much too obvious. Instead, they did their trial runs with cars parked on spurs right next to the track. It wasn't the perfect setup, but they all knew it was as good as it was going to get.

"Like to do it one more time, at least," Reif said after the last run.

Ralph Wheeler was already shaking his head. "Can't. I throw any more problems at the main line over such a short time period, they're going to bring people out to take a look. And you know what they'll find? Nothing. When that happens, they'll start asking questions and looking at me, which means they'll be looking at everyone here, including you and your boys. Don't think you'd want that."

Reif and Wheeler had developed something of a detente over the last few weeks. They didn't exactly trust each other…much less like each other, but they both knew the other man's limits and abilities. That led to a certain level of respect, which put them both in a position where they were listening to the other instead of always pushing back.

"No, I wouldn't," Reif admitted.

"Your first one was a little rough, I'll grant you that. But the last one was damned near perfect."

Reif nodded. It *had* been damned near perfect…but that was simply another way of saying it wasn't quite good enough. He said as much to Wheeler.

"I hear you. But remember, in a few days when the

genuine article rolls through here, a brake line is going to get cut. My maintenance guys can patch a cut line in thirty minutes. That's more than twice the amount of time you're going to need...more time than you've had on the practice runs. Don't overthink it."

Reif knew the old man was right. They'd done all they could do. It'd either go off without a hitch, or the entire plan would go to shit. There simply wasn't much of a middle ground. He put the odds of success at about eighty-five percent. Not too bad, but not great, either. "Okay," Reif said. "It is what it is, I guess. I'm going to walk the yard."

Wheeler grunted at him. "Again?"

"What's the downside?" Reif and his crew had been free to roam the yard for weeks. It gave them the chance to get the lay of the land. Now, with only days to go before the shipment came through, they knew the maintenance yard like the backs of their own hands. They'd be able to maneuver throughout the yard blindfolded if need be. Not only that, they could park equipment in places that would suit them when the time came to take the material.

And it was almost time.

Gibson was helping Murton build the bomb that would hold the nuclear material. Murton kept the explosive material out...not for safety, but for show. Reif had been watching him like a hawk ever since he'd arrived. Now, this morning, Reif insisted that they take a small portion of the C-4 far out into the countryside and detonate it. Murton argued it was a waste of time and resources, but Reif wasn't having it. "I want to see it go off. I need to know this shit is the genuine article."

Fortunately for Murton, Gibson had anticipated Reif's desire to ensure the material was real, because ninety-eight percent of the C-4 was nothing more than green clay, wrapped up and stamped with all the appropriate markings. A small section of one of the bricks had a tiny hash mark on it, nearly invisible to the naked eye unless you were looking for it.

Murton knew what he was about to do was a risk, but he'd been around guys like Reif most of his career. They didn't trust anyone. So when he grabbed one of the bricks, he purposely chose the one that was completely fake, took out a knife and moved to cut a piece off the end.

Reif stopped him. "Not that one."

Murton let out a sigh and allowed his shoulders to slump like he was weary of the whole thing. "Why the hell not?"

Reif got down in his face. "Because I said so."

His gamble paid off. Murton stared at him for a moment, shrugged his shoulders, then sliced off the actual explosive part of the other brick. He had all the other materials he needed and an hour later had a crude miniature bomb. Reif, who knew nothing of explosives watched him every step of the way. They took it far out in the hills where Murton inserted the detonator then set a digital timer for three minutes.

"What now?" Reif asked.

Murton gave him a blank stare, then pressed the button on the timer. "I suggest we get back in the car and get the hell out of here."

"I want to see it go off," Reif said.

"Then give me the keys. I'll drive. But the clock is ticking and I'm going. If you don't do the same and do it now, you'll have a front-row ticket on the express train to hell." To emphasize his point, Murton turned and ran to Reif's SUV.

Reif followed. He actually beat him back to the vehicle. He tossed the keys to Murton, climbed in the back seat and watched out the rear window as they drove away. "Hey, slow down a little," Reif said. "And don't get too far away. I want to be able to—"

They were less than a quarter-mile away when the bomb went off. Not only did Reif see it, both men felt the pressure of the blast as it rocked the SUV. Murton accelerated hard to put as much distance as possible between them and the blast site.

Reif turned and stared at Murton. "Holy shit. I saw how much of that brick you sliced off. It was only a sliver."

"Are you satisfied now?" Murton asked, his voice calm.

Reif clapped him on the shoulder. "I am. Nice job. You know, when we're done with all this, I could use someone like you."

Murton caught Reif's eyes in the rear-view mirror. "I work for myself. And take your hand off my shoulder."

CHAPTER TWENTY-EIGHT

Virgil caught up with Becky at the bar and she filled him in on the latest reports Lawless had sent over. They'd slipped him inside Radiology, Inc. as planned without a hitch where he worked as a shipping clerk. He had access to every record and bill of lading for all scheduled shipments of nuclear material both in the past, and more importantly, the ones scheduled to go out over the next twelve months. The only problem was, he'd found exactly nothing out of the ordinary. The upcoming shipment had been manufactured and was going through the complex packaging system prior to transport. Everything was right on schedule, and the manufacturing and inventory management logs matched, right down to the fraction of an ounce. Short of weighing the material himself, which wasn't even remotely possible, there wasn't anything else he could see or do.

"What about the thumb drive?"

"Program's still running."

"Any idea how much longer?"

"Nope. And no, I can't make it go any faster, so don't ask."

"I wasn't going to."

"Uh-huh."

"Clearly, we're missing something," Virgil said. "That shipment goes out tomorrow."

"What about security?" Becky asked.

"I've thought about that, and it's an extremely tough call, Becks. I could get Mok and his SWAT crew on the train, but what if I do and it somehow screws up Murt's operation? Gibson has a plan of some sort. The problem is, we don't know what. If Mok and his men are on board, it could ruin an operation that has so far cost Murt almost a full month of his life."

Becky gave him a hard stare. "And what about the rest of his life, Jonesy? I wasn't kidding. I think somewhere in the back of his mind he thinks…he knows that you're going to be there for him when he needs you the most. Lawless is watching things on Radiology's end. He says everything looks exactly right. I say we get the word federal out of our vocabulary and do what we do best."

Virgil thought about it. "I'll run it by Mok and see what he thinks. In the meantime we need to figure out what's going on." He stood from his seat and walked behind the bar. He filled both their cups with fresh coffee and turned to put the pot back in the brewer.

The brewer triggered a memory of his father behind the bar in the exact spot where Virgil now stood. The front door opening…Amanda Pate walking in…his father yelling the word 'gun'…Sandy pulling him to the ground as she fired her weapon…Mason bleeding out in their arms. It all happened so fast, so…unexpected. They never saw it coming.

And then…

He was back. Becky was next to him, behind the bar, one hand on his shoulder, the other around his waist. "Hey, Jonesy? You okay?" She took the pot from his hand and placed it back in the brewer.

Virgil turned and looked at her. "Yeah, sorry. I was thinking about something."

She punched him in the shoulder. "Well, quit it. Jeez, I thought you were having a stroke or something."

They moved around to the other side of the bar, back to their seats, then Becky said, "What were you thinking about?"

"Ah, nothing. It doesn't matter."

She put her hand on his arm and held it there until he looked at her. "I think it does. The last thing you said was, 'clearly we're missing something' and then you went away for a minute. Now tell me."

He smiled at her. "You're the best, Becks. You know

that don't you? You sound like Sandy." Then, "Although she doesn't punch me nearly as often."

"If you don't tell me, I'll punch you again. Let's have it."

"I had a little flashback, is all. I was thinking about the day my dad died. Something about that coffee brewer triggered the memory. He was standing right next to it when he got shot."

Becky thought about it for a minute. "So we are missing something."

"Yeah, I think I already said that."

"That's not what I mean. When you had your little flashback, what was the main part of it?"

Virgil thought about it for a minute. "I don't know. The whole scene just replayed in my head. It happens every once in a while."

Becky nodded. "I understand what happened." She paused for a moment, then tried again. "Remember that day when you asked me to come and work for you and Murt? We were sitting right where we are now. You told me you don't miss much and then you proved it. That always impressed me."

"Thank you," Virgil said. "But I don't understand what you're getting at."

"I'm asking you to think about what was *behind* the thoughts you had."

Virgil tipped his head back and closed his eyes. He was quiet for almost a full minute and when he spoke his voice was distant, his speech rutted and slow. "We thought it was over. Samuel Pate and both the Wells were dead. We thought everyone who mattered was out of the picture. But we were wrong. I tried to tell Elliott that something felt wrong, but he wasn't listening. He wanted my paperwork turned in so the case could be cleared and everyone could move on. But after my dad was killed, I remember thinking when it was all over that it was a failure of imagination on my part. I was already feeling the effects of the pills. My thinking wasn't what it should have been. No one bothered to look at Samuel's wife, Amanda. We… missed it. I missed it." He opened his eyes and looked at Becky. "That's what was behind the thought. It was there all along and I missed it."

"So what, or who, are we missing now?" Becky asked. The question was full of urgency. "Murt's career, hell, his life is on the line here, Jonesy."

Virgil's phone buzzed at him before he could answer the question. When he saw who it was he let out a little groan. Cal Lipkins.

He gave Becky a 'just a second' look, picked up the phone and pressed the answer button. "Hey, Cal. What's up?"

VIRGIL LISTENED FOR A FEW MOMENTS, THEN SAID, "I thought we did that already. Isn't that what all those forms were for?" He listened again, then said, "No, I don't have time to come and sign another. I've got a job to do."

Becky stared at Virgil until she had his attention, then pointed at the upstairs office and mouthed 'be right back.' Virgil nodded at her and went back to his conversation with Lipkins. "Look, Cal, I'm not trying to be difficult, but I'm too busy. If you lost one of the forms, you're either going to have to find it, or fax another one to me."

"I guess that'd be okay," Lipkins said. "But we need it as soon as possible."

Virgil gave him the fax number at his house, waited until Lipkins read it back to him to make sure he had it right, then asked a question. "Listen, I don't want you to take this the wrong way, but I sort of thought any back and forth would be between me and Carl Johnson. The way the deal is set up…"

Lipkins cut him off, his voice layered with exasperation. "Yeah, yeah, I know what you're getting at. But I run the Co-op, which means I'm responsible for making sure everyone has everything they need. Johnson farms the land, is all. But in order to do that, we need fuel, seed, fertilizer and the like, and that all comes through the Co-op. You're the landowner, so we need your signature on the requisitions for your acreage."

"Okay, whatever." Virgil didn't really know all the ins and outs of the operations and didn't care. "Send it over and I'll get it back to you."

"Today?"

"As soon as I can."

"Today would be best. Land's being tilled as we speak. Gotta be ready."

Virgil pulled the phone away from his ear for a moment and rubbed his face with his free hand. When he spoke, he had to make a conscious effort to keep his teeth from coming together. "I'll have my wife sign it and send it right back."

Lipkins wasn't having it. "I've been doing this a long time, city-boy. Has to be the landowner."

"Would you please stop calling me that? I live in the country. The land is held in a trust, Cal. The trust is in both our names." When Lipkins didn't respond, Virgil thought the call had been dropped, or that Lipkins had hung up on him. "Cal?"

"I really wish you hadn't told me that, though for your sake, I guess it's a good thing you did."

"What are you talking about?"

"All those papers you signed last month? If your wife is an owner of the land, she's going to have to sign them too."

Virgil squeezed his phone so hard he thought he heard a little crack. "When?"

Lipkins must have heard the frustration in his voice. "Look, if you can get me the form back by the end of today with both your signatures, we should be okay. We'll get to all the other ones that need your wife's signature later. Next few days or something. How's that sound?"

Lipkins was trying, or at the very least, sounded like he was trying. Virgil wasn't sure which. By then he didn't care. "Alright, I'll make it happen." Virgil told him to fax the document to the bar instead of his house. He'd sign it, send it over to Sandy then she could sign it and shoot it back to Cal. "How's that sound?"

"That's fine." Then Lipkins softened even more and said something that made Virgil feel like an ass for being so frustrated with him. "Listen, let me know when you're coming. Bring Jonas with you, Sandy can sign the other paperwork, and we'll give them a tour. You can drive your boy around on a tractor. He'd probably get a kick out of it. What do you say?" Cal Lipkins suddenly didn't sound like a crusty old farmer…he sounded like somebody's grandfather.

Virgil said he'd do that. When he finished the call though, something was tickling the back part of his brain. Something Cal had said. He replayed the conversation a few times trying to figure it out, but it wouldn't come.

He signed the form without really looking at it then sent it off to his house. He called Sandy. "How's it going, baby?"

"It's going well. I'm in the middle of feeding our little guy."

"How's he doing today?"

"He's doing great. I, on the other hand, feel like a milk machine."

Virgil knew better than to address the latter part of her comment. "You're the best, baby. I love you, and the kids do too."

"Whoops, hold on, I've got to switch to the other side or I'll be lopsided for the rest of the day." Virgil heard her set the phone down, then a series of ruffling noises. A few seconds later she was back. "So, what's up?"

When you get a chance, would you grab a fax from the machine? It's from the Co-op. It needs your signature. Once you sign it, fax it back to Cal."

"Sure. Why does it need my signature?"

Virgil sighed. No time like the present, he thought. "As it turns out, that isn't the only form you have to sign…"

He told her what Lipkins had said about all the forms and how they required both their signatures.

"That's no problem, Virgil. I can sign a few documents."

"You might think otherwise once you see the stack. There's only about a billion of them."

She laughed and said, "Don't worry about it. We'll get it worked out." Then the tenor of her voice changed and there was no mistaking the level of concern set within in her question. "Where are you guys with Murton?"

"Doing everything we can, which, unfortunately, unless he makes contact with us, isn't much. We're stuck between trying to help and staying out of the way of an ongoing federal operation."

"I'm starting to get a really bad feeling about all this, Virgil. It's time for you to do what you do best. I say screw the feds. Find your brother and bring him home." Then, "Ouch. Hey, I've got to go. Wyatt's done eating. Now he's biting."

Virgil told Sandy he loved her, set his phone down on the bar, and tried once again to figure out what it was Lipkins had said that bothered him. He didn't get very far because his morning suddenly went a little further south and the thought, whatever it was, left him.

CHAPTER TWENTY-NINE

Delroy came in through the back and when Virgil saw the look on his face he knew something wasn't quite right. Jamaicans move with a rhythm all their own, one that exemplifies the heritage and cultural conditions of their small island nation. In other words, they move at a pace that is often slower than most people are accustomed to. But when Delroy came through the swinging doors he was moving faster than Virgil had ever seen, like maybe the kitchen might be on fire. In addition, he looked a little…disheveled. He straightened his shirt and glanced at Virgil, then tipped his head back toward the kitchen. Just as he did, two men followed him through. Delroy hadn't hurried through the door on his own. He'd been pushed through.

Virgil recognized them immediately for what they were, or more accurately, who they represented.

Feds.

They both wore dark suits, white starched shirts, and plain, dark neckties. Their haircuts were high and tight, their faces clean-shaven and they both wore mirrored sunglasses even though they were inside. One of the men had a clear coiled wire poking out of the collar of his shirt that led to an earbud tucked into his right ear. But it was the other man who caught the bulk of Virgil's attention. Both his hands, his neck, and a portion of his jaw were spotted white, all the pigmentation gone from the affected areas of his skin. The colorless blotches were irregular in size and configuration. Some looked like misshapen bleeding hearts of white, others more like rivulets that seemed to flow upward toward his neck and face, as though gravity had no role on his person. The white areas were much more prominent than his regular skin tone.

Virgil winked at Delroy, then turned his attention back to the two men who were now standing next to him on the patron side of the bar. "It's a little early guys. Bar's not open yet. But I'd be happy to make an exception for federal agents as soon as you tell me why you've been man-handling my bar manager."

The suit with the earbud spoke first. "We're not here to place an order, or to explain ourselves." He reached into his breast pocket and pulled out his ID. "I'm agent Robert Thorpe, Department of Homeland Security, Portland, Oregon field office." He tipped his head to the right. "This is Agent Chris Dobson with ICE."

"That stands for Immigrations and Customs Enforcement," Dobson said.

"I know what ICE is," Virgil said, trying to keep the sarcasm out of his voice. "Seems like you're quite a ways from home."

"One of us is," Dobson said.

"What's this about?"

"Are you Virgil Jones?"

"I am. I'm also an officer with the state police, currently assigned to the MCU. That stands for Major Crimes Unit. Now, how about you stand down and answer the question. What's this about?"

Before either of them could answer, Delroy moved enough to catch Virgil's eye. He looked quickly at the kitchen doors, then right back to Virgil.

Thorpe opened his mouth to answer, but Virgil beat him to it. "Excuse me for a moment. I need to have a word with my man behind the bar here." He stood from his stool but Dobson moved to block his exit. When Virgil tried to step around him, Agent Dobson grabbed Virgil by the wrist.

"We need to speak with you now, Detective."

Virgil looked at his wrist, then turned his face up to Dobson. "Take your hand off my person immediately. It's not a request and I won't say it twice."

Dobson's eyes narrowed as he squeezed Virgil's wrist tighter in an effort to show who was in control of the situation.

Virgil almost laughed at him. "Did you know that grabbing someone's wrist without cause or permission is considered a form of battery in the state of Indiana? Pretty much everywhere else too, if I'm not mistaken, which I'm not. As a federal officer, you should know that. It's also the least effective means of restraint available. Here's why."

Dobson expected him to try and pull away. Instead, Virgil stepped forward, let a natural bend form in his own elbow, then rotated his arm in and down, all while rotating his hand in the opposite direction. The leverage he'd created caused Dobson to lose his grip and Virgil now had a firm grasp of Dobson's wrist. When Dobson tried to pull away, Virgil stepped into the momentum, spun him around and twisted his arm behind his back. He bent him over the bar, then looked at Thorpe. "I don't like to get railroaded in my own bar. Are we going to have a problem here, or are you going to let me talk to my bartender?"

BECKY WAS UPSTAIRS IN THE OFFICE, CHECKING ON THE password crack for the thumb drive. Then she thought about Lawless and the logs he was monitoring at Radiology. That gave her an idea. She pulled up a directory of files she kept on a hidden partition of her hard drive and rooted around for a few minutes until she found exactly what she wanted. She copied a bit of code, sent it to

Lawless via email along with instructions on how to use it. She was waiting for his reply when she happened to turn in her chair and glance down at the bar through the window. She saw Delroy behind the bar, along with Virgil and two other men she didn't recognize on the other side. When one of the men reached out and grabbed Virgil's wrist, she forgot all about the thumb drive and the email she'd sent Lawless. But she did remember something she and Murton had discussed a few months ago when Decker was on the loose.

WHEN THORPE DIDN'T ANSWER, VIRGIL REACHED INSIDE Dobson's jacket and pulled his weapon free. He kept it pointed down and away from Thorpe, but it didn't matter. Thorpe took his weapon out and pointed it at Virgil.

"We're federal agents. Drop that weapon and release Agent Dobson immediately." Thorpe was so focused on Virgil and Dobson he made a mental mistake and let his situational awareness slip.

"And we're state agents with the Major Crimes Unit," Becky said. She'd positioned herself at a perfect angle behind Thorpe, with Virgil out of her line of fire. When Thorpe refused to look her way, Becky pumped the action on the shotgun. The sound was unmistakable; a metallic reverberation that carried a sense of weight and power… the first two parts of an unfinished three-part crescendo.

"Put your weapon on the bar and slide it to the end. Do it now."

Thorpe hesitated for a beat, then let his shoulders slump. He set his gun on the bar and slid it to the end.

"Atta boy," Becky said. "Now, take out your handcuffs and shackle both hands around the bar rail."

Thorpe looked at Virgil. "How about we start over?"

"Your boy here made the play, not me," Virgil said. "I'd do what the lady says if I were you. She's a force of nature even without the firepower."

Thirty seconds later both men were cuffed to the brass rail that fronted the bar.

"You're making a colossal mistake," Dobson said.

"It wouldn't be the first time. Probably won't be the last either if this is the best the federal government has to offer. Take a seat. We still might be able to work this out, but right now, I need to speak with my bar manager." He turned around and nodded to Becky. "Keep these two company for a few, will you?"

"My pleasure," Becky said. Then, "A force of nature, huh?"

Virgil looked around the bar. "Where's Delroy?"

"I'm down here, mon," Delroy said. He'd dropped to the floor behind the bar. "It safe to come out now, me?"

Becky had the shotgun leveled at the two federal agents. She laughed out loud at Delroy's statement and when she did, Virgil suddenly realized how much he missed Murton.

CHAPTER THIRTY

Virgil still held Agent Dobson's weapon. He collected Agent Thorpe's gun and set both weapons on the table next to Becky. Then he and Delroy walked outside and sat down on the employee picnic table.

After a beat: "What wrong with people these days, mon?"

Virgil didn't have an answer to his friend's question. "Tell me what happened, Delroy."

"They were on me as soon as I got out of my car. Da one with the antenna in his ear never said a word. Da one with the spots back me up against the wall with his arm across my throat. Said if I didn't tell him where Murton and dat Gibson fellow at, they deport me back to Jamaica. I say: Go ahead and try. I'm an American now, like you. Jamaican too. I got dual citizenship, mon. I'm at home no matter where you try to send me. It probably didn't help that I smiled when I tell him dat."

"He put his hands on you? You didn't do anything to provoke him?"

Delroy was flapping his arms. Virgil had never seen him so agitated. "No, mon, no. Right away had me up against the wall. Then he pushed me through the kitchen door. You know Delroy don't move that fast."

"I'm going back inside," Virgil said. "I don't want you in there right now, understand?" He stood and moved to go back in the bar.

"What you do, you?"

Virgil turned. "Delroy, give me your word. You'll stay out of the bar."

"Yeah, mon. It's a beautiful day, no? Let's not ruin it over some red stripe who don't know the meaning of respect."

"That's not up to me," Virgil said. He took out his phone and punched in a quick text as he walked back into the bar.

When he got back inside, Virgil discovered three weapons on the table next to Becky. He looked at her and let a question form on his face.

"Guess who had an ankle piece?" she said. "Looks

like a throw-down, too. Maybe not, but the serial numbers are filed away."

"Becks, you shouldn't have tried to take it away. It's too dangerous."

Becky batted her eyelashes at Virgil, then tipped her head at Dobson. "You think? Take a closer look at Spot. He might be peeing red for a few days."

Virgil looked at Dobson. His body was bent at an awkward angle as he tried to massage the area around his left kidney.

"You'll be in federal lock-up before the end of the day, princess," Dobson said. "I personally guarantee it. In fact, I know a couple of bull-dykes who'll give you a guided tour of places the guards won't go without full riot gear."

"Bring it, sunshine," Becky said. "You think this is our first encounter with assholes like you? Take a look around. This place is wired ten ways from Sunday. The outside too. We've got the whole thing on high definition video, all backed up to the cloud and delivered to computers here, at my house, and to the operations center at the MCU. Oh, I almost forgot. Right here to my phone, too." She held up her phone and wiggled it back and forth. The video of Delroy pinned against the wall by Dobson was playing on a loop. "Hey look, Facebook is asking me if I want to share an update." She looked at Virgil. "What do you say, Boss? A little social justice goes a long way these days. Federal cops pinning an innocent black man against the wall of his own business establishment? I'll bet it makes the evening news."

No matter the seriousness of the situation, Virgil simply couldn't help himself. He smiled.

Then Miles, Rosencrantz, and Ross walked through the door. Thorpe looked at the three men, then at Virgil. "Really, I was serious a few minutes ago. How about we start over?" He looked at Dobson. "My first interaction with this asshole was about an hour ago when he picked me up at the airport."

VIRGIL CAUGHT RON'S ATTENTION. GIVEN THE NATURE OF the situation it wasn't very difficult. They moved to the front of the bar, out of earshot of the others.

"I appreciate you getting here so fast, Ron."

Miles sucked in a cheek and gave Virgil a look. "Let's come to an understanding. You and I have known each other a long time, Jonesy. I've always considered you a fine cop and a good friend."

"Me too, Ron."

"But we have two very different styles, don't we?"

Virgil nodded. "I guess we do."

"How about we decide to let them compliment each other instead of working against each other? Because that's what I'm trying to do right now. When one of my team members sends a text that says 'get to the bar - 911,' I drop everything and come."

Virgil put his hand on Ron's shoulder. "I appreciate it, Ron." Then he took his hand away and chose his words with care. "The tension between us has been my fault. I'm going to let that go. The hard part for me isn't that you have my old job, it's that Murt and I are operating on a different level. It wasn't my idea. It was Mac's. I know you know that."

Miles nodded, then squinted and Virgil caught it. "What?"

"You had Becky do an end-run on the subpoena for Doyle's account information."

"That's not entirely accurate, Ron. We were waiting on you to push the paper through."

"And I did. But that sort of thing takes time. I got my ass handed to me by one of Apple's lawyers, by the way."

"How'd they know what we were doing?"

Miles ran a finger inside his shirt color and tugged. "How the hell should I know? They've probably got a team of interns who do nothing but keep an eye out for that sort of thing."

They were sliding backward, the exact opposite of what Virgil wanted. "You're right. I'm sorry. We should have waited before we did anything. I thought it would come back on me, not you."

Miles shrugged. "Anyway…" He tipped his head to the other end of the bar. "Mind telling me why Becky has what looks like two feds cuffed to the bar with a shotgun pointed their way?"

"The short answer is aggravated assault on Delroy, and battery on me."

Ron turned and looked at the men cuffed to the bar. "Both of them? Without cause?"

Virgil shook his head. "No cause whatsoever. The one holding his kidney tried to brace Delroy outside. Had him pinned against the wall. When they got inside, the same one—Dobson's his name, by the way—tried to restrain me."

"It doesn't seem to be going their way."

"No, it doesn't." Then: "Listen, don't ever mess with Becky. She's sort of like a mini-Murt or something."

Virgil outlined the rest of it for Ron, then they walked back and joined the others. Rosencrantz asked Becky to put the shotgun away. She stuck her tongue out at him, then walked the gun back up to the office.

"Who's that?" Ross asked. He was interested.

"Nobody you'd ever want to mess with, kid," Rosencrantz said.

"Still, she's pretty hot."

"You know who Murton Wheeler is, right?"

"Yeah, of course. Haven't met him yet, though. We

both worked the op at Decker's trailer a few months back, but never had the chance to talk."

"You will. That's his girlfriend."

"Gotcha," Ross said, his disappointment almost evident. "So. Now what?"

"Four things: Sit down, be quiet, watch, and learn. You're about to get a first-hand glimpse of how things get done at the MCU. It's a gas."

CHAPTER THIRTY-ONE

Virgil removed the cuffs from Thorpe's wrists and led him to a booth at the other end of the bar, away from Dobson. Miles, Rosencrantz, and Ross joined them.

"Hey, if you're having some sort of management meeting, I'd like to attend," Dobson yelled over his shoulder.

Ross stood from his seat and said, "Don't start without me." He walked back over to Dobson, leaned in close and whispered in his ear. The look on Dobson's face as Ross spoke was not unlike that of a submariner watching the crush panels collapse one by one inside his ship as it exceeded its maximum depth rating. When he returned to the booth Miles asked him what he'd said.

"I told him what I did prior to joining the MCU. I may have also let it slip that I once hit the X-ring from fifteen hundred meters with a five-mile-per-hour quartering crosswind. The message was you never see the one that gets you."

Rosencrantz turned in his seat and looked at Ross. "Think he got the point?"

"I doubt it, but a guy's gotta try. I think he might have some dry rot in the foundation of his cerebral architecture." When Rosencrantz didn't respond, he added, "Hey, no disrespect. I'm sitting, I'll be quiet, I'm watching, and learning. I am a quick study though."

Rosencrantz looked away. He didn't want Ross to see his smile.

Virgil looked at Thorpe. "What's going on here, Agent Thorpe? Why come in here like Butch and Sundance and put my manager up against the wall?"

Thorpe visibly swallowed. "I was telling you the truth earlier. My first encounter with that idiot was when he picked me up at the airport. You should have heard him on the drive over here. He wouldn't shut up about immigrants. I had no idea he was going to brace your manager. To tell you the truth, I don't think he did either. Turn his kind loose on the streets and they see targets of opportunity at every turn. With the political climate around the world these days it's open season for guys like him."

"You didn't try to intercede," Virgil said.

Thorpe had his elbows on the table. He turned his palms up. "It was a fluid situation. It was also over almost as soon as it started."

Virgil wasn't having it. "Bullshit. I watched my bar

manager get shoved through the door. I almost immediately identified myself as a police officer. That didn't stop him from trying to restrain me, and it didn't stop you from pointing your weapon in my direction either." Virgil was getting wound up.

"How about we all admit the whole thing could have been handled better," Miles said.

"That certainly works for me," Thorpe said. Then to Virgil: "I'm sorry, okay? Really. But tell me you wouldn't have done the same thing if our situations were reversed. Someone has your partner face down on the bar holding his weapon and yours doesn't come out?"

Virgil let it go…partly because Thorpe was right. "Okay, okay, whatever. Why are you here? More specifically, why is a DHS field agent out of Portland looking for one of their own?"

"Not just Gibson. We're looking for Wheeler too."

"Still doesn't answer my question."

"It's classified," Thorpe said. But when he saw the look on Virgil's face he changed his mind about the nature of the classification system. "The truth is, we've lost contact with Gibson. The entire operation has spun out of control. This was supposed to be a simple sting operation. We handle these things every day. That's not an exaggeration."

"C'mon, Thorpe," Virgil said. "We can start telling each other the truth, or we can end this conversation right now. You want us to believe that hijacked nuclear material by home-grown terrorists is an everyday occurrence for DHS? Peddle that crap to someone else."

Thorpe's mouth formed a thin line, the corners of his eyes crinkling tight. "You know about the nuclear aspect of the operation?"

"Of course we know," Miles said. "This is the MCU."

Rosencrantz and Ross looked at each other, their expressions identical. Thorpe caught it. "Maybe everyone isn't quite up to speed. Which one of you is Rosencrantz?"

"I am."

"You caught the double down in Jeffersonville…at the quarry?"

"What about it?"

"They were two of a five-man crew. We know who they are, but not who's running the crew, or how and why two of them ended up on the buffet table for the local wildlife population."

"I can give you the how," Rosencrantz said. "They were both shot to death. One with a high-powered rifle, the other up close and personal."

"Any other valuable information?"

"Is that a genuine question?" Rosencrantz asked. "Or are you being facetious? Because your tone suggests—"

Thorpe interrupted him. "No, no. I'm asking a genuine question. I need all the information I can get."

Rosencrantz bit into his lower lip and gave Thorpe a hard look. "That's about all we have as of now. The shooter or shooters picked up their brass. The M.E. said one was shot with a high-powered rifle, the other with a handgun, up close and personal. There were footprints and tire marks, but they won't tell us anything because the crime scene techs say there are too many. All different kinds of vehicles. The quarry seems to attract kids who go there for sex. The local sheriff says it's a hotspot for dopers and degenerates of all kinds. Don't ask me why."

"How did you connect them to the rest of the crew?" Miles asked.

"One of the quarry victims…Fischer, was involved in a gun heist in Northern California. We got a hit on his DNA. Good old fashion detective work gave us the rest of the crew, all the way up the ladder. Their leader is a guy named Armon Reif. He's got dual citizenship…here and in Canada. That's why dipshit over there is involved." He jerked his thumb at Dobson. When he did, the other men naturally turned their heads that way. It was just in time to see Delroy push through the kitchen door and smash Dobson's forearm with a baseball bat.

THE BAT CRACKED DOBSON'S ARM AND HE SCREAMED IN pain. The other men rushed out of the booth and over to the bar. Virgil saw that one of the cuffs had been unlocked, the key lying on the floor at Dobson's feet.

"He was trying to get away," Delroy said.

Dobson's arm was clearly broken. It looked as if he had two elbows. Virgil turned to Ross. "Get an ambulance started."

Ross nodded and made the call. Miles took the bat from Delroy, then led him to a table and sat him down. When Miles turned and looked at Virgil, his expression was flat, the intent in his eyes clear.

And Virgil thought, *Oh Delroy, what have you done?*

CHAPTER THIRTY-TWO

WHILE VIRGIL WENT INSIDE THE BAR TO CONFRONT THE two agents, Delroy lit a cigarette and sat on the employee picnic table and wondered at the complexities of human desire. The federal agent had attacked him for no other reason than he felt he could. What kind of person did that? One who had no respect for his fellow man, that's who. He was probably rotten to the core.

But his Jamaican upbringing wouldn't let him dwell on the actions of others, particularly ones who held no sway in his life. He'd told Virgil it was a beautiful day and it was. Why spoil it with thoughts of a heavy-handed *borosie* when there were more pleasant things to consider.

Like Huma Moon.

He'd not been so taken with an American woman for as long as he could remember. He'd had plenty of offers from other women ever since he started working for Virgil and Mason. He'd even followed through on a few of them, though they were nothing more than brief encounters. But Huma had captivated him from the moment she walked in. In many ways, it surprised him.

Delroy was so caught up with his thoughts of Huma and wondering when he might see her again that he forgot his promise to Virgil. He crushed out his cigarette and entered the bar, ready to set up for the day.

Robert kept a baseball bat in the kitchen, right next to the swinging door that gave way to the bar area. To the best of Delroy's recollection, it'd never been used. One of the better parts of being partnered with a police officer was the simple fact that there were always a lot of cops in the bar. Arguments were rare. Fights were almost nonexistent.

The swinging door had a square window at eye level. Delroy made it all the way to the door before he remembered that Virgil wanted him to stay out of the bar until he'd resolved the situation with the federal officers. Did being in the kitchen violate that promise? Delroy thought not.

Then he looked through the window at the man who'd attacked him earlier. He was bent over in an awkward position, his arms extended on either side of the railing, his jacket pulled askew on his torso. He took something out of his pocket and turned his back to Virgil and the other men. Ten seconds later his wrists were free. When Delroy saw what was happening, he grabbed the bat and slipped through the door, only a few feet away from the man who'd pinned him against the wall outside, his forearm pressed tight across his throat.

Dobson was doing his best to be as quiet as possible. The guns were right behind him on the table. But the timing didn't work in his favor. As he freed himself from the bar the other cops happened to turn and look his way. At the same exact moment, Delroy swung the bat, maybe a little harder than he intended.

Dobson screamed in pain and Delroy winced when he heard the bone let go. Then Virgil and the others were there and it was all over.

Miles collected the guns, looked at Virgil, and tipped his head. He wanted a word. Virgil asked Delroy to take a seat and told him not to say anything. Delroy nodded, his eyes clear, his face calm.

"You realize that everyone in this room saw Delroy assault a federal agent."

"I don't see it that way, Ron," Virgil said, even though technically, Miles was correct.

"The man's got an extra elbow, Jonesy. How do you think this is going to play out?"

Virgil felt a bubble of anger inflate inside his chest. "I'll tell you exactly how this is going to play out, Ron. We're going to have a little talk with Dobson and explain his options to him."

Rosencrantz and Ross had made their way over to where Virgil and Miles stood. Thorpe was standing between Delroy and Dobson. Dobson held his broken arm by the elbow—the natural one—and stared at his shoes. Virgil thought it looked as though he might vomit.

"And you think that's going to make all of this go away?"

"Make what go away?" Ross said. "The man saved our bacon."

Miles looked at Ross. "Shut up. You're the new kid in town and right now, I'm not interested in your version of events."

"You should be," Rosencrantz said. "Ross and I had our backs turned. I didn't actually see anything except the aftermath. How about you, Ross?"

Ross nodded at Rosencrantz, then squared off on Miles. "Same here. I might be the new guy on the squad but there's no doubt in my mind that Delroy probably saved someone from getting shot. Dobson was two steps away from a table full of guns. You'd think the senior officer on the scene would have thought to secure them." Then to show he wasn't one to be pushed around by anyone, he put a finger in Ron's face and added, "Boss or not, don't ever tell me to shut up. If that doesn't fit your management style, you can go fuck yourself."

Ron's neck and face turned a deep red, the cartilage in his jaw corded with tension. "Get your finger out of my face." When Ross lowered his hand, Miles reached behind his jacket, pulled out a set of handcuffs and walked over toward Delroy. He leaned over and said, "I've never in my life had the kind of friends you have here. It's probably my own fault." Then he walked over to Dobson and cuffed his uninjured wrist to the bar railing. "You're under arrest for aggravated assault, attempted assault, assault on a state police officer, interfering with an ongoing state investigation, attempted evasion, and anything else I can think of between now and the time the medics are done with you. You have the right to remain silent. Anything you say can and will be used against you…"

Rosencrantz looked at Ross. "I'm telling you right here and now, that took some major balls, kid."

Ross looked at Virgil. "Miles should save his breath. That guy will be cut loose by lunchtime. Besides, he probably thinks Miranda is Spanish for an STD." He looked around the room then let his gaze settle on Rosencrantz. "Man oh man, I think I'm really going to like it here. You weren't kidding, were you? This shit's a gas."

The medics came in and looked at Dobson's arm. Virgil walked over and said, "How's it look?"

"Broken," the medic said, his voice flat, his face expressionless. He glanced at Dobson's other wrist still shackled to the bar rail. "If this guy's under arrest or being detained in any way, someone is going to have to ride in the back with him."

"I'll take it," Miles said. He looked at Ross. "You and I might have to have a conversation sometime soon."

Ross shrugged a single shoulder. "Right is right. How about we have it now? I've spent the last five years knocking down doors without knowing what was on the other side. I've been shot at, stabbed three times, beat in the back with a lead pipe, had uncut coke thrown in my face, and bitten by more Pit Bulls than I can count. I've also had to park a few rounds into someone's squash on different occasions from a hundred yards or more. One guy had a gun to someone else's head. Another time some asshole was running down the street with a shotgun blasting away at anything that moved. What I'm trying to say here is this: I've seen the very worst of people. You want to chew me out for standing up for what's right, bring it. I'm all ears. The man was going for the guns. It'll be in my report. I don't know what else you want."

"I want you to show some respect. That's what I want," Miles said. He was hot.

Ross looked at Delroy for a moment, then back at

Miles. "Looks like we want the same thing then. We're all on the same team here, right?"

Miles and Virgil looked at each other without saying a word.

BECKY HADN'T BEEN KIDDING WHEN SHE TOLD DOBSON the bar was wired to the gills. She got the whole thing on video. She pulled Miles and Virgil upstairs and pointed at the monitor. "It does look like he was going for the guns," she said.

"And any lawyer could make a case that he had every right to," Miles said. "It was his gun."

"Federal officer or not, he was being lawfully detained," Virgil said.

"Can't anything be easy anymore?" Miles said. "You know, back in the day, when I was on the beat, you didn't see this kind of shit. Everybody stayed between the lines. Now it's hard to tell the good guys from the bad."

Virgil thought Ron needed a friend. He threw his arm around his shoulder. "We're the good guys, Ron. And it's not because we have badges. Cut Ross a break, will you? I'll talk to him about how he might dial it back a little. What do you say?"

Miles turned his body and released himself from Virgil's grasp. "Don't you dare. What he said was true. I should have made sure those guns were secure. I guess Rosencrantz was right."

"About what?"

"That kid's got a certain testicular fortitude. Except it's not very pleasant when it's pointed your way."

The medic jogged up the steps and popped his head in the door. We're ready to roll."

Miles turned to leave. Then he looked back and asked a question Virgil couldn't answer. "You think Murt's okay?"

CHAPTER THIRTY-THREE

THE SAME MORNING REIF AND HIS CREW WERE FEELING cramped. Reif was again telling everyone about the test bomb. They were all a little tired of hearing about it. He exaggerated the size of the blast and how close they'd been. Murton let him. The cramped feeling made them want to get out for a while. Maybe get something to eat. They tried to talk Murton and Gibson into joining them, all pals now that Murton had proved himself.

"No thanks," Murton said. "We like to keep a low profile. The feds aren't stupid. You know how they catch guys like you? They know you have to eat and that you probably like to drink. They've got more manpower than you can imagine. They're going to interview every restaurant and bar employee in three states no matter how long it takes. The liquor stores too. Someone will remember your faces, or you'll get caught on camera. It might take them two years to get through it all, but one day you'll be sitting at a Denny's somewhere and before you know what's happening you'll be swarmed by guys wearing blue windbreakers with big bright yellow lettering on the back. I'll let you imagine what the letters might be. We've got one day to go. My advice? Stay put. There's plenty of food in the kitchen."

Reif laughed at Murton's speech. "Someone's been watching too much TV. When this thing is over we'll be so far gone they won't even know where to start looking."

Murton reached into his pocket and pulled out two twenties. "Have it your way then. Bring us back something from a drive-through. I don't care what."

Reif laughed and took the money. "You worry too much."

After Reif, Chase, and Stone had gone, Murton asked Gibson about his father's involvement. Gibson's answer was simple and straightforward.

"If I'd have told you your father was working as a confidential informant for DHS, you'd have called it off on the spot. Tell me I'm wrong."

Ralph Wheeler had made contact with a group of Russians while in prison. They offered him protection in exchange for favors once he was out. Ralph Wheeler had delivered on his promise, occasionally rerouting various shipments of goods on the rail line whenever the Russians asked. When they asked for a shipment of nuclear material from Radiology, Inc. to be rerouted, Ralph Wheeler knew he was in over his head. He contacted Homeland Security and told them everything in exchange for immunity. DHS agreed, and Gibson was put on point.

Murton was weighing his options. He could walk away right now and leave Gibson to clean up his own mess. But if everything he said was true, there was simply too much at stake. Plus, Gibson had compromised the governor by having him present when Decker was killed and disposed of. If Murton walked away, the governor might have some difficult questions to answer. "I'm telling you that it looks like my old man is a little more than a basic C.I. I'm also telling you it would have been nice to have a little warning he was going to be here the night we arrived. You're losing your edge, Paul."

"Look Murt, I had no idea he was going to be here. How could I? We're working with limited resources."

"And why is that?" Murton wanted to know. "You've got a group of people who are trying to put their hands on nuclear material to build a dirty bomb. You'd think we'd have a little more help. It looks to me like you're trying a little too hard to make a name for yourself within the agency. I know you like it fast and loose, but this is over the top."

"We've got all our bases covered and I have the full

support of the agency. We shut down assholes like this all the time."

"Then why are we here? Wait, don't bother answering. I already know why. I used to be a fed, remember? You get your hooks into someone and squeeze them for all they're worth."

"That's a little bit of a stretch, Murt. I wanted you on this operation for two reasons: Your knowledge of demolitions because they're going to need an explosives expert, and because your old man is the wild card. You know him better than anyone."

"I don't know him at all. I haven't seen him in nearly forty years."

"Still better than anyone we've got."

"That's horse shit, and you know it, Paul," Murton told him. "What's the real reason I'm being pulled through the mud on this one?"

Gibson let out a heavy sigh. It was time to come clean, and he knew Murton wouldn't like it. "I'm trying to protect your family, Murt."

Murton barked out a laugh. "My family? My mom died when I was a kid. You think my old man is family to me? I don't give two shits about him. He's been dead to me for decades. So you know what that means? It means I don't have any fam—"

Then, the change that occurred on Murton's face was one that defined the rage he'd kept hidden for so many years. The blood drained away from his face until his skin was colorless and his lips curled back, showing his teeth. If he'd have seen himself in a mirror that very moment, he would have thought he was looking at his father forty years ago. "You're talking about Jonesy and Small, aren't you?"

Gibson nodded. "They're in trouble, Murt, and they don't even know it."

CHAPTER THIRTY-FOUR

After Miles left with Dobson, Virgil thought about what his father had said to him…that Murton had made a statement of some sort the day Cora and Gibson showed up at the bar. He turned to Becky. "Will you do something for me?"

"I think you meant to say 'something else.'"

Virgil ignored her remark. "Would you pull up the tapes from a few weeks ago…the day Cora and Gibson were here?"

"Tapes? Sure. Let me dust off the VCR and get it set up."

"Becky, this is important."

"I know. I'm simply making a point. What was the date?"

Virgil didn't know off the top of his head. Becky rolled her eyes at him and pulled up the calendar on her phone. "Okay, I've got it. Let me go through the computer logs and pull the file. What are we looking for?"

"I'm not exactly sure. I'm hoping I'll know it when I see it." He walked to the door. "Shout at me when you've got it. I have to finish up with Agent Thorpe."

Thorpe, Ross, and Rosencrantz were seated at a table in the center of the bar area. Delroy was still sitting alone at the table near the kitchen entrance, the baseball bat propped up in the chair next to him.

Robert arrived to get the kitchen going, stuck his head through the door and said hello. Then, "What my bat doing out here, mon?"

Virgil handed the bat to Robert and told him he'd explain everything later.

Robert twirled the bat in his hand like a baton then looked at Delroy. "Yeah irie, mon?"

Delroy looked at Virgil, then at Robert. "Yeah, mon. Maybe touch and go there for a few minutes. No worries, though, right, Virgil?"

Virgil nodded, though he thought in one form or another, they'd not seen or heard the last from Agent Dobson. Delroy may have opened a door and let the wolf in. It'd be something they'd have to keep an eye on. But why worry someone whose innocence, decency, and goodwill toward others was their calling card? "It'll all work out, Delroy, I'm sure."

"Looks to me like it already has, mon."

I hope you're right, Virgil thought. He excused himself and joined Rosencrantz, Ross, and Thorpe. Virgil noticed that Thorpe's weapon was back in his possession. He pulled out a chair, looked at Thorpe and said, "I'd like to take you up on your offer. How about we start over?"

"Works for me," Thorpe said. He got right to it. "I've brought your men up to speed on the nuclear aspect of the situation. I think we need to put the rule book through the shredder on this one."

"Sounds like we're all on the same page then," Virgil said. "You indicated that Gibson's op had gone off the rails. I'd like to know more about that."

Thorpe chuffed. "Great choice of words. I've been coordinating with Gibson for months on this one. The difficulty we faced from the start was we simply didn't know who we were dealing with. The discovery of the bodies down in Jeffersonville changes all that. Now that we know who they are it's a snake hunt."

Virgil didn't want to hear about snakes, even metaphorical ones. "But you don't know where they are?"

Thorpe tipped his head, an admission of sorts. "Not exactly. After the riot at Sheridan—that was planned, by the way, even though it got a little out of hand—Gibson was supposed to report back with a location. We were going to put the whole thing under surveillance and take it from there. Wheeler was flown to Louisville and our agents on the plane confirmed that Gibson picked him up right on schedule. But where they went from there is anybody's guess."

Virgil shook his head. He was irritated with himself. He was certain that Gibson and Murton were at the address Murton had been watching for weeks. The problem was, he'd never told any of them—not even Becky—the actual location. Virgil saw the address exactly once when Murton showed him the picture of his father. But he was so focused on the photo, he paid no attention whatsoever to the address when it was right in front of him, on paper. If he had, they might have all the answers they needed to bring the entire operation down.

"How does the shipment get from Radiology to the train?" Ross wanted to know. "Is it trucked over or something?"

Thorpe shook his head. "There's a spur that runs right to their facility. The shipment is loaded directly on the train…sort of like a major lumber yard or an automotive manufacturer. More cost-efficient and more secure."

"Any stops along the way?" Virgil asked.

"Never. Not when there's nuclear material on board. This shipment goes straight to Purdue university."

"Well that doesn't make any sense," Rosencrantz said. "You're saying they have what? An engine and one train car that makes a run from Kentucky all the way up to West Lafayette?"

"No, no," Thorpe said. "It's a regular train. But for security purposes they simply schedule it so their first stop is at the university. It goes on from there up through Gary and into Chicago."

"I'll tell you what I'd like to do," Virgil said. "I'd like to put our SWAT team in place on that train before it ever gets to Radiology's pick up. Stick them in an empty boxcar or whatever and let them make the entire ride."

"You're talking about putting state agents outside their jurisdictional boundaries."

"You did say something about shredding the rule book on this one, didn't you?"

"Yeah," Thorpe admitted. "I guess I did. But what happens if something goes down right there at the loading point, in Kentucky?"

"What are the chances of that?" Virgil said. "They're right across the river. We'd only have to worry about it for ten minutes. Once they cross into Indiana, we're good." Then another thought occurred to him. "If you're on the train with SWAT, that makes it federal jurisdiction."

Thorpe smiled. "That's exactly what I was thinking. By the way, I understand you've got someone on the inside at Radiology?"

Virgil looked at Thorpe for a moment before he said anything. "How, exactly, do you know that?"

"Don't be so surprised, Detective. It's your federal tax dollars at work. Simply put, it's an HR function. Companies like Radiology who deal with nuclear material have to file a report of any new employees. Your man Lawless popped up the moment you put him inside."

Virgil was impressed. "Huh."

"Said never said anything to you about it?"

Virgil shook his head. "No, but I'm not surprised. He's got a trainload of nuclear material getting ready to roll out of there. I'd say the man's had other things on his mind over the last few days."

Virgil's statement turned out to be more accurate than he knew.

Becky walked up to the table and touched Virgil on the shoulder. "I've got that file you wanted to see ready to go."

"Thanks, Becks. I'll be right there."

Becky turned to go back upstairs but Virgil had a thought. "Hey Becky, can you get me a map of train routes from Louisville up through Indiana that run through West Lafayette?"

Becky walked back over to the table. "Let me see your phone."

Virgil handed her his phone. Her thumbs moved across the keypad in a blur and she handed the phone back. "Here you go. Anything else?"

Virgil looked at his phone. It showed all the train

routes for the state of Indiana. He tipped his head up at her. "How did you do that?"

"Google, sharp stuff. I'll be upstairs."

Virgil stared at the map for a few minutes. "What are you thinking, Boss?" Rosencrantz said.

"Give me a minute, will you? There's something I have to look at."

Virgil went upstairs and sat down in front of the computer. Becky brought the video up. She pressed a button on the keyboard and the video began to play. They both watched it all the way through.

"I don't get it," Becky said. "What are we looking for?"

"I'm not exactly sure. It was something Murt said." Virgil watched for a few seconds. "This is the wrong part of the video. I need to see it right from the moment Gibson and Cora got here."

"That's what we watched, Jonesy."

"No, no. Not from when they came up here. When they walked in downstairs. They weren't up here yet, but we were still talking. Roll it back. There's a point where Murt and I are both looking out the window."

Becky reversed the video until Virgil said, "Stop. Right there. Play it from there." Becky pressed the play button on the keyboard and they both watched the scene unfold.

They saw Murton walk over to the window and look out over the bar. Then they watched Virgil turn and look through the glass as well. Virgil heard himself say 'What the heck are they doing here?'

Then they both heard Murton say, 'It's all connected, brother.'

"That's it," Virgil said.

Becky didn't understand. "What?"

"What Murt said. 'It's all connected, brother.'"

Virgil…starting to put it together…

CHAPTER THIRTY-FIVE

VIRGIL WAS SO MAD AT HIMSELF HE WAS HAVING TROUBLE getting the words out. "We never got a hit on Ralph Wheeler."

"No, we didn't," Becky said.

"Except we've had the information all along, Becky. Little pieces here and there we simply didn't connect to each other."

"I guess I'm still not putting them together. What are you talking about?"

"What Murt said. 'It's all connected.' And what Gibson told us, about Murt's dad being a CI for DHS."

Becky looked away for a moment, her mind racing. She tugged at her lower lip, exposing her bottom row of teeth. "Tell me more of what you're thinking, because I'm not getting it."

"Ralph Wheeler did time at Sheridan. He had protection on the inside. But when he gets out he's suddenly off the grid."

"We already know that."

"You're right, we do. But Gibson put Murton inside the same facility with an alias."

"Yeah, he'd have to. If they used his real name, he'd pop up as a former federal agent, not to mention a current state cop."

Virgil nodded. "That's right. So, two sides of the same coin. Gibson said there were guards at Sheridan that'd take a payoff. But he also said they had their own people inside as well. Essentially two groups working against each other at the same time."

"You're losing me here, Jonesy."

"If Murt couldn't use his real name but still needed to be known as Ralph Wheeler's son, we shouldn't be looking for Ralph Wheeler."

Becky covered her mouth with her hands. "Oh my god," she said through her fingers. "We should be looking for someone named Weller."

"That's right. Remember at the meeting when Gibson asked me about Jonas?"

"I remember you knocked him on his butt."

"Yeah. At the time it went right past me, but I think he was telling me the same thing Murt was. That it's all connected. My knee-jerk response was he was threatening my family…my son. But the more I think about it, I'm starting to believe he said what he did because he wanted me thinking about *fathers and sons*." Then Virgil thought about what his father had told him and when he spoke again, it was more to himself than to Becky. "But why would he say they aim to take everything away from me?"

Becky didn't understand the last part of his statement. "What was that? Take everything away?"

Virgil waved it off. "I don't know. Maybe nothing. I'm working with limited information on that."

"From who?"

Virgil didn't answer. "Let's go talk to Thorpe."

HE WENT BACK TO THORPE. BECKY WAS RIGHT THERE with him. They'd had the entire month to figure it out and it had been staring them right in the face the entire time. When Virgil spoke, the frustration in his voice was evident. He looked at Thorpe. "You said you've been working this with Gibson for months?"

Virgil was standing over him and Thorpe had to crank his head sideways and up to answer. "That's right, why?"

"And how exactly did Ralph Wheeler make contact with Agent Gibson?"

"You've got it backward. I'm sorry, I thought you knew that. Ralph Wheeler didn't make contact with Gibson. Gibson made contact with Wheeler."

"That's not what he told us," Becky said.

Thorpe visibly swallowed. "I'm not sure why he'd do that."

"Is there any reason to believe that Agent Gibson is compromised?" Virgil asked Thorpe.

"None that I'm aware of."

"I'm not sure it matters," Virgil said. "Murton was trying to tell me something. Gibson was too. Murton's father…he's using the name Weller, right?"

Thorpe nodded. "Yes. Ron Weller. Why?"

Virgil looked at Becky. "Go run it. Murt's dad spent his entire life doing one thing. He worked for the railroad. I'll bet Ron Weller comes back as a railroad employee."

Becky ran back up the stairs.

Virgil pulled out his phone and made a call.

The phone was answered on the second ring. "I'm Cool," Cool said. "What's happening, Jones-man?"

Virgil didn't beat around the bush. "Where are you?"

"Sitting on my back patio, enjoying my day off."

"That's about to change. I need you standing by and ready to go."

"Where?"

"Hold on a second." He took the phone away from his ear and looked at the railroad map again for a few minutes.

Virgil brought the phone back up. "You still there, Cool?"

"Yeah, I'm here. Where are we going?"

"South. How many people can you fit in that chopper?"

With Cool set to go, Virgil was getting ready to make another call…this one to Sandy to tell her what was happening and that it would most likely be late by the time he got home that evening. He never got the chance. Becky came back downstairs.

"You're right, Jonesy. Ralph Wheeler, aka Ron Weller, works as a maintenance supervisor for the Jeffersonville rail yard. It took about thirty seconds to get the hit." Then her phone buzzed at her and she said, "Huh."

"What?" Virgil asked.

"Not sure yet. Give me a minute." She turned and ran back up the stairs.

Virgil turned back to the table. "Okay, here's how this is going to go." He started to lay out his idea and how they would position themselves at the Jeffersonville train yard when Becky came out of the upstairs office and yelled from the top of the steps. "Jonesy. I need you guys up here. We've got a problem."

Ralph Wheeler's job at the yard was almost finished. He'd put in for the time off over a month ago, but it was only for appearances. He didn't want to be on the schedule when the shipment rolled through. With a little luck, he wouldn't even see Reif or the rest of his crew ever again. Those boys were in for a little surprise, they simply didn't know it. He checked the routing schedule and saw that the next train through was the one out of Louisville. He took a section of the main track off-line, sent the notice to central dispatch, then left the yard.

He got in his car and headed toward Louisville. He had a busy day ahead. He spent the time thinking of the final question Reif had asked him. It wasn't the question itself, but what it represented: The downside, Reif had called it. Ralph Wheeler knew what the downside was and the bottom line was this: He didn't care.

Ralph Wheeler blamed his entire adult life situation on exactly four people: Two of them were his long-dead wife who didn't know how to keep her mouth shut, and that asshole former sheriff, Mason Jones. He'd finally gotten his wife to shut the hell up, but her death—in Ralph's mind anyway—had been an accident. Yes, yes, he'd smacked her around a little. How else were you supposed to keep a bitch in line? Was it his fault she didn't know how to take a fall? Hardly.

Then when Mason Jones showed up and took his boy away and ran him out of town, it changed everything. He could have molded Murton into a real man. Someone like himself. Someone who knew how to kick ass and take names, not kiss ass with a pair of knee pads always at the ready.

He thought back to the night Murton had tried to take a hammer to him. No one messed with Ralph Wheeler and walked away. No one. He had two in the box and by his score, there were only two more to go.

His idiot son, Murton, and Virgil Jones.

THE THOUGHT OF IT, WHAT HE WAS DOING DIDN'T SCARE him. The truth of it was, it was supposed to have been done for him. Lipkins was supposed to take care of everything, but he'd screwed that up so bad you'd need a spreadsheet to keep track of his mistakes. And now the people who'd protected him in the joint expected him to come through…to finish the job that started months ago. They offered him everything he needed: A job at the rail yard, help from Reif and his crew, a backwater fed who thought he had the governor under his thumb, a payout he could retire to the islands with, and best of all, a chance to get even with his past.

There was, Ralph thought, a certain symmetry to it all…yet another Jones had taken another man's son away, like it was open season on young boys with a sad story. So. It was time to cut the cord. The Russians had made that much clear. They didn't care how he did it, but they wanted that land opened up for fracking. And given Ralph

Wheeler's history, all the way back to that night his nut job wife told him that some perv had tried to smoke his kid's bone, he finally knew his path was clear, his choices practically preordained.

Virgil spun around and said, "What?"

Becky gave him a look, one he could read all the way across the bar. Virgil and the other men went upstairs. Once they were in the office, Becky puffed out her cheeks and said, "I took a little initiative and sent a piece of computer code to Lawless."

"Code for what?" Virgil asked.

"Code that would give him access to Radiology's mainframe. Everything he's been looking at is tied directly to shipping. But he wasn't getting anything because his access was restricted. I thought maybe if we had a little room to maneuver we might be able to dig around and figure out who altered their records and why."

Virgil made a twirling motion with his hand.

"Please don't do that," Becky said. "Anyway, we don't know why, but we now know who altered the records."

"Who?"

"It was Said."

Virgil couldn't quite believe it. "Said? Why would he do that? It's his company."

"I already told you I don't know. But I've got full

access to their system." She pointed to her computer. "There are clearly two sets of records."

"Where's Lawless?"

"Still at Radiology."

"Better pull him out, Boss," Rosencrantz said.

Virgil was nodding. "I know." He looked at Becky. "Get him on the phone, right now."

"There might be more information to be gained," Becky said.

"As a member of the MCU, he's a sworn officer, Becks. But as a crime scene technician he's in over his head. And Said knows who he is. If he finds out that we know who altered the records, Lawless could be in real trouble. He's not armed."

"Becky's face went pale. "Jeez, I never thought of that." She reached for the phone and punched in Lawless's number.

CHAPTER THIRTY-SIX

After Sandy had Wyatt fed, she bathed him and got him dressed, then put him down for his nap. She made sure the baby monitor was on, then closed the door to his room and went into the kitchen for a snack. The breastfeeding zapped her…left her feeling depleted. She rooted around in the fridge for a few minutes, but didn't find anything that appealed to her.

What did appeal to her, she thought, was motherhood. It suited her. She'd decided that the first moment she woke in the hospital four months ago and saw her beautiful baby boy. Then she thought, no, that wasn't quite right. It was decided the moment Jonas had entered their lives. Wyatt had simply solidified the feeling.

When she looked out the kitchen window, she saw Jonas and Huma down by the pond. Huma was sitting in one of the chairs and Jonas stood between her and Mason's cross. He kept turning back and forth between her and the monument, moving his arms in an exaggerated manner. Though Sandy couldn't hear what he was saying, she had a good idea what was being said. He was in all likelihood telling her yet again of the night he got to say goodbye to his parents, Ed and Pam Donatti. When he knelt by the cross then slowly raised his arms and mimed a big circular motion, she was sure of it.

She was about to go out and join them for a few minutes when she remembered she was supposed to sign a fax and get it back to the Co-op. She went into the office, picked up the papers and looked them over. She read the cover letter and in doing so discovered much of what Cal Lipkins had told Virgil earlier. There was, it seemed, a stack of papers that needed her signature, and by the tone of the cover letter, sooner rather than later. She signed where indicated and then fed the paper back into the machine and sent it on its way.

Then another thought, one she'd been unwilling to address with anyone, much less herself. Had she been focusing too much of her attention on Wyatt and not enough on Jonas? Huma was doing a fine job, no one could deny that. But a new baby is a new baby, and the older child sometimes got inadvertently set aside, something the What To Expect bible had warned them about. Had she been doing that? What's more, had she been letting Huma be a mother by proxy? She thought it over for a few minutes and decided not, but then she also thought there was nothing wrong with getting ahead of the curve. She made sure the fax had gone through, then grabbed her car keys and walked down to the pond.

Huma could take care of Wyatt for the day. She and Jonas would go get a bite to eat then take a drive down to Shelby County and kill two birds with one stone. She could sign the forms Lipkins needed and Jonas would get a first-hand look at his inheritance. Maybe get a ride on a tractor or something.

Lawless used the code Becky sent him. In truth, he thought maybe the whole thing had a whiff of bullshit to it. A little busy work to make him feel like he'd accomplished something when clearly he hadn't.

He knew computers as well as the next guy, but he wasn't a programmer or coder or whatever they were called. So he wasn't sure it'd work, or if it was even real. What he was sure of was this: He was the new guy with the MCU and he wanted to make an impression. When they asked him if he'd be willing to take an undercover position, he jumped at the chance. Besides, it really wasn't that big of a deal. He was acting as a shipping clerk. It really wasn't even undercover work. Sure, he'd had to tell a few polite little fibs to some of the other people in the shipping department, but the owner of the company knew who he was, so there was a bit of a yawn factor to the whole thing. It wasn't like he was a DEA agent infiltrating a drug cartel. A shipping clerk? It was almost embarrassing.

The instructions Becky sent him were as basic as they could be. Step one, click the attachment she'd inserted into the email. Step two, none. The program would do the rest. He'd done that first thing in the morning and so far nothing had happened. He wondered if the program was functioning properly. He was about to take his lunch break when he saw three security men enter the shipping area. They climbed the steps up to the shipping manager's office and entered without knocking.

The manager's office was a glass box that overlooked the entire shipping and receiving floor. The whole area was about the size of a football field. If the manager's office was in the end zone, that put Lawless about twenty-yards away, right in the red zone, near the twenty-yard line.

Lawless might not have been a cop, but he wasn't an idiot. The sight of the security guards had him on edge. He stood from his desk, stretched, and rolled his head, never taking his eyes off the guards. They were roaming around the manager's office, animated in their gestures, looking over their shoulders at the area below. Then the manager stood from his desk, walked to the window and pointed directly at Lawless. The look on his face was clear. The three security guards ran through the door and started down the steps, their eyes glued to their target.

Lawless started to run for the exit. If he could make it to the door before they got to the bottom of the steps, he had a shot. He had a twenty-yard head start, with eighty-yards to go. He felt his phone buzzing in his pocket.

CHAPTER THIRTY-SEVEN

He's not answering," Becky said. The fear on her face was real. Had she inadvertently put Lawless in some kind of danger?

"Becky, get me the phone number of the fire department closest to Radiology. I can't use nine-one-one. C'mon, quickly now."

Virgil spun around and looked at Thorpe. "Give me your phone."

Thorpe was going to ask why, but when he looked into Virgil's eyes he reconsidered and handed the phone to him.

Becky had the number twenty seconds later and Virgil punched it in. When the call was answered, Virgil put some urgency in his voice. "This is Agent Thorpe with the Department of Homeland Security. I'm undercover near Radiology, Inc.'s manufacturing facility. There's smoke pouring out of that building. You better get everything you've got headed that way. Everybody in town knows what they make out there. You guys are about to have a hell of a mess on your hands. You might have to evacuate the entire city."

There was a slight pause, then the man on the other end of the phone said, "We know. The alarm already came through. I sent everyone out. They should be rolling up any second now. I'm the station chief. I'm heading out there myself. Why didn't you call nine-one-one? What'd you say your name was again?"

He hung up and tossed the phone back to Thorpe. Atta boy, kid, Virgil thought.

Lawless turned around and saw that the men were gaining on him. Not only did he have to make it to the door, he also had to get to his car. At the rate they were closing, he wouldn't even make it out of the building. Then he noticed the fire alarm box along the wall, right next to the door. He put his head down and gave it everything he had. When he reached the door he yanked the handle on the fire alarm and burst outside.

"What's happening," Becky asked.

"Either I'm psychic or Lawless is one step ahead of

us. I think he's been made though. He's probably on the run. Keep trying his phone."

Becky dialed again and got the same result as before. Four rings then voice mail. She shook her head at Virgil.

"Okay, leave it alone for a few minutes. I think he's busy."

Becky was almost panicking. "We can't just sit here, Jonesy. We've got to do something."

"He's over a hundred miles away, Becks," Rosencrantz said. "I think we're going to have to wait this one out. We've done all we can do."

Thorpe was dialing his phone. "This is one of those rare occasions when the statement 'I'm from the government and I'm here to help' is actually true." Then, into his phone, "Yeah, Bob Thorpe here. Who do we have in Louisville? Good. Where are they? Are you shitting me? No, no, it's perfect. Okay, I'm going to send you a picture. He's running out of an undercover op that went bad over there. He's at imminent risk. Let's get him picked up. And remember, he's one of us. Okay, let me know."

Becky had been listening and sent a photo of Lawless to Thorpe's phone. Thorpe sent it to his people and looked around the room. "What? This is what we do." Then to Becky: "Would you mind explaining how you have my phone number, young lady?"

Becky opened her mouth to answer, then decided not to. Thorpe, who was generally a good guy, let it go.

When Lawless pulled the alarm three things happened almost at once. An alarm started to sound—a loud *claack-claack-claack*—the sprinkler system kicked in, and people began pouring out of the building from every available exit. The sprinkler system and the mass of people exiting the building slowed the security guards, but they refused to give up. By the time they made it outside, Lawless had increased his lead to more than fifty yards.

But he wasn't out of the woods yet and he knew it. His car was at the far end of the lot, on the other side of the building. Since he'd exited at the end—the facility was essentially one big rectangle—it was a shorter run to the other side but still a long way to go to his car. When he turned the corner he saw people coming out of a side door right in front of him. Since he knew he wouldn't make it to his car, he did the only thing he could think of to lose the guards.

He ducked back inside. Off in the distance he heard the sirens from the fire trucks.

He stayed close to the open door and watched as the security men raced by. Once he saw them go past, he stuck his head out to make sure they weren't going to double back. They raced to the other end of the building and turned the corner. When they did, Lawless exited the building and turned to run back the other way.

And when he did, he ran right into Rick Said. "I've been looking for you," Said said. He grabbed him by the arm. Lawless tried to pull free, but Said twisted his arm behind his back and pushed him flush against the side of the building. "My tech people said you've been operating outside your area. You've got no idea what's at stake here, what you may have just done."

Said felt the barrel of a gun at the back of his head. "I don't care what you think is at stake here, mister. But I know this: That young man you're holding is with us. Let him go."

Said released Lawless and turned around. When he did he found himself face to face with two armed men, their weapons pointed straight at him. "Who the hell are you?"

"We're agents with the department of homeland security. And you're under arrest."

The other agent looked at Lawless. "You're Lawless, I hope."

"I am. Boy am I glad to see you guys."

"You did good, kid. Come on, let's beat feet before those security guys show up. If I have to shoot someone there's about three days worth of genuine Grade-A United States federal government paperwork that needs to be filled out. It's a drag."

Ten minutes later they had him on speakerphone. "Are you all right?" Becky asked. She stepped right in front of Virgil, the first to say anything. It'd been her idea and she'd almost gotten him hurt…or worse.

Lawless seemed fine, his voice calm, his speech steady. "Yeah, I'm good. It was a little iffy there for a second. I had to make a run for it. To tell you the truth, I sort of thought that email you sent me wasn't doing what it was supposed to do. I mean, nothing had happened all morning, then suddenly there were, like, three security guys in the shipping manager's office. They zeroed in on me like I was a bank robber or something. The fire alarm slowed them down, but if those homeland guys hadn't shown up…"

Virgil leaned over Becky's shoulder and said, "Listen, kid, you did good. Where are you now, right this second?"

"Standing in the employee parking lot. The homeland guys are still here. They've got Mr. Said in handcuffs in the back of their car. He's not too happy, I can tell you that."

"Okay, listen, your part of this is over. Have them escort you past the security gate then drive back up here."

"What about Said?"

"Leave that to us," Thorpe said.

"He's right," Virgil said. "We'll take it from here. Come on home."

"Well...okay, I guess."

Virgil could hear the disappointment in his voice. He understood, mostly because he'd experienced it himself on other cases. A rush of adrenaline, then nothing. It was the police procedural version of thank you very much, goodbye. "You're working out of state, Chip. We'd like to get you across the river as soon as possible. Get back, take the rest of the day and get with Mimi tomorrow. She'll have your next assignment."

They ended the call and Virgil looked at Thorpe. "Sounds like you've got more assets in place than we were aware of."

Thorpe let the corners of his mouth turn down. "It's the federal government. We're everywhere these days." Then, to drive home his point. "Good thing too, huh?" His phone rang before Virgil could respond. He held up a finger and picked up the phone. "Thorpe." Then, "Hey Franklin. How's Kentucky?" He verbally emphasized each syllable of the state's name, the implication clear. "Good question. Hold on a second." He put the phone to his chest, looked at Virgil, and said, "Franklin wants to know what to do with Said. The only reason they have him detained right now is because he had your man up against the wall."

Virgil thought about it for a moment. They'd thought all along that someone had been messing with the shipping records at Radiology...except they never imagined it would be the CEO. But that created a problem in itself. If

Virgil had DHS detain Said, then there was a good possibility that the shipment wouldn't go out as planned. Would Murton be compromised if that happened? He didn't know. On the other hand, Said was clearly involved in a crime, one which could ultimately result in the detonation of an explosive device laced with radioactive material. He didn't like it, but the choice was clear. He looked at Thorpe. "Have your men get him to the airport. We'll be there inside of two hours."

Becky stepped between Thorpe and Virgil. She turned to Thorpe, put a finger in his face and said, "Wait." There was no mistaking her tone. She spun and looked at Virgil. "You'll be hanging Murton out to dry. He's hooked into these terrorists or whatever they are, and if they don't get their hands on that shipment, they're going to wonder what went wrong. How do you think that's going to play out for him…the guy brought in at the last second to build the bomb? Do you think these are the type of people who are going to walk away and leave Murton, not to mention Gibson hanging around?"

"Becks…"

Thorpe had the phone back up to his ear, nodding as he listened.

"Don't, Jonesy. Don't you dare leave him out there to fend for himself. When was the last time he did that to you?"

"Never."

Thorpe leaned sideways and got Virgil's attention. "My guys say Said wants to speak with you."

Becky was visibly shaking with fear. When she spoke again her voice was full of dread. "Murton Wheeler is your brother."

"I know that." He snapped it at her. He closed his eyes for a brief moment before he looked at Thorpe. "Put him on speaker."

Thorpe pressed a button on his phone then told Franklin to put Said on.

Said's voice was frenetic, his words coming fast, full of anxiety. "I didn't have a choice."

"A choice about what?" Virgil said.

"Everything. All of it. They made me do it."

"Who?"

"I don't know who they are."

"Mr. Said, maybe if you start at the beginning…"

Said was choking back tears. They could all hear it over the phone. "It's too late, it's too late. I should have said something earlier."

"I don't understand, Mr. Said. Too late for wha—"

"Patty Doyle is my niece. She's my niece and they've got her." He screamed at them over and over until the phone was taken from him.

"Get him to the airport," Virgil said. He was speaking to Thorpe, but he was looking at Becky when he said it.

Becky sat down at her desk and stared at her lap.

CHAPTER THIRTY-EIGHT

Virgil hated to do it, but Ross and Rosencrantz had to stay behind. When he told them, Rosencrantz nodded like it was nothing. Ross wasn't pleased.

"Look Jonesy, no disrespect. I know I'm the new guy here and all that, but I'm also former SWAT. I could be a big help on this."

Virgil shook his head. "I want you guys here, with Becky. We don't have all the facts yet. Everything is a little too fluid. And the hard reality of the situation is this: There's simply not enough room for everyone on the chopper with Mok and his crew. It'll be a tight fit as it is."

Ross didn't like it, but what was he going to do? Make a stink about it? He'd been chewed out by Virgil before and didn't want that to happen again, and he was already on thin ice with his real boss, Ron Miles. "Okay, okay."

Virgil looked at Becky. "Get everything you can on

Said. Start with the records from Radiology and take it from there. And I need to know what's on that thumb drive."

Becky didn't answer him. She simply brought up the proper programs on her computer and got to work.

Virgil and Thorpe left and headed for the airport. When Virgil tried to reach Sandy she didn't answer. He left her a brief message saying it might be a late night.

ON THE WAY TO THE AIRPORT, THORPE GOT FRANKLIN ON the phone again. Said had calmed down, mostly, and was able to tell them his story…the meat of it anyway.

"I don't know who he was. I only saw him twice. An older guy. Mean. He showed up one day at my home and handed me an envelope. This was about a week after Patty went missing." He had to pause for a moment to collect himself. "It was a photo of Patty. She was lying at the bottom of a stairwell. Her arms and legs were bound with tape and she had a gag tied around her mouth. I don't even know if she was alive."

"Would you recognize this man if you saw him again?"

"Yes, there's no doubt. I'll never forget him."

"He wasn't disguised in any way? No mask or anything like that?"

There was a pause before Said answered. "You're

saying she's already dead, aren't you? He wouldn't let me see his face if they were going to give her back, would they?"

That's exactly what I'm saying, Virgil thought. "It's not helpful to speculate on those types of things until we have all the facts, Mr. Said. Now please, tell me exactly what they wanted you to do. Mr. Said?"

"They wanted me to swap the loads."

Virgil didn't understand. "What do you mean, swap the loads?"

"I'm not the bad guy here."

"Get to it, Said."

"We manufacture exactly two things. The main one is our radioactive dye for medical procedures and research functions. The other is a non-radioactive dye that contains harmless biological nano tracers. It's a new technology. It hasn't caught on yet, but it's getting some traction. When it does, the radioactive dye will be obsolete."

"Yes, yes," Virgil said. "I don't need a summary of the company brochure. Answer the question. What's this about swapping the loads?"

He heard Said sigh into the phone. "I'm simply trying to give you some perspective. The logs were altered. I did that. I admit it and I'll take full responsibility for it. But the bottom line is this: I tried to play both sides against the middle. I'm sorry. I was only trying to get my niece back. She's like a daughter to me."

"Here's what I need to know, and I need to know it right now, Said. Where is the nuclear material?"

Said waited a long time before he answered.

Reif, Chase, and Stone were almost finished with their meal when Reif's phone buzzed at him. He looked at the screen. It was Gus. "Yes, sir?"

Chase and Stone stopped eating to listen. There was only one person on the planet Reif addressed as sir. There was a long pause, then Reif said, "I understand, sir. The fact is they were both in a position to compromise us. I felt there was no other choice. Yes, sir, I'm glad you understand."

Then Chase and Stone watched as an odd expression passed over Reif's face and he was quiet for a long time. "You're sure? That seems rather…extreme. No, of course, it's your call. I'll take care of it right away. Yes sir."

Chase and Stone looked at Reif, their expressions blank, their eyes unblinking. Reif threw a wad of bills on the table and stood. "Not in here," he said. "We've got some things to talk about."

They went out to the SUV, Chase at the wheel, Stone in the passenger seat. Reif climbed into the back.

Chase looked at Reif in the rearview mirror. "That was Gus, right? What'd he say?"

Reif looked out the front window of the SUV. "Take a right up here, through the alley. We need to get out of sight for a minute."

Stone kept his eyes straight ahead, but he let his right arm drift down along his thigh. He began to pull his right leg back toward the seat.

Chase made the turn. A picket fence ran along one side of the alley, a row of brick buildings without windows on the other. They were isolated and alone, the alley deserted.

"Okay. Stop here," Reif said. "We've got to talk."

Chase put the truck in park and left the engine running.

"That was Gus. He's not too happy with us, me in particular. A couple of kids were out at that quarry and found Fischer and Reed. They got hits on the DNA and they've traced everything all the way up the chain. We won't be seeing the northwest anytime soon, if ever."

"Are the feds in on it?" Stone asked.

"Gus says yes. ATF and ICE."

"ICE?" Chase said. "What are they doing on this?"

"That's on me," Reif said. "Those boys did their homework. They know I've got dual citizenship. They've turned the whole thing over to DHS. Gus says they've got someone at ICE who might be able to help, but I'd rather we handled things ourselves."

"What about the job?" Stone asked.

"It's still on. But there have been a few changes. We also now know where we're taking the load."

"Where?" Stone asked.

"To the Shelby County farmer's Co-op. We've got a little cleanup that needs to be addressed first. Let's get back to the house."

Chase put the SUV in gear and drove out of the alley. Stone slipped the gun back in his ankle holster.

Murton got right in Gibson's face. "What kind of trouble, Paul?"

Gibson held his hands up, his palms out. "Listen, sit down and we'll talk about it." Murton gave him a hard stare then sat back down at the table.

"We think your old man is playing us. In fact, we're sure of it. You know how many times a bad actor working with the feds has some sort of agenda of their own?"

"Yeah, I do," Murton said. "This isn't new information to me, Paul, for two reasons: One, I used to be a fed, and two, I know what that man is capable of. I barely survived it. So how about you get to the point?"

"The point is this: The people who set up the fracking deal in Shelby County are out for one thing and one thing only. They want the gas under the ground and they don't care what it takes to get it. Remember when I said we had people on the inside at Sheridan? It wasn't only for your protection. It's a big part of how we get our intel. Your old man's been running his little side operation ever since he got out of the joint, all backed by the people who helped protect him on the inside. He needs to get out from under their thumb. Working for us was a good move on his part. We've agreed not to pursue charges against him for crimes committed since he's been out in exchange for his assistance. The problem is your old man has the impression that being a C.I. for DHS means it's open season to operate outside the lines."

"What does any of that have to do with Jonesy and Small?"

Gibson rubbed his temples. "Think it through, Murt. When you and Jonesy worked the Shelby County case, everyone thought the fracking deal was on the up and up, like it was Exxon Mobile or any other Fortune Five Hundred company backing the play down there, but it wasn't. It was a Russian company. Westlake failed to get everyone on board and they got rid of him like he was yesterday's toilet paper. Gordon too. And you took care of Decker for them."

"I took care of Decker for other reasons, and you know it."

"Fair enough. But none of that changes anything, Murt. There's money under that land…billions of dollars worth. People will go to extraordinary measures to take it out of the ground once they know it's there. This bomb you're putting together? It's not meant to destroy a city. It's meant to destroy the land, specifically the land that Virgil and Sandy own. Once a radioactive bomb goes off the land will be worthless, unless of course, you make a deal with a group of big oil executives who know how to get the gas out."

Murton laughed at him. "And you think my old man set up a deal like that all by himself? No way."

Gibson was shaking his head. "No, we don't. He's had help the entire time."

"Help? From who?"

Reif, Chase, and Stone came around the corner. Reif had his gun pointed straight at the back of Gibson's head. "I can answer that for you."

Gibson and Murton both froze. "Hands on the backs of your heads, boys. C'mon, don't make me repeat myself here."

Gibson and Murton brought their hands up and locked their fingers behind their heads.

"Chase, get their weapons. Stone, get the Flex-cuffs."

"What's going on here?" Gibson said, his voice calm.

"This, asshole," Reif said. He swung the butt of his gun against the side of Gibson's head, knocking him to the floor. The blow left him dazed and bleeding from a gash above his ear. Murton dropped his hands and moved to stand, but Reif was right there, his gun now pressed against the back of Murton's head.

"Try it," Reif said. Murton knew his options were limited. He put his hands back. Stone came back with two sets of cuffs and restrained both men with their hands behind their backs.

"Time for a little truth-telling, boys," Reif said. "I had something of an unpleasant conversation with my boss. Want to guess what he told me? No? Okay, I'll fill you in anyway." He looked at Murton. "It seems your old man might be a little smarter than he likes to let on."

Murton laughed without humor. "My old man couldn't find his ass if someone handed it to him. If you think you're being played by him you might want to check your sources."

"My source is good. That's the one thing I'm sure of in all of this."

Just keep them talking, Murton thought. He'd been in worse situations than this before. Get their thinking twisted up. Turn it back around on them. It was undercover-101. "So where's all this help coming from? I'd like to know myself. We're all on the same side here."

Reif ignored him and waved his hand in the general direction of Gibson, who was still on the floor. "Chase, Stone, get him in the chair and hold him there."

Chase and Stone grabbed Gibson and set him in the chair, their hands on his shoulders. They looked at their boss.

"Want to know where the help is coming from? I'll show you." He stepped clear of Murton, swung his gun over and pointed it at Gibson. Then before Murton could do anything, Reif fired two quick shots in a row.

The first shot killed Chase. The second killed Stone.

Murton tried to remain calm. Why had Reif killed his own men? They weren't working against him. He'd have known about it if they were. Gibson was still only half-conscious from the blow he'd taken to the side of his head. When he tried to look up he could only hold Murton's gaze for a few seconds before his chin dipped back down against his chest.

"You're wondering why I killed my own men, aren't you?" Reif said to Murton. "We've all been compromised. It was Fischer's fault really. But the people I work for don't like to leave loose ends. They also don't like undercover feds sticking their noses into their business. It's getting harder and harder to trust anyone these days." He brought the gun back up and pointed it a Gibson. Murton closed his eyes.

The gun went off again and Murton opened his eyes. When he saw Gibson's dead body, he knew he was at his own end. Reif was looking right at him. "Why so glum? Things just got a whole lot easier. C'mon tough guy." He grabbed Murton's arm and hoisted him out of the chair. "Time for a family reunion. Your old man seems to be running the show. For now, anyway."

"Where are we going?"

"All the way to hell, I'm sure. Gotta make a little run north first."

Murton's wheels were spinning. North? Then Reif clubbed him hard on the back of his head and Murton was out.

Reif bound his ankles, knees, and thighs and placed a hood over his head. Then he loaded him into the back of the SUV and hit the road. He had the detonator and bomb Murton had built.

The old man had the nuclear material. Time for a little trade.

Some kind of jacked-up family, Reif thought.

CHAPTER THIRTY-NINE

FOUR HOURS AGO

CAL LIPKINS WAS ALONE AT THE CO-OP, GOING OVER THE paper. The Co-op property was quiet this time of year. Not much going on except the delivery of fuel, seed, fertilizer, and other basic necessities to get the crops in the ground, and all of that had already happened. The activity picked up around harvest time of course, but that was months away, and if things went according to plan, there wouldn't be a harvest this year. There wouldn't, in fact, be any harvests ever again. Not for the Co-op, anyway.

When Lipkins looked out the window he saw the truck coming down the road. He went through the back of the building where the maintenance shop was located and opened the overhead door. Wheeler turned into the lot and drove the truck into the shop. Lipkins hit the button and the door began to lower.

Both men walked to the back of the truck and opened the rear doors. They stood and stared at the contents for a moment. Two large shipping crates sat on pallets at the very back of the truck. Both containers were covered with placards and warnings, the contents obvious even if you didn't know how to read.

"The other truck ready?" Wheeler asked.

Lipkins pointed at another box truck, almost identical to the one with the nuclear material. "Yep. Fertilizer and fuel are already packed inside. You know the best part?"

"What's that?"

Every drop of fuel and every ounce of fertilizer was ordered with Virgil Jones's name on it. When the feds come knocking, they'll be pulling him out of his office in handcuffs. C'mon, get that door opened and I'll move the load over."

"Be careful with that lift," Wheeler said. "That's one load you don't want to topple on you."

Ten minutes later with the nuclear material locked up in the truck with the fertilizer and fuel, Wheeler got back in the Radiology truck and pulled out of the shop. He was almost to the end of the Co-op's drive when he saw a car turn in, coming right at him. When he saw who was driving he knew he'd have to improvise…revise his plan a little.

Fact was, his job just got a little more interesting.

Sandy let the GPS on her phone guide her to their destination. Jonas was strapped in the back in his car seat. When she pulled in at the Co-op, she had to make a tight turn and stay close to the shoulder of the drive, as a large box truck approached from the opposite direction. When the truck passed she glanced at it in the rear-view and saw its brake lights flare as it pulled to a stop at the intersection.

"That's a big truck," Jonas said.

"Sure is, big guy."

Jonas laughed. "I'm big guy and Wyatt's little guy."

Sandy smiled at him. "You'll both be big guys someday."

"Then what will you call us?"

She reached behind the seat and found his leg. "Probably call you both trouble. What do you think of that?" She tickled him and Jonas laughed.

Then he pointed out the window. "That building looks funny."

"It's called a Quonset hut."

He pointed out the side window and Sandy caught it in the rear-view mirror. "What are those big things?"

"Those are silos. That's where they keep all the crops after the harvest."

"Then what happens?"

Good question. "I'm not sure. But I'll bet we can find

out." She parked the car away from the Co-op's main building. She wasn't sure how things worked around here, and she didn't want to be in the way. Besides, there was only one other vehicle in the lot—a pickup truck—and it was parked some distance from the building as well. She picked up her phone and noticed the battery indicator was in the red. The phone was about to die. The GPS had drained it. She plugged it into the charger and left it on the passenger seat.

"Come on. Mommy's got some paperwork to sign. Let's see if we can find somebody named Mr. Lipkins. He's supposed to help us."

SANDY AND JONAS WALKED INTO THE CO-OP AND FOUND Cal Lipkins sitting at a desk that fronted a window at the side of the building. He looked up from the paperwork, a mask of irritation on his face. "Hep ya?" He practically spat the words at them.

Sandy caught the irritation but tried a friendly grin anyway. "Are you Cal Lipkins? I'm Sandy Jones, Virgil's wife. This is my son, Jonas. I guess there's some forms or something I need to sign?"

Lipkins glanced out the window and saw Wheeler's truck coming back up the drive. What the hell was he doing? This wasn't part of their plan.

"Are you Mr. Lipkins?"

Lipkins turned away from the window and gave Sandy an awkward smile, his irritation replaced with something he couldn't quite get straight in his own mind. "I'm sorry. Yes." He walked from behind the desk and greeted her with a gentle handshake. Then he squatted down and offered his hand to Jonas. "How are you doing, little guy?"

Jonas stuck his entire arm straight out, the way young boys do when they shake an adult's hand. "I'm big guy. Wyatt is little guy. He's at home because he's still a baby. Wyatt's my little brother. That's how come I'm big guy because he's little and I'm bigger. So I'm big guy."

Lipkins laughed and rubbed the top of his head. "Wow, that's a mouthful. Big guy it is then." He stood up and glanced out the window and watched the other truck as it drove past, around toward the back of the building.

"Is this a bad time?" Sandy asked.

Depends on your perspective, I guess, Lipkins thought.

"I'm sorry?"

"I said, no, it's fine. I wasn't expecting you quite so soon, is all. I may have overstated the urgency about the forms and such to Virgil when I spoke with him last. Here, have a seat at the table and I'll get the paperwork. There's quite a bit of it, but it should go pretty quick unless you want me to go through it all like I did with your husband."

"I don't think that will be necessary," Sandy said.

"Fine, fine," Lipkins said. He sounded relieved.

"You'll need to sign next to your husband's signature on each page. We'll have you out of here in no time."

"That's no problem," Sandy said. "We've got plenty of time." She sat down. Jonas ran over to the window to look outside.

"I'll be right back," Lipkins said. "Let me have a word with that truck driver, then I'll get you the paperwork. That be all right?"

"Sure."

"Okay, don't leave."

Sandy said they wouldn't. Then she thought, that was sort of an odd thing to say. Why would they leave for Pete's sake? They'd just arrived.

Lipkins hustled out the back and caught Wheeler climbing from the cab of the truck. "What are you doing? Do you know who that is in there?"

"Damned right I do," Wheeler said.

"Then turn that truck around and get out of here. Let's stick to the plan."

"The plan has changed. Those two are mine."

"Yours? What the hell are you talking about?"

Wheeler got right up against him and when he did, Cal Lipkins felt something he'd not felt in a long time from another man. Fear.

"That cocksucker Jones and his family ruined my life

a long time ago. Ruined yours too. Isn't that what you told me? Time for a little payback."

"I ain't hurtin' some little kid," Lipkins said.

"Didn't seem to bother you when we took the girl."

"She was practically grown. Besides, we didn't kill her. We left her with supplies and everything."

"And you think she's still alive after all this time?" Wheeler laughed at him, a cruel, contemptuous bark. "Time to get your big-boy britches on, Cal. That girl is dead. If she ain't, you better go back and finish the job. If you don't, I will. Same goes for those two out there. When that bomb goes off and the land gets contaminated, I'll be gone and you'll get that drilling deal you've wanted for so long now. So what's it gonna be?"

Cal tried to hold Wheeler's gaze but felt his eyes slip away.

"That's what I thought. Now get back in there and find a way to separate them. Send the kid outside or something. I'll take it from there. It'll be like you had nothing to do with it. You can convince yourself of that, can't you?"

Lipkins turned and walked away. It felt like the whole thing was suddenly coming undone. But it wasn't sudden, was it? How had he let himself get to this point? The land was his. So was the gas under it. All he wanted to do was find a way to get it out. But he'd let it turn him into something he wasn't. He'd let his single-minded objectiveness get the better of him. It was like he had gas on the brain or something. He hadn't seen things clearly. He'd taken part in a kidnapping? What was he thinking? He wasn't a monster. He was a farmer.

That's what he kept telling himself. *I'm just a farmer. I'm just a farmer.*

When he returned to the office, Cal Lipkins held a stack of papers in his arms.

When Sandy saw the size of the stack her eyes widened. "Boy, Virgil wasn't kidding. That's a lot of paper."

Lipkins set the stack down on top of the table. "Yeah, there's a mess of it alright." He glanced at Jonas who was sitting in a chair at the end of the table, his little legs swinging back and forth. Somewhere in the back of his mind he realized that he'd deluded himself into thinking the college girl would be okay. Or had he? They hadn't bothered to hide their identities. If she lived, she'd be able to pick him out of a line-up with little difficulty. Whether he wanted to admit it or not he'd known all along that she was going to die one way or another. He hadn't cared at the time. Why should he care now? What was wrong with him? Why did he suddenly feel this way? He didn't have the answers.

"Mr. Lipkins? Are you okay? You look a little pale all of a sudden. Maybe you should sit down."

Lipkins looked at Sandy and shook the feelings away. "I'm fine." But he went on to correct his own statement without realizing it. "I'm tired is what I am." He pointed to the side of his head. "Up here I think I'm still young, that my whole life is still ahead of me, like the road is wide open. But it's not. I'm old and I'm tired. Farming will do that to a man…make you feel young and old at the same time. When I was younger, after a hard day's work, I used to think of it as a blessing. Now it's a curse, or more like a cruel joke where you end up as your own punch line. Sometimes I wonder if I'm a fool. Other times I'm certain of it." Then as if he'd not spoken his thoughts aloud he said, "Here, let me grab you a pen."

HE GOT SANDY STARTED ON THE FORMS. THEY SAT quietly for a few minutes as she fixed her signature on the paperwork. The battle that raged inside his own mind was so violent he couldn't contain it any longer. *Now or never*, he thought. "Say, how about I take your boy for a ride on a tractor or something? Think that'd be okay?"

She'd barely started on the forms when Lipkins asked about taking Jonas outside. She didn't want to offend him, but she wasn't about to let Jonas roam around the countryside with someone she'd only met a few minutes ago. When Sandy looked up to answer she noticed that Lipkins wasn't looking at her. He was looking through a doorway that led to the back of the building. She turned her head and looked in that direction. The hall lights were off and she couldn't see more than two or three feet past the door frame. Or could she? She thought she sensed some movement. Was there someone else at the back of the building, standing in the shadows? When Lipkins turned back and looked at her, Sandy knew something wasn't quite right, though if pressed, she would have had a hard time defining what it was she felt in the moment. They were safe here, weren't they? They were members of the Co-op.

Then Lipkins did something that surprised her. He reached across the table and grabbed her by the wrist and pulled her close, a few of the forms scattering to the floor. "Take your boy and get out of here. You're in danger. Do you hear me? You've got to go right now. There's someone here who means to do you harm. I'm afraid I can't stop him." He released her wrist and when the door at the back of the building slammed shut they both turned and looked that way.

Jonas said, "Mommy?"

Sandy stood so fast she sent her chair sliding across the tiled floor. Jonas grabbed her hand and they hustled out the door. Cal Lipkins, the farmer, ran with them.

CHAPTER FORTY

When Virgil and Thorpe pulled up to the hangar they saw Cool and Mok standing next to the state's helicopter. Virgil saw that Mok had six men with him. *Too many people*, he thought.

Cool said as much as soon as they were out of the truck. "I can take six people, Jonesy, that's it. There are only seven seats in this thing and one of them has to be mine. I'll let you guys figure out who stays and who goes." He gave Mok a sideways look and went about his preflight activities.

Virgil looked at Mok and raised his eyebrows at him. "You're not trying to piss off the pilot are you? That's a little like arguing with your brain surgeon right before they put you under. This is Agent Thorpe with DHS, by the way. Agent Thorpe…Jon Mok, SWAT commander."

Mok nodded to Thorpe. "I guess that gets us clearance

to operate outside the state…in theory anyway. What are we up against here, Jonesy?"

"On one hand it's not as bad as I thought. On the other, it's much worse."

"Which hand do I have?" Mok asked.

"The not so bad one. You'll be going up against three men somewhere between Louisville and West Lafayette. Our best guess is the Jeffersonville rail yard. So it could be a pretty short ride."

Mok didn't like it. "One of the things that makes us successful is an overwhelming show of force. We'll use ten guys to make an entry where we know they've only got two people. If I can only take three of my guys with me, that's four against three. Not very good odds."

"You'll have Agent Thorpe with you as well."

Mok looked at Thorpe. "Any tactical training?"

"I did two years in Bogotá with the Company."

Mok canted his head. "CIA, huh? I guess I can see that. You've sort of got the Company look. Let me ask you this: Were you slinking around La Candelaria in the cafes, or out in the jungle?"

"In the jungle." He said it so calmly that Mok believed him. So did Virgil. "I can handle myself."

Mok called three of his men over and told them they could stand down and take off. "Jackson, give Agent Thorpe your vest."

The cop named Jackson slipped out of his tactical vest and handed it to Thorpe. Five minutes later they were airborne, headed to the Louisville airport. Virgil briefed them in the air.

Lipkins scooped up Jonas...took him right out of Sandy's grasp as they were running to her car. "What are you doing?" she shouted at him.

"Helping you. He's slowing us down. C'mon, get in your car and get it started." Sandy ran around to her side of the car while Lipkins, holding Jonas like a football, ran to the passenger side and got the back door open. Jonas was crying.

"It's okay, big guy," Lipkins said. "You're going to be okay. You're going to be all right. You're a big guy, remember? C'mon, in you go."

Jonas crawled away from Lipkins and climbed into his car seat. Lipkins hadn't seen a car seat in years and didn't know how to operate the complex buckling mechanism.

"Never mind that," Sandy said. "I'll get it when we get out of here." Lipkins slammed the door.

"Go, go, go." He waved her away. Sandy buzzed the window down on the passenger side. "What about you?" That simple act of Sandy doing what she did best by showing concern for others cost them all. A look of horror fell across her face and Cal Lipkins never got the chance to answer. He spun around in time to see the giant box truck coming at him full bore. Sandy tried to get the car in gear to get out of the way but it was much too late for any type of evasive maneuver. The truck hit the car square in the side, pinning Lipkins between the two vehicles, killing him instantly. The force of the collision flipped the car completely over and spun it around. It landed back on all four tires facing the opposite direction. It had been one short and violent ride.

Lipkins had been crushed to a bloody pulp and was under the truck. Radiator fluid poured out of the engine compartment and covered his body. Neither Sandy nor Jonas had been buckled in. The impact had tossed them around the inside of the car like ball bearings inside a blender.

Ralph Wheeler climbed out of the truck and walked over to the car. He pried open the back door and pulled Jonas out and tossed him on the ground like a rag doll.

Then he went for Sandy.

CHAPTER FORTY-ONE

The state helicopter was a Bell 407GXP. It had a top speed of one hundred sixty-one miles per hour. Cool had them in Louisville in less than forty-five minutes. The DHS agents, Franklin, and his partner, Greg Parr were waiting with a handcuffed Rick Said when they landed. Said, who was seated in the back of the DHS vehicle tried to get Virgil's attention. Virgil saw him and ignored him.

He introduced himself and Mok to the two agents. Then he looked at Franklin. "I never did get your first name."

"Yeah you did," Parr said.

Virgil looked at Franklin and reddened a bit. "Jeez, I'm sorry. That's a little embarrassing. I've been referring to you as Agent Franklin."

"That's his name," Parr said.

Virgil thought Parr seemed to be enjoying himself. Then he put it together. "So…you're Franklin Franklin?"

"My parents thought it was hilarious."

Virgil opened his mouth to respond then closed it. He looked around. "Is there someplace we can set up for a full brief? We're a little tight on time."

"We're already set up in the hangar," Franklin said. "This way."

They left Said in the car.

When he saw the men walk away he let his head rest against the car window.

Franklin and Parr were good, Virgil thought. In movies, television, and crime novels, officers of the federal government were often portrayed as either bumbling bureaucratic idiots who couldn't catch a criminal if they woke up and found themselves shackled to one, or non-cooperative, aristocratic self-absorbed narcissists who placed personal appearance and career advancement above criminal apprehension.

Franklin and Parr weren't like that. They struck Virgil as good cops who were well prepared. A table had been set up with folding chairs. There was a whiteboard on an easel, a map of Indiana's rail line taped to one side. The bottom of the map contained a view of the greater metropolitan Louisville area on the other side of the river.

"We've got the train stopped here," Parr said. "About three miles short of the line that runs by Radiology. We've briefed the railroad company, and they've informed the engineer what to expect. There's no good place to land but the line of sight overhead is clear." He turned and looked at Virgil. "I take it your men are briefed on their responsibilities?"

"They are," Virgil said. "They're going to capture Reif and his men if and when they make a move on the train. We fully expect it to be at the Jeffersonville rail yard. I'll be in the chopper providing air support and communications to Mok and his men." Virgil looked at Mok, who simply nodded.

"This is mostly your show," Parr said. "Radiology is back up and running. The whole thing was written off as a false alarm. With all the commotion, we're certain Said was extracted without anyone noticing. But I'm advising you to get your team out to that train so they can get on board. Sooner the better. We don't want any delays. " He looked at Cool. "Is any of that going to be a problem for you?"

"Just another day," Cool said. "They'll be able to step off the skid and on top of any car they choose. Take me four minutes to get them on-site, thirty-seconds to let them out, and another four to get back here."

Virgil looked at Thorpe, Mok, and his men. "Go. Cool, see you in ten minutes."

They turned and left. When Cool walked past Virgil he

said, "That'd be eight-and-a-half minutes, Einstein. You can set your watch to it, guaranteed."

Cool got the chopper fired up, and after a few seconds it lifted off, spun ninety degrees to the left, and flew out of sight. Virgil checked the time.

They watched the helicopter until it was out of sight on the other side of the hangar. Franklin made a clicking noise with his tongue after the heavy beat of the rotor blades had dissipated. "He's sort of a cool motherfucker, isn't he?"

"I'll tell you a story sometime," Virgil said. "You don't know the half of it." Then his own statement reminded him that his father had used the very same words when they'd spoken about Murton.

As Virgil stood in the hangar he was less than five miles away from where Murton had been and never knew it, the distance between them growing further and further with each passing minute. He took out his phone and tried to call Sandy again. Still no answer. He'd already left her a message, so he simply ended the call. His phone buzzed at him before he got it back in his pocket. Becky.

"Hey, Becks. I'm in a briefing with the DHS guys. Things are ramping up. Can I get back with you?"

Becky didn't beat around the bush. "No. You're going to want to hear this. I've got access to the thumb drive."

When Sandy finally came around, she felt as though someone had taken a club to almost every inch of her body. She couldn't move her arms or legs and momentarily panicked. What had happened? Then it came flooding back. The bizarre statements from Cal Lipkins. His frantic effort to get them out of the Co-op…the truck smashing into her car and sending them rolling across the parking lot…Lipkins's body being crushed between the two vehicles. Then she remembered Jonas. That panicked her more, but in a different way.

When she opened her eyes she discovered she was in some sort of container. The container had an opaque roof made out of thick plastic. The roof let in enough light for her to see. The walls of the container were sided with pieces of plywood that were smooth to the touch. There was a roll-up door at the rear. The inside handle had been removed. Her hands were bound behind her back. Not cuffs, she thought. Duct tape. She could feel the thick adhesive against her skin as she tried to pry her wrists apart. She called out quietly to Jonas as she tried to free her hands. He was nowhere in sight. Each time she called his name she said it a little louder. Eventually, she began screaming his name.

Jonas never answered. He wasn't there.

Then she smelled the nitrogen and the diesel fuel. She saw the marking on the crates that indicated they contained radioactive material. Suddenly she was glad

Jonas wasn't there. She knew she was sitting on a dirty bomb. A big one.

Virgil took a few steps away from the table inside the hangar and turned his back to the federal agents. When he spoke he kept his voice low. "I'm with two DHS agents. Is this something we want them to hear?"

"Based on what I've seen so far, I'd say no."

"Okay, hold on a second." He put the phone to his chest and said, "Hey guys, I've got a personal situation here. Why don't we wait for Cool to get back before we get any deeper into this."

Franklin and Parr looked at each other and shrugged. "Like I said, it's your show," Parr said.

"Thanks, I'll be right with you." He stepped outside the hangar and out of earshot of the agents. To Becky: "Tell me."

"I hate to admit it, but you were right."

"About what?"

"It's mostly Word files and spreadsheets."

"What have you found?"

"I went through the table of contents before I called. There's stuff on here I probably shouldn't be looking at. I don't know what most of it even means."

Virgil was standing within sight of the vehicle where Said was locked up in the back seat. When he looked at him, Said banged his forehead against the side window, then opened his eyes wide. He jerked his head in a manner that indicated he wanted to say something. Virgil turned away from the car. Didn't need the distraction.

"Oh boy," Becky said.

"What?"

"Just a minute."

"Becky…"

"I'm pulling something up right now. Hang on a second."

Virgil scratched the back of his head and looked down at the ground. He was about to risk Becky's wrath and prompt her again when she came back on the line.

"There's a file in here…it's a spreadsheet actually. Practically every county in the state is listed."

"I'm not surprised," Virgil said. "According to Nicole Pope, the drive was background intel on Pearson's political maneuverings."

"It might be a little more complex than that. I'm looking at the one for Shelby County right now. Guess whose name is mentioned more than anyone else's?"

"Who?"

"Cal Lipkins."

"What?"

"It looks like Pearson was positioning himself to be a part of the fracking operation in Shelby County."

"That's not possible," Virgil said. "Pearson was

already dead when the fracking deal was brought to the Co-op members."

"That's what we were told, anyway."

"You're saying Lipkins had been working this deal with him before Pearson died?"

"It sure looks that way. There are copies of emails, meeting notes, and about a billion links in here that lead all over the place. I'm going to have to study it some more, but…oh no."

"What?"

"Jonesy…they knew about Jonas.

"What?"

"Hold on."

Virgil heard a series of frantic clicks as Becky worked the information. When she came back on the line the words came so fast Virgil could hardly keep up with her.

"There's a whole section in here that talks about how Ed Donatti wasn't Jonas's biological father…that Pam had an affair…that Decker was the real father. There's a grid or flow chart or whatever you call it. It's all mapped out, Jonesy. They were planning Ed's assassination. They'd had it planned for years."

Virgil sat down on the tarmac and brought his knees up, his chest pressed against his thighs. His mind was racing. Becky was still speaking but he couldn't hear what she was saying, the blood pounding through his head so hard and fast he could hear his own heartbeat.

Then it hit him. He knew what was bothering him

about the last conversation he'd had with Cal Lipkins. He'd told Virgil to bring Sandy and Jonas to the Co-op. He hadn't said bring your wife and son, he'd said bring *Sandy and Jonas.* He'd called them by name. "Becky, keep going through everything. Stay by the phone. I've got to go."

"Jonesy wait. There's one more thing."

Virgil heard the beat of rotor blades as Cool made his approach back to the airport. "Make it quick, Becks."

"Sheridan was built and run by Pri-Max…Pate's company. That place is infested with people who have probably known from the start that Murton wasn't who he said he was. This one is getting away from us, Jonesy. I'm starting to get really scared."

So am I, he thought. He hung up on Becky and tried to call Sandy again. Still no answer. Cool was bringing the chopper in over the hanger and the noise was deafening. He ran back to the hangar to get away from the noise and dialed Huma at the house. He covered his other ear with his free hand. When Huma answered, he could barely hear her.

"What's that noise?"

Virgil ignored her question and shouted into the phone. "Where's Sandy?"

Huma answered, but he couldn't make out what she said, the noise from the chopper drowning out her words. "Say that again."

"I said she took Jonas and they drove down to the Co-op to sign the papers for Mr. Lipkins."

Virgil shouted to Franklin and Parr. "Keep Said locked up." He made a twirling motion with his arm and ran toward the helicopter. Cool had the engine back up to full operating speed when Virgil yanked open the door. "Shelby County, Cool. Right now. Go, go, go…" Cool pulled on the collective and they were airborne before Virgil had the door closed.

CHAPTER FORTY-TWO

Virgil got his phone back out and used an app that let him check Sandy's location. It showed her at the Shelby County Co-op. He put a headset on, gave Cool the coordinates, and watched as he plugged them into the helicopter's nav unit. "How long?"

"Half hour," Cool said. When he saw the look on Virgil's face he increased his speed. "Maybe a little less."

"Are you armed?"

"Always. Talk to me, Jonesy."

"I think Cal Lipkins has Sandy and Jonas."

"Who is Cal Lipkins?"

"A farmer," Virgil said.

Cool made a few minor adjustments to the controls. The airspeed indicator was pegged solidly in the red. Virgil could feel the aircraft buffeting against the strain. He tightened his belt. When he looked at Cool, Virgil could see the cartilage in his jaw as it flexed with tension. Cool had saved Sandy once before. His own blood still ran through her veins.

They were eighty miles away.

Sandy heard a door open and the rattle of a Diesel engine. So…not a container after all. She was in the back of a truck. She should have known, she thought. But the panic and fear had kept her mind occupied with other thoughts. She was going to call out, but thought better of it. If her captor knew she was conscious, it could be trouble. She ached with the knowledge that Jonas was scared and alone, but she had to put that aside for now. She couldn't help him if she couldn't get to him. And that's what she intended to do.

The truck began to move and the smell of the chemicals and fuel became much stronger as they sloshed around inside their containers. She had to find a way to free herself from the back of the truck, or be ready to fight when her captor opened the door, whichever came first. She knew she couldn't do either of those things with her hands bound tightly behind her back.

One thing at a time, and right now, it was time to get her hands free.

Reif called the old man. "I told you the first time we met that no one has ever been able to get on top of me. I had the feeling you weren't listening then. Maybe you'll listen to me now."

Ralph Wheeler put the truck in low gear and turned down a dirt path. It was slow going. He didn't want to bounce the load around too much. "You know what the trouble with people like you is? You think you always know what the other person is thinking. That means you've already had the entire conversation in your head before you ever open your mouth." Then, as if they were still on the same page, "You set up at the yard?"

Reif laughed at him. "Hardly. That part of the operation is a bust. Why do I think you already know that?"

"Probably because we work for the same people. Except the way I hear it, they don't seem to have much faith in you anymore."

"That's not necessarily true. You see, I'm a good soldier, and when they tell me to do something, I do it. You and I need to meet."

"I don't see why," Wheeler said.

"I've got the detonator and the bomb."

This time Ralph Wheeler laughed. "Your bomb's a dud, you idiot. It was never going to be the bomb. You got played like a fiddle, boy. I've got tons of fertilizer and fuel oil packed into a truck. I've got the nuclear material too."

"I've still got the detonator…and maybe something else you might want."

"Oh yeah? What's that?"

"I've got your boy."

"Where are you?"

"Check your rearview mirror, smart guy."

Ralph Wheeler looked in the mirror and saw the SUV about one hundred yards back. "How'd you know where to find me?"

Is this guy for real? Reif thought. "We're working for the same people. They're not going to let anything get in the way this time. They've kept me informed every time they told you to do something. Been watching your every move all along."

Wheeler had the truck in position…or close enough anyway. He hit the brakes. "Get up here then. And remember what I said…I ain't afraid to die."

"Quit being so dramatic. We're on the same side."

SANDY SEARCHED AROUND THE CRAMPED QUARTERS OF the truck trying to find something she could use to cut her hands free. The containers that held the fuel and fertilizer were big plastic barrels. The walls and the floor were constructed of plywood with tightly fitted seams. The roll-up door was made from pressed boards and used rounded carriage bolts. She looked for any type of sharp edge and found none. There was nothing.

Then she looked at the pallets where the chemical barrels were secured. One of the pallet's cross members had cracked near the edge and a single nail stuck out at the corner, very near the spot where the floor met the sidewall. Sandy crawled over and backed up next to the pallet. She laid down on her side and got her wrists up against the nail.

She began to saw back and forth, slowly and carefully. Tiny little nicks. If the nail broke free, it'd be useless to her. The angle was difficult and she had trouble keeping her wrists steady. She felt the nail scratch and puncture her skin, the blood streaming across her palms and fingers.

She thought about Jonas and kept picking away at the bindings.

Reif pulled up behind the box truck and met Wheeler between the two vehicles. He looked around at the vastness of the area. "Seems like a waste of a good bomb, you ask me."

"That's because you don't know what's going on. You and your boys thought that bomb was going to take out a city block or something, didn't you?"

"We weren't told," Reif said. "Although there was

some hope that might be the eventual outcome."

Ralph Wheeler laughed at him. "That was never the plan. The bomb is going to ruin this land. Where's the detonator?"

Reif tipped his head back toward the SUV.

"Get it up here, then. Everything is wired up through the cab."

Reif got the detonator Murton had built and together the two men hooked it to the explosives. The detonator was nothing more than a simple battery pack with an electronic timer. The countdown would begin once they powered up the device.

Ralph Wheeler thought of his son. It'd be just like him to set the timer at zero so when they pressed the button the bomb would go off instantly, killing them both.

"What is it?" Reif asked.

"I'm wondering how long the timer is set for."

"The last one was only a few minutes."

"The last one?"

"I had your boy build a test bomb to make sure he knew what he was doing. Why are you looking at me like that? I thought you weren't afraid to die."

"I'm not," Wheeler said. "That doesn't necessarily mean I want to." He looked at the SUV. "Where's my idiot kid?"

"Wrapped up in the back," Reif said.

"Let's get him up here. He can press the button. If he hesitates, we'll know he tried to fuck us."

Sandy heard two men speaking at the rear of the truck. When she heard their voices she froze. She had to stop working on the bindings. They were right on the other side of the door and she was afraid they might hear her. Then she heard the front doors of the truck open and she could hear the men speaking in the cab. They were worried about the timer.

So was she.

She continued to pick at her bindings as quietly as possible.

They pulled Murton out of the SUV and dragged him up to the front of the box truck. Ralph Wheeler and Reif each held a gun pointed at Murton. They dropped him on the ground and Reif cut the ties from his hands. "Get up."

Murton was still hooded and couldn't see his surroundings. He rose slowly, the task complicated because his legs were bound together. Once he was upright, Reif yanked the hood from his head. "Surprise. Time for a little family gathering."

Murton stared at his father and didn't say a word.

"Here's what we're thinking," Reif said. "Your old man and I had a conversation and we don't trust you. We think you might have built the detonator to blow the minute the damned thing is activated. How long of a delay did you set?"

Murton grinned at them. "Press the button and find out," he said.

"Good idea, Son."

"Don't call me that. You don't ever get to call me that."

"Boy, the two of you sure do have mutual hard-ons for each other, don't you?" Reif said. "No matter, it's still a good idea." He pushed Murton forward and slammed him into the side of the truck. Then he yanked the door open, grabbed the timer and put it in Murton's hands. He pointed his gun at him and said, "Press the button."

Murton looked at his father. "I always knew it would come down to something like this between you and me. So sayonara, hasta luego, or whatever." He winked at his father. "See you in hell, old man."

Then he pressed the button.

Ralph Wheeler knew the look in his son's eyes. It was the same one he'd seen over forty years ago when he'd tried to attack him with the hammer. When he saw him wink, Ralph Wheeler shouted, "Wait!"

But he was too late. The timer made an audible click, then showed 29:59. Murton had set the timer for thirty minutes when he built it, but more importantly he'd scored a victory in much the same way Patty Doyle had. He'd tricked his father into showing fear in front of someone else, making him an unwilling participant of his own humiliation.

He tossed the timer on the seat, looked at both men, opened his eyes wide and said, "Boom."

Reif spun him around and secured his wrists with a pair of plastic cuffs. Then he looked at the old man and said, "It's your call. You want to take him out now, pull the trigger. Otherwise, let's get him in the back. When this thing blows it'll scatter his ashes across half the county."

Ralph Wheeler looked at the gun in his hand, then at his son. "Put him in the back."

Murton laughed without humor and spat at his father's feet. "Jonesy will square this. I've known him my whole life. I know what he's capable of, even if you don't. You won't even see it coming."

Ralph Wheeler kicked Murton's feet out from under him, then looked at Reif. "Got any more of those plastic ties?"

SANDY HEARD SOMEONE SAY 'PUT HIM IN THE BACK.' A few moments later she heard the lock mechanism on the door ratchet out of place. She had just enough time to let her body go limp. If they knew she was conscious, it wouldn't go well for her.

The door rolled up and Reif and the old man tossed Murton inside next to Sandy. Five seconds later the door was back down, the lock clicked back in place. Sandy opened her eyes and saw that Murton was bound with his hands behind his back and his feet pulled up behind him, his wrists and ankles held tight against each other by the plastic cuffs. His back was arched so severely she thought his spine might snap. They were face to face. "Oh, Murton," she said, leaning forward and pressing her forehead against his.

Murton pulled back and looked her right in the eye. "Shh. Wait till they're gone," he whispered. He said it so quietly Sandy had to practically read his lips to understand. A few moments later they heard two doors slam as the other vehicle backed up and drove away.

"Can you roll over?" he asked Sandy.

It took some doing in the cramped quarters but Sandy managed to wiggle herself around until she was facing away from Murton. "Now what?"

"Inside my right boot."

Sandy arched her back until she thought her own spine might snap. She couldn't see what she was doing and every time she turned her head it pulled her hands further away.

"Don't try to look," Murton said. "Close your eyes and do it by touch. My right leg."

She closed her eyes and reached his leg. She worked his pants out of the way then slid her fingers down inside his boot. When she had the knife free she said, "Got it."

"Are you taped or cuffed?"

"Taped. I've been picking at it with a nail."

"Put the knife in my hands."

Sandy rolled and Murton grabbed the knife. He pressed a button and the blade clicked open. Sandy wiggled up against him. "Okay, carefully now," he said. "This thing's like a razor. I want you to slide your wrists right up to the blade and then—"

Sandy pulled her hands apart and ripped the remaining tape from her wrists. "We gonna talk about it or we gonna do it?"

"I guess we're doing it." She took the knife from Murton's hands and cut the bindings from his wrists. Then she handed him the blade. A minute later he had himself free as well.

Sandy stood slowly, still sore from the beating she'd taken in the crash. "Murton we've got to get out of here."

"No kidding."

"Can you kill the timer?"

Murton stood next to her. The look on his face was hollow, as if someone had vacuumed his expression away. "No. The detonator has a fail-safe built into it. I can't shut it down. We've got a little less than thirty minutes."

Sandy grabbed him by the arms. "It's not us I'm worried about, Murt. It's Jonas. They've got Jonas."

CHAPTER FORTY-THREE

Virgil leaned forward in his seat, his shoulders rounded, his neck extended, as if the act of doing so would help the helicopter go faster. He looked at Cool. "How long?"

Cool glanced at the nav unit. "Fifteen minutes."

Virgil shook his head and Cool caught it. He inched the speed up a fraction. Any more and they'd come apart in the air. They were already well past the design limits.

Virgil watched the countryside slide by. It felt like they were crawling.

Murton climbed on top of the containers, laid down on his back and punched his knife through the roof of the truck. The material wasn't very thick, but it was tough. He began sawing through the plastic with as much speed and efficiency as he could manage. Every time he made a cut, little bits of the material shredded away and fell onto his face and into his mouth. He spit the pieces out and said, "Tell me."

Sandy watched Murton work on the roof and realized this was a side of him she'd never seen, one she'd only heard of, fragments that had been pieced together over the years. Gone was the smiling face, the carefree attitude, the facade that told everyone he couldn't be touched. Murton was working with a single-minded objectiveness, one that had no equal. He was calm, driven, quietly optimistic, determined, and curious all at once. "Small?"

Sandy told him all of it. How she and Jonas had gone to the Co-op to sign the paperwork, the odd and mercurial way Cal Lipkins had behaved, the antithetical nature of his remarks, the duality of his actions, and ultimately how he died trying to save them. "I'm not sure what's going on, Murton. He was up to something, I'm sure of it. I think he was trying to separate me and Jonas. Then at the last minute it was like he had a change of heart."

"Guys like that don't have hearts, Small." He made another cut in the roof. Then he added, "I should know."

"Murt?"

He looked down at her, still sawing frantically through the roof. "What?"

"That other man? That was your father, right?"

"What of it?"

Sandy thought of her own father and how he'd died saving Virgil, how she'd never had the chance to know him as a person or a man. She thought of second chances and how she almost had the opportunity to regain what she'd lost through Mason and how that had been taken from her as well. It was as if the universe never intended for her to have a father. "Promise me you won't do anything you'll regret."

He punched a giant section of the roof away and stuck his head through. They were alone. He crawled out and laid down on top of the roof and stuck his hand through the hole. "C'mon. Let's go get your boy."

Murton had his hand wrapped around Sandy's bloodied wrist. He pulled her up on top of the crates and through the hole as if she weighed no more than a child. What he said next shouldn't have surprised her, but it did. "Is Becky okay?"

Surprised or not, it didn't get past Sandy that Murton had refused to address her request regarding his own father. "You tell me," she said.

THEY CLIMBED DOWN FROM THE TOP OF THE TRUCK AND looked around. They were in the middle of an empty field. The soil had recently been turned and the dirt smelled fresh and alive.

"Where are we?" Sandy asked. "Do you have any idea?"

Murton held his hand up to his forehead and shielded the sun from his eyes. He saw the moon off in the distance, a faint thin arc of a thumbnail, perched upright and low on the horizon, hung across the underbelly of a thin layer of Cirrus clouds. Below the moon was the squat rounded structure of the Co-op building. "Standing on your land, I'd say. Look behind you. The Co-op is about a half-mile that way," he said pointing across her shoulder. "That's also the direction the tire tracks lead. We're unarmed, probably outnumbered, and we don't know when or if any backup will arrive. Are you up for this?"

"Like you wouldn't believe," Sandy said. "I'd go alone if I had to." She started running toward the Co-op.

I know you would, Murton thought. He yanked open the cab of the truck and checked the timer. When he saw how much time they had remaining he began to run as well.

Reif and Wheeler were back at the Co-op, neither of them quite sure they were far enough away. "I don't know about you, old man, but I think I've done all I can do here. Maybe it's time to put the pedal to the metal, if you know what I'm saying. What about the kid?"

"What about him?" Wheeler said. "He's an insurance policy."

Jonas was lying on the table, surrounded by the paperwork Cal Lipkins had brought out for Sandy to sign. He wasn't injured very badly despite the severity of the crash. He had some bumps and bruises and a few minor cuts, but he'd sort of shut down mentally. He was curled into a fetal position, his hands clenched in fists and stuck between his little legs.

"More like a liability, if you ask me," Reif said.

"I told you not long ago that there was a debt that needed to be paid." He tipped his chin at Jonas. "That boy's father is on his way here, I'm certain of it. After he's taken care of we can be on our way. How long now?"

Reif looked at his watch. "Four minutes. It's time you'll be spending alone. Any debts that need to be paid or collected are yours, not mine. I'm out of here."

Virgil looked at Cool again. "How long?"

Cool checked the nav unit. "Four minutes."

Sandy and Murton had worked their way around to the back of the Co-op building. The SUV sat in the parking lot, Cal Lipkins's body still under the truck that had smashed her car. Her son was inside the building, she was sure of it. Then, as if Murton had somehow taken up residence inside her own skin, as if their thoughts had become symbiotic in nature she thought to herself, *time to dance, motherfuckers.*

She put her hand on the back door of the Co-op and quietly pushed it open. All of a sudden, as if her hearing had been clicked on, she heard the thunderous roar of rotor blades pounding a rhythmic beat in the air. She glanced up at the helicopter as it made a sweeping pass and settled down in the gravel. When she turned around, Murton was nowhere in sight.

CHAPTER FORTY-FOUR

FOUR MINUTES AGO

Reif was getting ready to leave and happened to glance out the front window of the Co-op right before he opened the door. He couldn't quite believe what he saw. Murton Wheeler stood in front of the wrecked box truck, his hands hanging down at his sides, his posture almost simian in nature. "Better come take a look at this," he said to the old man.

Ralph Wheeler walked over to the window and peered through the glass. "I'll tell you something," he said to Reif. "I always thought the better part of that kid went running down his momma's leg. But I've got to hand it to him, he doesn't have much quit in him."

Whatever, Reif thought. It was time to put this particular titty-baby to bed. He took out his gun and said, "I'm going to do you one last favor, old man. You can thank me later, if we ever meet up again, which I sincerely hope we do not."

"What do you intend to do?" Wheeler said.

"What you should have done a long time ago, from the looks of it."

Reif stepped outside, his gun hanging down along the side of his leg. He moved forward, expecting Murton to run or duck in cover. But none of that happened. Murton stood perfectly still and waited until Reif was less than ten yards away before he spoke.

"You big on history?"

"Not particularly," Reif said. "Why?"

"Because it's how we learn from our mistakes."

Reif pulled the hammer back on his gun. "What mistakes? Or are you trying to delay the inevitable?"

"The inevitability is yours you pathetic piece of shit."

Reif stepped closer and raised the gun. "Say that again."

"I would, but I'm not big on wasting my breath with people who were dropped on their heads as infants. Somehow the information never takes hold. You want a history lesson? Here's the last one you're ever going to get. I told you I didn't kill that prison guard. Want to know what your mistake was?"

"What's that?"

"You didn't believe him," Jack Grady said. He stood at the opposite corner of the Co-op building, his weapon pointed at Reif. When Reif turned his way, Grady pulled the trigger. The bullet ripped through the side of Reif's head and he dropped to the ground, dead inside a pool of his own blood.

When Reif hit the ground a helicopter roared overhead, its skids clearing the roof of the Co-op building with less than two feet to spare.

Cool began to throttle back on the power as he put the chopper into a nosedive. "Keep the power to it, Cool," Virgil said.

"I can't," Cool replied, his voice overly calm the way pilots are when placed in a stressful situation. "We'll break apart. I've got to bleed off some speed if this is a landing you want to walk away from."

Virgil looked out the front window. He never saw Murton, his view blocked by the wrecked box truck in the parking lot, but when they crossed over the top of the building he saw Sandy. She turned and looked behind her as if she expected someone to be there. Then she disappeared inside the building.

Cool brought the helicopter in hard and fast, the skids grinding along the hard gravel pack before it finally came to a rest.

"Keep it running. We're going to have to get out of here in a hurry. I need your weapon." Cool reached into the side pocket of the door and handed over his service revolver. Virgil climbed out, ducked the rotor, and followed Sandy in through the back door.

MURTON GRABBED REIF'S GUN AND RAN OVER TO GRADY. He saw Cal Lipkins's body under the truck. He didn't know what to make of it. "Stay out here and cover the front. I don't know who else is in the area or what's in play. I'm not taking any chances." Grady nodded and said he would. Murton released the magazine, checked the number of rounds and slapped it back in place. He ran up the steps and inside the Co-op building. What he saw caused his throat to constrict and for a moment he wondered if his heart still beat in his chest.

His father sat at the end of the meeting room table, Jonas in his lap, a gun pressed to the side of his head.

Murton pointed his gun at his father, drew his mouth into a tight line, then immediately lowered his weapon. He couldn't risk a shot without injuring or possibly killing Jonas.

"Let him go, Pop."

"So, you can call me pop but I can't call you son, is that it?"

"I said let him go."

"Now why would I do that?" Ralph Wheeler said. "Looks to me like I've got everything I wanted. Or at least

I will when that asshole buddy of yours shows up. I know he's here. I heard the back door open after that helicopter set down." He glanced toward the hallway that led to the back of the building. "Come on out, Virgil. It's time to get reacquainted. Bring your bitch with you too." Then he looked back at Murton. "Mine's already here." He cocked the hammer on his gun and placed it against Jonas's ear. "Set your gun on the table, boy, and slide it down here to me or I swear to Christ I'll scatter this little fellow's grits across the cinderblocks."

Murton felt like he didn't have a choice. He set the gun on the table and slid it down to his father. Ralph Wheeler looked at the gun, a Heckler & Koch P30-S and said, "Nice piece. Those Germans really know how to make them. Better than the piece of shit I'm holding. He laid his own gun on the table and pointed the weapon at Murton. "I'll bet you could find a hammer in the back, if you wanted one. You do, don't you, boy? I can see it in your eyes. Now sit the fuck down."

Virgil caught up with Sandy and pulled her back. He had no doubt that she would have rushed headlong into the meeting room of the Co-op and charged Wheeler, forcing him to shoot at her. When she tried to yank free he grabbed both her arms and spun her around. "We've got to be smart here, baby."

"He's got our son, Virgil."

"I know. And I'll get him back, I promise. Look at me. I promise I will do whatever I have to do. *Anything*. Are you with me?"

Sandy nodded. Virgil handed her Cool's service weapon. They crept forward through the shop, and into the hallway that led to the meeting room. When they got to the end of the hall they heard Ralph Wheeler say, 'Come on out, Virgil. It's time to get reacquainted...' Virgil held his hand out, an indication for Sandy to stop. They were pressed up against the wall, right around the corner of the door frame. Virgil's .45 was in his left hand, pointed down at the floor.

"If you're trying to be quiet, you're failing miserably," Ralph Wheeler said. "I've heard less noise from circus monkeys on the business end of a training stick. Step out here now before I lose my patience." He looked at Murton and said, "Move one single muscle and this kid won't see tomorrow." He stood from the chair and dragged Jonas with him until they were positioned directly behind Murton. He moved the gun away from Jonas and pointed it at the back of Murton's head.

Virgil and Sandy stepped into the room, Virgil's gun coming up as he rounded the door frame.

CHAPTER FORTY-FIVE

FOUR SECONDS AGO

Virgil held the Glock with a firm grip, his hands steady, the barrel pointed straight at the other man's head, a choice now, and without question, a price to be paid. He leaned forward, his knees slightly bent, his weight rotated up on the balls of his feet. When he slipped his finger into the trigger guard he asked for forgiveness, though he didn't know to whom he was speaking, or if they were even listening.

He took a breath, the inhalation something like acid in his lungs and when he could inhale no more he locked eyes with his best friend and brother, Murton Wheeler. The look on Virgil's face remained a conveyance of everything that couldn't be said aloud, a lifetime of memories, brotherly love, their victories, their mistakes, and now...

This:

Murton nodded at Virgil, his mouth a thin hard line, his jaw flexed tight. The nod was nothing more than a quick tip of his head, one that said, get on with it, then.

When Jones pulled the trigger, Ralph Wheeler's head jerked away and he fell to the ground, dead before he hit the floor, his body bent in an awkward position, blood leaking from the gaping hole in his forehead. His eyes remained open and seemed to register surprise, as if maybe the last thought his brain processed was disbelief that his death would come from the hand of the one person he least suspected.

But it had, and in that instant Virgil knew in many ways his life would never be the same. He'd been prepared to shoot, had even begun to tighten up on the trigger. Another half-pound of pressure and his gun would have fired.

But Sandy beat him to it.

When Virgil looked at Sandy she was still in a shooter's stance. He took the gun from her hand, the barrel warm to the touch. She released her grip on the weapon and ran to Jonas, scooping him into her arms. She glanced down at the man she'd just killed and for some reason thought of her own father. Murton stood from the chair and looked her in the eyes, his face as blank and expressionless as a dime-store mannequin. There was no contempt in his voice when he spoke, but there may have been a touch of cynicism.

"I promise," he said. He touched the back of Jonas's head and brushed his fingers through his hair.

Grady came through the front door. He glanced at Ralph Wheeler's dead body, then at Murton. "You okay?"

Murton opened his mouth to say something, but the words, whatever they may have been, were lost in what happened next.

There was a brilliant, almost blinding flash of white light. Virgil and Murton looked at each other and together they pulled Sandy and Jonas to the floor as a thunderous boom rolled over the building and blew out the windows. Once the glass stopped flying Virgil ran out the back in time to see the small mushroom cloud forming. He yelled to Sandy, Murton, and Grady. "C'mon, we've got to get the hell out of here."

Twenty seconds later they were on the helicopter and moving away from the Co-op and the blast site. When they were a safe distance away Virgil said something to Cool who nodded, then maneuvered the chopper into a hover and spun it back around. They hung there for a full minute and looked out the windows and watched as radioactive dirt and dust rained down over their farmland.

When Virgil turned in his seat and looked at Sandy he

saw her holding Murton's hand. Jonas was in her lap, his little hands reaching up, wiping the tears from her face. Murton stared straight ahead, his eyes fixed on nothing at all.

Cool spun the chopper around and flew a few miles away before setting down right in the center of the main intersection that led to the Co-op. Once they were all out of the helicopter, Virgil took out his phone and called Cora. How do you tell your boss that a dirty bomb had been detonated on your own land, threatening the entire county? Virgil wondered.

As it turned out, he didn't have to.

Murton walked away and made a call to Becky. He sat down in the dirt and told her everything.

Virgil didn't have to explain the dirty bomb to Cora because just as he was getting ready to call his phone buzzed at him. Franklin.

"You better talk to Said," Franklin said. "He's literally been bouncing off the walls trying to make his point. I don't know how much of it is bullshit, but—"

"But what?"

"Here, I'll let him tell you. Hold on."

Virgil waited a beat and then Radiology's CEO was on the phone. Said finally had his say. He told Virgil what he wanted to tell him, had been trying to tell him back at the airport. He finally told him the whole truth.

It had happened like this:

When Ralph Wheeler entered the rear of Radiology, Inc.'s shipping area, Said had been right there waiting for him. Wheeler gave him a hard stare. "The truck ready?"

Said tossed a set of keys to Wheeler and pointed at a box truck with his chin.

"Keep your mouth shut and everything will work out fine. We clear on that?"

"How do I know she's still alive?"

Wheeler tipped his head in what he hoped was a thoughtful manner. "I guess you'll have to take my word for it because the bottom line is this: you don't."

Said took a step forward. He might have looked like a writer or an anthropologist, but he wasn't a pussy. "Then maybe I'll walk inside and do what I should have done all along. Maybe I'll go inside and call the cops."

Wheeler laughed at him. "Go ahead. She's your niece, not mine. But I'll tell you something, if this truck doesn't end up where it's supposed to be she will be dead. That's a fact. So you're left with two choices, smart guy. Do nothing and hope everything turns out all right for your niece, or go make the phone call and ensure that it doesn't."

Said knew he didn't have any choice at all. In fact, he knew his life was over the moment they'd taken his sister's child. He'd never had children of his own, and Patty had always been like a daughter to him. He'd helped raise her and even paid for her education. When the old man showed Said the photos weeks ago he broke down and cried right in front of him. Wheeler had laughed, Said's fear and anguish a source of wicked pleasure.

Now Wheeler climbed in the truck, started the engine and lowered the window. He let his arm rest on the side of the door. "By tomorrow it'll all be over and you'll have your precious niece back, safe and sound. Stay by the phone and you'll get a call."

Said watched the truck drive away, his heart beating like a kettle drum. He knew if they found out what he'd done it would be the end of Patty's life. Still, he knew he had to do it. As much as he loved Patty, he couldn't allow the material to get loose. There'd never be a call and he knew it.

He told Virgil as much. "I didn't think I had any other choice."

"I don't know exactly how all this is going to play out for you, Mr. Said. You've put yourself, your company, and your niece at grave risk. If you'd have called us at the beginning we might have been able to save her."

Said didn't respond, and Virgil wasn't surprised. "Give the phone back to Agent Franklin."

A moment later Franklin was on the line. "We'll be up there as soon as we can."

"Bring him with you," Virgil said. "If he tries to lawyer up or anything like that, explain the situation to him."

"That won't be a problem, "Franklin said. "We're talking about nuclear material. Ever hear of the Patriot Act?"

"Ah, go easy on him," Virgil said. "We're talking about a guy looking out for his family. The nuclear material is safe. You might want to call Thorpe and get him and Mok off that train. If they have to ride that thing all the way to West Lafayette I'll never hear the end of it."

What about the other guys…the ones who were going to take the material off the train?"

"According to our people here, they're off the board. Said outplayed them all. He'd kept the nuclear material crated away and altered the logs. Both the train and the truck were loaded with the nano particles, which are supposedly harmless. If he's telling the truth, and I think he is, the radioactive material is still at the plant. If you guys could verify that then get him up here, I'd appreciate it."

"Do that," Franklin said. "See you in a few hours."

Virgil then spoke at length with Cora and brought her up to speed on what had happened. He finished with, "So, hell of a blast, but no radiation…I hope. It'd be nice if someone brought a Geiger counter for verification though."

"That's already being handled. The ATF is on the way as we speak," she said. "So is the EPA, the Nuclear Regulatory Agency, the FBI and probably a bunch of three-letter agencies no one has ever heard of because they don't officially exist. By the time it's all said and done, I think it's going to look like federal alphabet soup out there. Boy, this isn't going to play well with the media."

"That's not really my biggest concern right now, Cora."

"Maybe it should be."

"I don't know what else you'd have me do," Virgil said. "We were working with limited information the whole time."

"Were you?"

Just then, Sheriff Benjamin Holden pulled up and parked his ancient station wagon right next to the helicopter. Virgil noticed the jackpot flasher had been replaced with a modern light bar. Holden stepped up to Virgil and said, "God almighty, what have you done now?"

Virgil ignored him. He and the sheriff had something of a tense relationship.

"Is that the sheriff I hear?" Cora asked.

"Yeah. He doesn't seem too happy to see me right now."

"Let me talk to him."

Virgil handed Holden the phone. "It's for you."

Holden gave him a quizzical look and put the phone to his ear. "Sheriff Holden, here. Who's this?"

Holden listened, his face growing redder by the second. When he was done listening, he said, "Yes ma'am," and gave the phone back to Virgil. Then he got back in his car and simply sat there, staring out the windshield.

"What'd you say to him?"

"Let's not sweat the small stuff, Jones-man. Stay put until the guard shows up, then get back to the city. I'll be in my office." Virgil heard a click and she was gone.

Small stuff?

SANDY TOLD VIRGIL EVERYTHING THAT HAD HAPPENED from the time she left the house with Jonas. "I didn't think anything of it. I thought we'd take a drive out to the country, sign a few papers and it'd be one less thing we'd have to deal with. I had no idea Cal Lipkins was a part of all this. I'm not sure what to make of it. In the end he tried to help. In fact, he gave his life trying to save us."

Virgil didn't know what to make of that either. He let it go. Jonas crawled into his arms and hugged him tight. "You okay, big guy?"

Jonas nodded at him.

Virgil was concerned that he'd not yet heard Jonas

speak. "You ready to get back home? Mr. Cool is going to take you for another ride in the helicopter."

"Can I sit in front?"

When Jonas finally spoke, Virgil was filled with relief. "Let's go find out."

"We got hit by a big truck," Jonas said, some normalcy creeping into his voice.

Virgil rubbed the top of his head. "You sure did. It's all over now though."

Except…it wasn't.

Virgil asked Cool to take Sandy and Jonas home then come back for him and Murton. Sandy walked over and Virgil hugged his wife and child, told them he'd see them as soon as possible, then helped them into the helicopter. He leaned up and pulled Sandy close. "Maybe get in touch with Bell."

She nodded at him. "I've already called him. Huma too. Bell's on his way to our place. So is Delroy."

Delroy was one of Jonas's favorite people. It'd be a good start. "I love you, Small."

"I love you too, Virgil." Sandy took a quick peek at Jonas. "I think he'll be okay. He's one resilient kid."

"He's been through so much in such a short period of time."

Sandy grabbed Virgil's arm. "We'll get him whatever help he needs. One step at a time. What about Murt?"

Virgil cocked his head. "He's the toughest man I've ever known."

"Me too," Sandy said. "And I just killed his father. I'm afraid I may have changed everything."

You did, Virgil thought. For the better.

"What was that?"

"I said just like Jonas…one step at a time."

Sandy let go of his arm, leaned forward and tapped Cool on the shoulder. Virgil closed the door and stepped away.

ONCE SANDY AND JONAS WERE ON THEIR WAY HE TURNED around and saw Jack Grady leaning down talking to the sheriff. He walked that way.

"What's up?"

Grady stood and looked across the top of the station wagon and said, "The sheriff is debating whether or not he wants to take us back to the Co-op."

Virgil leaned down and looked inside the vehicle. "Sheriff?"

"How many bodies are out there this time?"

Virgil wasn't having it. "Look, Sheriff, I didn't create this situation any more than you did. Why not holster your moral authority and help us do our jobs?"

"Your job seems to be to create chaos everywhere you go. Either that or it follows you around like a swarm of gnats."

"What did my boss say to you?"

Holden turned his head and looked Virgil straight in the eyes. "Ask her. Can't say that I enjoyed it, but I'll tell you this: If that's how she looks after her people, I wish she was my boss too."

Virgil stared at him without speaking.

"You coming or not? I'm running low on gas."

Murton walked over and they all got in the station wagon.

Holden took them back to the Co-op. They parked near the wrecked box truck and Sandy's smashed car. When Virgil finally got a look at the condition of the vehicle he knew how lucky they'd been. The car was totaled, the passenger side completely caved in. If it weren't for the airbags...

Virgil stopped himself. Didn't want to go there. They were safe, and that's all that mattered.

The sheriff was squatted down next to the front of the box truck. When Virgil walked over Holden stood and squared off with him. "That's Cal Lipkins under that truck, isn't it?"

Virgil nodded. "I'm afraid so."

Holden looked at Reif's body on the ground less than ten yards away. Half his head was blown apart. "What the hell happened here?"

Virgil was about to tell the sheriff how Lipkins had been involved with Ralph Wheeler and their attempt to contaminate the land with radioactive material by detonating a dirty bomb. Instead, he told him something he hoped would be much more palatable. "I only have part of the story, but from what I understand Cal gave his life in an effort to save my wife and son."

Holden looked at Virgil for a long time before he spoke. "Of course he did. Cal Lipkins was a good man." His words came out as a challenge.

Virgil didn't take the bait.

CHAPTER FORTY-SIX

When Virgil went inside the Co-op building he found Murton sitting in a chair, his father's dead body near his feet. His back was rounded, his shoulders hunched, his forearms resting on his thighs. When Murton looked up at him, Virgil feared whatever words might be said next would be ones that redefined not only their relationship, but the rest of their lives.

Maybe Murton did too. He must have, because neither of them said anything. He stood from the chair and they walked out of the building together. A short time later Virgil realized that if he had any doubts about what Cora had said regarding the arrival of the federal government en masse they were soon put to rest. The ATF was first on the scene, followed by Franklin and Parr representing DHS. When the FBI showed up, things got a little heated between Virgil and one of the agents when they discovered that Sandy had left the scene without permission from any of the federal agencies.

"She was the shooter. She should have stayed until she gave a formal statement and was officially released."

Virgil got right in his face. "She was also the one who saved my partner's life. Our child was here. She saved him as well. Our first priority was to get our boy to safety. She's an officer of the state. She'll make a formal statement as soon as possible." Virgil started to walk away.

"That's not good enough."

Virgil spun around, his fists clenched, his body taut with tension. Murton stepped in front of him and looked at the agent. "Throttle it back, dude. He's right. You have kids?"

"No."

"Thank God," Murton said. Then he looked at Virgil. "Where's Grady?"

Virgil turned and looked around and spotted Grady leaning against the side of the Co-op building. He pointed with his chin. "Why?"

Cool brought the chopper in and landed behind the Quonset hut. "Because our ride's here."

The agent wasn't having it. "Hey, you guys can't leave. Where do you think you're going? Hey!"

Franklin heard the commotion and intercepted the FBI agent. "Homeland has the point on this. Back off." The FBI agent didn't like it, but he went away. Franklin looked at Virgil. "Said's in the car. I'm willing to entertain suggestions on what to do with him. All the nuclear material is accounted for. It's still at their facility. I'm not sure altering the logs of your own company's shipping manifest is considered a crime. Though from what I understand he did lie to you and officer Grady regarding the nature of those alterations, which technically is a crime, so…your call."

"Let me talk with him," Virgil said.

"Be my guest," Franklin said. "He's sitting in my car. He tossed Virgil the keys.

Virgil got Said out of the car and let him know he wouldn't be charged.

The statement had little impact on him. "I don't care about any of that. All I ever wanted was to get my niece back safe and sound." Tears streamed down his face as he spoke.

Virgil put his hand on Said's shoulder. "Listen, I need you to do something for us. It won't be easy, but I need you to take a look at a body. See if you can positively identify the man that made contact with you. It could help us recover your niece's—" Virgil caught himself a little late. Said finished it for him.

"Remains, right? That's what you almost said, isn't it?"

Virgil didn't answer. "Let's go take a look." He walked Said over to the Co-op building. Said never made it through the doorway. Ralph Wheeler was in plain sight and when Said saw him he simply nodded and stepped back off the porch.

"He's the only one you ever saw?" Virgil asked.

"Yes. Where did he live?"

"Down near Jeffersonville. We've got state agents searching his home right now. I'm sorry to say they've found nothing that indicates Patty was ever there. C'mon, let's get you out of here. We'll give you a ride back to Kentucky in the helicopter. About your niece…I'm sorry. I really am. If things had gone differently we might have been able to—"

So much had happened in such a short amount of time that Virgil failed to notice something that was right in front of his face.

Cal Lipkins's truck.

It sat in the Co-op parking lot and was identical to the picture he had from the post office security footage.

Virgil ran over to the truck and yanked the door open. He pulled the registration from the glove box and ran toward the helicopter. Murton and Grady were already there.

Said didn't know what was happening, so he ran that

way too. By the time he reached the chopper Cool had the engine running and was ready to lift off. Said yanked the door open and looked at Virgil. "What is it?"

"Maybe nothing," Virgil said. He had to yell over the sound of the jet engine and the beat of the rotor blades.

"Patty?" Said yelled back. "You're going to look for Patty?"

Virgil nodded. "Stay put. We'll let you know what we find."

"To hell with that. I'm coming with you. Try and stop me." When he climbed in the helicopter, no one did.

Virgil gave Lipkins's address to Cool and they headed out in that direction. They were there in a little over ten minutes. When Cool touched down Virgil turned to Said. "You are going to wait here with the pilot. That's not a request. This is part of an active crime scene and you are not allowed inside. Tell me you're hearing me on this, Mr. Said. I'll arrest you if you don't follow my instructions."

"Yes, yes," Said said. "Just go. Go find her."

Virgil glanced at Cool who gave him a nod. When he was sure Said was going to stay put, Virgil, Murton, and Grady climbed out and headed for the house.

VIRGIL WAS READY TO KICK THE DOOR, BUT MURTON grabbed his shoulder, then stepped in front of him and twisted the knob. He pushed the door open and gave Virgil a look before going inside.

The house was a two-story, square orange brick box, the kind you see everywhere in the countryside. Grady took the upper floor, and Murton took the main level. That left the cellar for Virgil. He descended the steps in the dark and when he reached the bottom got hit in the face by a pull string that hung from a light fixture. The fixture contained a single bare bulb and when Virgil pulled the string his heart sank.

Other than the furnace, water pump, hot water heater, a few pieces of old furniture, and a row of canned goods that might have been twenty years old, the basement was empty. When he looked at the floor Virgil could see his own footprints in the dust. No one had been down here for a long time, he thought. He checked every inch to be sure, but it was hopeless. Patty Doyle wasn't there. She never had been.

When he returned to the main floor Murton and Grady were waiting for him. They both shook their heads. "You sure?"

"Checked every room and closet," Murton said.

"Same here," Grady said. "Even looked under the beds."

"Attic?"

"Completely empty. Besides, if she'd been here, after all this time, you know as well as I do we'd have smelled it the minute we walked in."

They went back outside and moved around to the rear of the house. The yard was neat and well-manicured. "What about a well, or a cistern?" Murton asked. They walked the entire lot and found neither.

On the way back to the helicopter Grady said, "This guy is a farmer, right?"

"Was," Virgil said.

"Then where's his barn?"

Virgil didn't hesitate. "Ah, it's a Co-op thing. They've got a maintenance shop over there. It's where they keep all their equipment. No need for a barn on the property."

They climbed into the chopper and gave Said the news. He looked out the window and didn't speak. Cool took off and flew south, toward Kentucky. They'd drop him off, then head back to Indy.

If Virgil hadn't been so quick to answer, if he would have thought about it like a real farmer, they would have found what was left of Patty Doyle in no time at all.

VIRGIL AND MURTON RODE IN COMPLETE SILENCE ALL THE way to Murton's house. When they pulled up, Becky was waiting on the front porch. Virgil put the truck in park, but left the engine running. "Is there anything you want to talk about?" Virgil said.

Murton waited a long time before he answered. "Yeah. But not right now."

"Are we okay?"

"Sure. Why wouldn't we be?"

"What about you and Sandy?"

Murton looked at his best friend and brother. "Small's my hero, Jonesy."

"You might want to tell her that."

Murton looked down at the floor of the truck. "When we were in the helicopter right after the bomb went off… did you see her holding my hand? Did you see Jonas wiping the tears from her face?"

"Yeah, I did."

Murton lifted his head and looked Virgil square in the face. He waited a beat, then tapped him on the thigh with his index finger and got out of the truck without another word. Becky ran off the porch and leapt into his arms. Virgil watched Murton carry her up the steps and inside their house, kicking the door closed with his foot.

He dropped the truck in gear and drove home.

CHAPTER FORTY-SEVEN

By the time he got home, Sandy told him that Dr. Bell had already come and gone. Jonas was okay, but Bell wanted him to go back to the child psychologist he'd seen after his mother died.

"What do you think?" Virgil said.

"I think it's a good idea. They know each other, and Jonas always seemed happy to go." Then, "How's Murton?"

Virgil thought about the question. No one knew Murton better than he did. "I think he'll be okay. He says you're his hero, by the way."

Sandy didn't want to hear it. She waved her hands in front of her face, as if the motion could erase the words from the air.

"What?"

"He told me that when we were in the back of the helicopter. I didn't want to hear it then and I don't want to hear it now."

"You saved his life, Sandy. That's no small thing."

"No pun intended, right?" There was a little bite in her voice.

"Hey, hey, what is it?"

"You mean besides the fact that I killed someone?"

Virgil knew Sandy appreciated straight talk more than anything else, so he didn't hesitate when he answered. "Yes. What's your point?"

"My point is exactly this, Virgil: Murton is your brother and that makes him my brother too. I love him with my whole heart."

"I know that."

"Just let me say it, will you, please? When we stepped into that room I did what I had to do to save our *son*. I saw that gun pointed at the top of Murton's head, and I saw his father holding Jonas. I didn't think twice. In fact, I didn't think at all. I stepped in, lined up the shot and took it before Ralph Wheeler could move that gun from his son to ours. In that moment I didn't care about Murton, I didn't care about myself, and I damned sure didn't care about Ralph Wheeler or the history between him and Murt."

"You did the right thing. I was ready to fire myself. You beat me to it is all."

"But that's not all, Jonesy, and I think you know it. I lost my dad when he saved your life. You lost your dad when I pulled you off that bar stool. Now Murton has lost his dad because of me. What is it with me and fathers?"

Virgil didn't have an answer for that. Who would?

THE NEXT TWO DAYS WERE SOMETHING OF A BLUR. THE loss of Patty Doyle haunted Virgil. He and Sandy made formal statements to every law enforcement agency that had either been a part of the investigation or present after the detonation of the bomb on their farmland.

The blast ruined about fifty acres of planted crops. Carl Johnson offered to run a dozer over the crater and fill the hole and replant, but when they talked about the cost, Virgil told him to forget it. Fifty acres out of two thousand wasn't worth it. They'd let it go for now and address it after the harvest in the fall. They were standing next to the hole when Angus Mizner walked up to them. "That's quite a hole."

Virgil looked at him. "It was quite a bomb."

"Anyway," Mizner said, "Me and Basil been talking about it and we need to run something by you, Virgil. You too, Carl."

Virgil and Carl Johnson looked at each other, then back at Mizner. "What is it?"

"We're going to buy Cal's land from his estate. It's all in the Co-op's charter so there won't be any other bidders and such."

Johnson shrugged. "Fine by me."

"Me too," Virgil said. "Heck, I'd go in with you if I could afford it."

Mizner had a toe-in-the-dirt look on his face. It was so obvious he actually kicked his toe in the dirt, a few pieces of rock and debris trickling down in the hole when he did. "Well, you see, the thing is…"

Virgil was instantly pissed. "That is absolutely unacceptable, Angus. I won't stand for it. Not for one single minute."

Mizner was nodding, almost like he was on Virgil's side. "I know you're upset, Virgil. I would be too if the situation was reversed." He didn't look at Virgil when he spoke. Instead he kicked a few more pieces of dirt into the hole.

"Except it's not reversed, is it?" Virgil said through his teeth.

Mizner had told them that as soon as he and Basil Graves took over Cal's land, they'd hold the majority of shares in the Co-op. The Co-op charter stated that the majority shareholders were allowed to set the rules regarding who could and could not be a member. Virgil and Carl Johnson were getting pushed out.

"Look, it's strictly a business decision," Mizner said.

Then, as if he couldn't live with the lie he'd told, he added, "Well, maybe not all business."

"Meaning what?" Virgil said. He was practically yelling at Mizner.

"Ever since you showed up here last fall, people have been dropping like flies." He ticked them off on his fingers. "Martha Esser, Charlie Esser, Vernon Conrad, a whole slew of people connected to the gas operation, and now Cal Lipkins. We're afraid if you keep hanging around one of us is going to be next."

"That's bullshit," Virgil said. "You make it sound like I killed them. I was down here doing my job."

Mizner tossed his hands in the air and let them flop down at his sides. "Dead is dead. The decision's been made. Ain't nothing said here going to change anything."

Virgil took a few deep breaths and tried to get his emotions in check. "Look, if you do this, you'll be hanging me out to dry. Carl can't handle this much land by himself." He glanced at Carl Johnson. "No offense."

Johnson waved it off. "You're right. I can't."

"So what do you suggest I do?"

"It's your land, Virgil. Anything you want. Me and Basil talked about it. We've agreed to let you stay on for the rest of this year. A commitment was made and it's one we intend to honor. But come next spring, you're on your own. Maybe you could sell the Esser house. That would hold you over for another year without planting a thing."

"Yeah, that's great advice, Angus. Thanks." Virgil turned around and walked away.

THAT NIGHT VIRGIL TOLD SANDY ABOUT GETTING BOOTED from the Co-op. Her reply wasn't what he expected. "Maybe it's for the best, Virgil."

"What? How? How could it possibly be for the best?"

Sandy knew her husband well enough to know there wasn't anything she could say in the moment to calm him. She kissed him on the cheek and told him she was going to bed. Virgil told her he'd be in later. He sat at his desk trying to figure out a way to keep himself financially afloat.

The land was going to be a curse...he just knew it. Maybe he'd be able to make a deal with one of the conglomerates after the harvest later in the year. He walked down to the pond and sat down in the grass, his back leaning against his father's cross. It wasn't very comfortable but at some point he fell asleep. Eventually, the stiffness in his back woke him. When he looked at his watch he was surprised to see it was almost four in the morning.

"I didn't think you were ever going to wake up," Mason said. He was seated in the chair where Virgil usually sat, his legs crossed, his fingers interlaced behind his head. "Lot of stuff on that thumb drive, huh?"

Virgil rubbed the sleep out of his eyes and stood up. His back ached. "Yeah, I guess so. Mind telling me why you waited so long to give it to me?"

"Boy oh boy, you sure know how to make a guy feel like he's his own victim sometimes."

"What?"

"If I'd have let you crush that drive under your boot like you wanted to, you never would have known what Pearson was willing to do to get rid of Ed Donatti."

"It still didn't save him."

"That's because he wasn't meant to be saved, Son. Jonas and Murton were. And the way it turned out, Jonas is right where he belongs…where he was meant to be. Always. Just like Murton, both years ago and right now."

"Then why'd you let me have it when you did?"

"Because there's information on there that will help you and others."

"Who?"

"You'll figure it out. By the way, getting kicked out of the Co-op was a gift. Bank on it, Virg."

"I don't see how."

"Stop seeing and start thinking, Son. Use your imagination. Dream big and all that jazz." Mason raised his wrist and tapped the face of his watch. "Still sort of bugs me that my watch doesn't work over here. Anyway, it's time, Virg."

"Time for what?"

Mason grinned at him. "The farm report. I'm sure

Mizner is watching. He gave you the answer you wanted. All you have to do is ask yourself the right questions. Don't let anything haunt you, Son. Ever."

And Virgil thought, *what?*

Virgil walked up to the house. He replayed the conversation he had with Mizner in his head. He'd been furious with him. Had he missed something? If he had, he didn't know what it could be. He went inside and plopped down on the sofa. He tuned into the farm report on television and watched the entire show. It was a painfully dry dissertation on weather conditions and forecasts that were no better than the regular morning news. He was about to turn the damned thing off when an editorial piece came on that spoke of old farmhouses and what a waste it was that the farmers were buying up the land and letting the houses go to seed. The counterpoint was that farmers were farmers, not landlords. They had neither the time nor the desire to maintain the houses and make them available for rent. Why bother with a few hundred bucks a month and the hassle of finding quality tenants when you could pull ten grand an acre out of the ground every year? Virgil could see the logic in the counterpoint. It simply wasn't worth it. He still hadn't done anything with the Esser house. He had neither the time nor the desire to be a landlord. Then he saw a commercial for a realty company that specialized in buying old farmhouses. He grabbed the remote and paused the screen.

Virgil replayed the conversation again. Mizner had told him to sell the Esser house. Virgil and Company owned the house as part of the inheritance, but they'd not yet done anything with it. It simply sat there empty. His father had told him to watch the farm report. He'd also said not to let anything haunt him. There were plenty of things that were bothering Virgil, but only one thing that was haunting him.

Virgil finally understood.

When he picked up the phone and called Becky, she was not happy.

"You can be pissed at me later, Becks. I need some information and I need it right now."

"At four-thirty in the morning? Why am I not surprised? Hold on a minute." She set the phone down—a little harder than necessary, Virgil thought—and was back a few moments later. "Okay, I'm at the computer. I can barely see, but I'm at the computer."

"How many separate plots of land did Cal Lipkins own that made up the entirety of his farm?"

"Hold on." Virgil heard a series of keyboard clicks he thought might never end. It went on for so long he began to picture Becky sitting in front of the keyboard, her head propped up with one hand, the other simply stabbing at random keys in an effort to appease him. Then the clicking suddenly stopped.

"Becks?"

"What?"

"Why did you stop?'

"Because I'm reading. Please be quiet for a minute will you?" Then a few moments later, "Okay, over the years it looks like he purchased twelve other farms that connect to his land in one way or another."

"Can you check the history of the assessed value? I need to know how many of them have or had farmhouses that were included in the sale."

The clicking started again. When it finally stopped, Becky said, "Oh man. That's beautiful."

"What? What's beautiful?"

"Murton brought me a cup of coffee. That never happens."

Virgil heard Murton in the background. "Yes it does. It happens all the time."

Becky ignored him. "Anyway, the tax records show only one of the twelve had a dwelling on it. Want the address?"

Virgil scribbled a note to Sandy and ran out the door. He punched the address into the truck's nav unit and once he was clear of his house he hit the lights and siren and pushed the Ford Raptor to its limit. When the speedometer hit one hundred twenty the front end started to wobble and Virgil had to back off slightly. It was still very early in the morning and he was able to hold the speed all the way down to Shelby County.

He turned off the highway and then followed the nav unit as it took him down a dirt road. There were no markings of any kind and when he sailed past the point where he was supposed to turn, the nav unit starting bitching at him. He skidded to a stop and put the truck in reverse. This time when the nav unit told him he was at the proper place he shined the truck's spotlight out the side window and saw a long drive that was nothing more than an overgrown trail. He turned down the dirt lane, taking it slow. He'd gone almost a half mile before he saw the structure. It was a broken shell of a house set off to the side at the far end of the lane. When Virgil saw it, he knew he was in the right place. What he didn't know was what he'd find, though in the dark rivers of his heart, he had a pretty good idea.

Patty Doyle had been missing for a long time.

Far too long.

EPILOGUE

When Virgil finally returned home, Sandy, Huma, Murton, and Becky were waiting for him. He got an earful from Sandy.

"We've been worried sick, Virgil. We had an agreement, remember?"

Virgil was in more than a little trouble and he knew it. He countered with his best diplomacy. He bit into his lip, closed his left eye and said, "I left you a note. Didn't you get it?"

Sandy walked over to the table, picked up the note and waved it at him. "You mean this?" She looked at Murton and Becky. "He left a note, he says. Here, let me read it to you."

Murton leaned in close to whisper something into Virgil's ear and got a whiff of the odor that hung on his brother. "Holy cow, dude, where the hell *have* you been?

You smell like death…and something else I can't quite put my finger on. Pickles, maybe? Anyway, she's read us the note about twenty times already."

Sandy pointed a finger at Murton. "Murton Wheeler, if you know what's good for you…"

Murton held up his hands and stepped away. "Don't worry. I don't know what's going on, but if I get any closer to him I'm going to need a respirator."

"The note says, 'I'll be back.' I'll be back? What kind of note is that?"

"Well, I am back. Besides, if you were that worried, why didn't you call?"

Virgil heard Murton say, 'Uh oh.' When he looked at him, Murton was staring at the floor, his hand shielding his eyes as if blocking them from the sun's rays.

"I did call, Virgil. Once. Want to know what happened?"

"Sure."

Sandy took out her phone and punched in Virgil's number. When Virgil heard his phone buzz he turned around and saw that it sat on his desk. When he turned back to Sandy she had her hands on her hips, her head tipped to one side, her mouth formed a tight line, her eyebrows arched. Virgil was mildly surprised she wasn't tapping her foot on the floor.

Delroy walked in, looked at Virgil and said, "Tank God. Where you been, you?" Then without waiting for an answer he walked over and kissed Huma on the cheek. "What'd I miss, me?"

Huma turned and kissed Delroy full on the lips. "That's a kiss." Then, "Not much. It's just starting to get good." She slipped her hand into his.

Virgil walked up to Sandy to give her a hug and apologize. Sandy, who was actually more relieved than mad would have let him if it weren't for the smell. She stepped back before he got any closer. "Dear God, what is that smell?"

Jonas ran into the room to greet his father. "Hi Dad. I tink Mommy's mad at you."

Delroy looked at Huma. "Hear dat?"

Huma grinned at him. "It sounds like the conversion process is taking hold."

Jonas looked at his father. "You smell like business." Then to Delroy. "Irie, mon?"

Delroy laughed his big loud Jamaican laugh and when he did it sucked most of the tension out of the room.

Sandy told Virgil to go take a shower before he stunk up the entire house. They'd waited this long. A few more minutes wouldn't kill them, especially since they knew he was safe. Once he was cleaned up they all sat down and he told them what happened.

"Okay, first of all, let me say that Becky knew where I was and—"

Becky wasn't having it. "No way, Jonesy. You're not going to drag me into this. You pulled me out of bed at four-thirty in the morning. I'd only been asleep for two hours."

Virgil looked at her. "Two hours? Are you usually up so late?"

Murton looked at Virgil and let his eyes fall to half-mast. "We had a little catching up to do," Murton said. "Besides, when Small finally got in touch with us we came right over. That was an hour ago. I was getting ready to head down to Shelby County when we saw you turn in the drive."

Virgil took a deep breath. "Okay, look, I'm sorry everyone. Really. I got the address from Becky. It was one of Cal Lipkins's properties. I had to take one more shot at finding Patty Doyle."

"But what took you so long?" Sandy asked. "Did you find her?"

Virgil couldn't help it. His voice got shaky and his eyes began to water as he told them the story.

The sun had yet to cross the horizon and it wasn't nearly bright enough for Virgil to see. He pointed his truck directly at the front of the house and hit the spotlight again. When he twisted the interior handle of the spot and manipulated the light, the house lit up like some kind of monster in the false dawn. He moved the light across the surface of the structure, watching the shadows dance and slither away with the movement of the light.

The gaping holes with broken windows were at once hideous and inviting, beckoning him to step inside. An entire section of the roof was torn off, its rafters exposed to the elements, as if a giant hand had reached out and simply ripped it away. A large tree stood close to the front corner, one limb hanging low by the remnants of the eve trough, then sweeping back upward across the peak of the roof, its finer branches like fingers of a hand. The whole thing looked like a giant arm, bent at the elbow. It didn't take too much imagination to envision the hand and fingers sliding across the shingles and tearing out the missing part of the roof.

The entire place looked…haunted.

Don't let anything haunt you, Son. Ever.

Virgil grabbed his flashlight, unlocked the shotgun from its holder and headed toward the house. The shotgun might have been a little much. But then again, the whole place gave him the willies.

THE MOMENT HE STEPPED INSIDE HE KNEW HE WAS TOO late. He'd smelled death before and there was no mistaking the overwhelming foul odor of decaying flesh. He immediately turned around and moved back out of the house. He sat down on the front step and let his head hang down. The house no longer seemed haunted. It just felt incredibly sad.

All of this because someone wanted to extract natural gas from under his land. How many more people had to die before the gas issue would go away? Why did it have to culminate in the death of an innocent and beautiful young woman in the prime of her life? Where did it end?

He walked back to his truck and put the shotgun back in its rack. He opened another box and took out a pair of latex gloves and a paper face mask. He slipped everything on and headed back inside.

Patty Doyle's body was in there somewhere. Like it or not, it was his job to find her remains and help put her to rest.

THE PAPER MASK DIDN'T HELP MUCH WITH THE SMELL AND Virgil found himself breathing through his mouth, the mask puffing in and out with each breath. He was only four steps into the damned place before he could taste death at the back of his throat. The floorboards under his feet creaked with every step and Virgil wondered if they'd be able to take his weight. They seemed solid, but he felt the sag with almost every step.

He shined his flashlight around the entryway and into what must have been the living room. He noticed a faint humming noise that seemed to grow louder with each step. When he stopped to listen the sound was more clear. He let his ears guide him through a doorway that led him into the kitchen and when he saw the dead body, his heart began to race.

It also gave him hope.

Virgil wasn't the least bit religious, but if he'd been listening just then, he would have heard himself saying, 'Please God, please,' over and over and over again, the face mask puffing in and out with each word, the crinkle of the paper and the sound of his breath like a backing track of a repetitive chant.

THE HUMMING NOISE WASN'T HUMMING AT ALL. IT WAS buzzing. The entire room was filled with flies. They swirled around him and bounced off his face and body like pieces of ice in a hailstorm. He tried to wave them away with his free arm but it was like trying to hold water in the palm of your hand. The flashlight drew them in and they looked like little bullets whizzing past.

The flies and maggots covered the body of a large deer that had crashed through the back kitchen door. The glass sliced the deer along the side of its neck and it had bled out while trying to free itself. The carcass hung suspended in the center of the door, the deer's eyes wide with fear and glazed with death.

He spun around in a circle to get the flies off himself and the beam of his flashlight caught the glint of the lock and hasp on the door. And Virgil thought: Basement.

He yanked on the lock but it held fast. He beat on it with the butt end of his flashlight a couple of times before realizing the only thing he was going to accomplish with that maneuver was the purchase of a new flashlight. He pounded on the door with his fist and kicked it with his boots, calling out Patty's name. When he got no response, he ran back out to his truck to get the shotgun to blast the lock from the door.

VIRGIL LINED UP ALONG THE EDGE OF THE DOOR, THE shotgun no more than two feet away from the lock and hasp. When he fired, the blast lit up the room and blew chunks of the door and frame away. He pumped the action and fired again. This time the lock and hasp flew away and clattered to the floor next to the deer's hooves. Virgil leaned the gun against the wall and yanked open the door.

And the smell slapped him all over again.

When he turned his flashlight into the well of the basement he saw the walls were covered with sound-proof foam. Despite the smell he ran down the steps, turned the corner, and stopped dead in his tracks. Virgil, who'd been a cop his entire adult life, who'd seen the worst of what other human beings could do to each other, who'd thought he'd seen it all discovered he had not. When he saw what was left of Patty Doyle, he couldn't help it. He dropped to his knees and choked out a sob.

Patty Doyle sat on a cot, munching on a pickle. "I've been locked down in this hole for over a month by my count," she said. "Can you get me out of here, please?" She threw the pickle on the floor and wiped her hands on her shirt. She was filthy, her clothes had turned to rags that barely covered her body and her hair was plastered against the sides of her face. Had Virgil not seen a picture of her, he would have thought she was someone else.

He pulled the mask from his face and told her who he was. "How did you survive down here for so long?"

She held up her wrist, the one that had been shackled to the chain. Her hand was swollen, her thumb wrapped in a homemade splint. "I ran out of food and water about two weeks ago. I'd been severely rationing it, but eventually it was all gone. I knew I had to get free or I was going to die, except I couldn't get loose from that steel band locked around my wrist. Then one day I noticed that I was losing weight. I was getting skinnier and skinnier, but not enough to get that damned band off."

Virgil looked at her hand. "You broke your own thumb? How bad is it?"

"It's pretty bad. Do you have any aspirin or anything?"

"Yeah. I've got a first-aid kit. C'mon. Let's get the hell out of here."

Once they were outside, Patty sat down on the front porch steps and Virgil brought the first aid kit to her, along with a bottle of water and a blanket. She took four aspirin and drank the entire bottle of water. Virgil carefully removed the homemade splint and taped a finger brace on her thumb.

"Not my best work," he said when he was finished. But it'll hold until you get to the hospital."

"Thank you."

"You said you ran out of food, but you were eating a pickle."

"Once I got free of the shackle the first thing I tried to do was break through the door. But I couldn't do it. I only had one good arm to work with and the door opened inward. I couldn't get any kind of leverage at the top of the steps. So I started looking around the rest of the basement and found a root cellar or whatever they're called. It was fully stocked. Unfortunately, it was fully stocked with pickles. I've been eating pickles and drinking pickle juice for almost two weeks."

Virgil thought if there were more young women like Patty Doyle around, the world would be a better place. "You ready to get out of here?"

"What do you think? Although I'd like to go a little slow if you don't mind. I need to get my head on straight before I go rushing back into the real world."

They got in the truck and Virgil took it slow down the long drive and off the property. He'd run her back up to Indianapolis and get her some medical attention…and a much-needed bath. Along the way they talked about Virgil's cases and he told her everything about how he tried to find her. He wanted to keep her talking…keep the conversation going so she wouldn't go into shock. He told her about the bomb and his land. He even told her about getting kicked out of the Co-op.

"That doesn't seem fair."

"It's not," Virgil agreed. "The truth of it is, there are tens of millions of dollars worth of natural gas out there, but I refuse to ruin two thousand acres of perfectly good land by pumping a bunch of poison into the ground to get it out." He pulled up to the intersection of the highway and stopped.

"What if you didn't have to…ruin the land to get the gas out?"

Virgil laughed. "That'd solve a lot of problems."

"So let's take a little drive. There's someone we both need to see anyway."

Virgil was confused. "Who?"

Patty seemed to consider her answer. "When I was locked down in that basement…I don't quite know how to explain this, but I knew you'd find me. Not you, specifically, but someone like you."

Virgil was interested. "What, exactly is someone like me?"

"Somebody who doesn't quit. Somebody who sees things sometimes that no one else can. Somebody who has faith, not only in himself, but others."

Virgil felt himself swallow.

Patty wasn't finished. "Turn left and we go to Indy. Turn right and we go to Kentucky and you can keep the faith. Radiology, Inc. isn't the only company my uncle owns. Ever heard of something called sonic drilling technology?"

Virgil had no idea what that was. "No."

"That's because it's brand new. My uncle, Rick Said? He holds the patent. It's going to change the way natural gas is pulled out of the ground."

Virgil was interested, but Patty was his priority in the moment. He turned on his left blinker. But when Patty spoke again she said something that changed his mind.

"I'll bet getting kicked out of that Co-op was a gift. In fact, I'd say bank on it."

Virgil looked her in the eye for a long time. Then he

thought, why not? He turned right. After a few miles of silence he said, "I'm sorry it took me so long to find you."

Patty scooted over as close as she could and leaned her whole person against Virgil. She grabbed his arm with both hands and began to cry. It was all coming out now, and Virgil knew in the moment it was exactly what she needed. He buzzed the window down. In the close confines of the truck her smell was so overwhelming he had to turn his head away and watch the road out of the corner of his eye.

Patty Doyle, still turning…well, you get it.

ACKNOWLEDGMENTS

Thank you for reading this story. As I've said before it is an honor to write for each and every one of you. I hope that means something to you. It certainly does to me.

I'd like to thank the following people for their help, support, and encouragement along the way:

Linda Heaton, my editor, whose enthusiasm, dedication, sharp eye, attention to detail, and patience have proved invaluable. I am amazed at what a great editor can do with a decent manuscript. I couldn't have done it without you, Linda. You have no idea how grateful I am that our paths crossed along the way. Thank you.

Carol Cline, Debra Hizer-Johnson, and Carolyn Pawluk: There's an old adage that says you can't play to your hometown crowd. There is some truth to that statement, but the three of you continue to chart a new course in that regard and I remain thankful I have the three of you in my corner, and in my life.

Sharon N. from Kansas, John P. down in Florida, Charlie H. for the numbers, Cris Brock who planted a seed and never knew it. You all keep me going and have in your own individual ways brought light into my work and my life. I couldn't be more grateful.

Betty Lawless, who graciously allowed me the use of her son's name. I know it wasn't an easy decision, Betty. Thank you.

To my wife, Debra: Your belief in me is like medicine for my spirit and soul. You have singlehandedly redefined the word 'abundance' for me, and countless others as we all sail into the mystic. Thank you, baby.

And finally to everyone of you who are reading this right now: You, my dear readers, are the backbone of every story I've written. Many of you have asked where my stories come from. My answer remains the same: *Me, trying to figure myself out.* I remain humbled by your trust, support, and generosity during our journey together. Thank you so very much. Send me an email if you get the chance. I'd love to hear from you. I really would. It's the best part of the whole gig.

...and the story continues.
Virgil and the gang are back in State of Exile.
As Delroy would say, "Yeah, mon!"

State of Exile - Book 5 of the Virgil Jones Suspense Thriller series

Virgil Jones knew it would come back on them one day. He just didn't think it would happen quite so soon...

When Immigrations and Customs Enforcement Agent Chris Dobson goes after one of Virgil's own, he does so in a horrific manner, one that leaves Virgil and his wife, Sandy in shock, and exiles two of their best friends at a time when they need them the most...

Three months ago, Virgil rescued a young woman, Patty Doyle, from certain death. As a result, Patty and her uncle, Rick Said, show their gratitude by using Virgil's Shelby County farmland as a testbed for their new natural gas extraction method, one that Virgil hopes will free him and his family from a major burden in their lives. But while extracting core samples for testing, Patty is once again forced to face her demons, all while making a discovery that will either save Virgil financially, or ruin him once and for all...

But Patty's discovery brings pure evil to light, and Dobson's thirst for revenge put forces in motion that changes everything. And when it does, not only does Virgil once again find himself and those he loves at the very center of terror, he makes an unexpected and perilous decision, one that will ultimately change his life forever, because for Virgil, all crossroads lead back to Shelby County.

>
> You've felt the Anger.
> You've experienced the Betrayal.
> You've taken Control.

You've faced the Deception.
Now…it's time to accept the Exile!

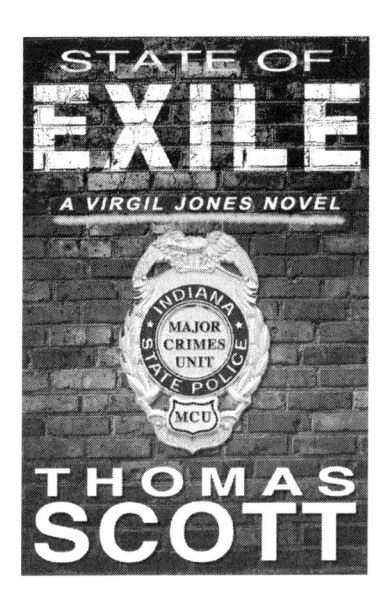

Get your copy of State of Exile today!

— **Also by Thomas Scott** —

The Virgil Jones Series In Order

State of Anger - Book 1
State of Betrayal - Book 2
State of Control - Book 3
State of Deception - Book 4
State of Exile - Book 5
State of Freedom - Book 6
State of Genesis - Book 7
State of Humanity - Book 8
State of Impact - Book 9
State of Justice - Book 10
State of Killers - Book 11
State of Life - Book 12
State of Mind - Book 13
State of Need - Book 14
State of One - Book 15
State of Play - Book 16
State of Qualms - Book 17
State of Remains - Book 18
State of Suspense - Book 19

The Jack Bellows Series In Order

Wayward Strangers - Book 1
Brave Strangers - Book 2

Visit ThomasScottBooks.com for further information regarding future release dates, and more.

ABOUT THE AUTHOR

Thomas Scott is the author of the **Virgil Jones** series, and the **Jack Bellows** series of novels. He lives in northern Indiana with his lovely wife, Debra, his children, and his trusty sidekicks and writing buddies, Lucy, the cat, and Buster, the dog.

You may contact Thomas anytime via his website ThomasScottBooks.com where he personally answers every single email he receives. Be sure to sign up to be notified of the latest release information.

Also, if you enjoy the Virgil Jones series of books, leaving an honest review on Amazon.com helps others decide if a book is right for them. Just a sentence or two makes all the difference in the world. Plus, rumor has it that it's good for the soul!

For information on future books in the Virgil Jones series, or to connect with the author, please visit:

ThomasScottBooks.com

And remember:
Virgil and the gang are back and waiting for you in State of Exile!

State of Exile - Book 5 of the Virgil Jones Suspense Thriller Series

Grab your copy today!

Printed in Great Britain
by Amazon